What the Hart Wants

Headstrong Harts, Book 1

by Emily Royal

ARE YOU SIGNED UP FOR DRAGONBLADE'S BLOG?

You'll get the latest news and information on exclusive giveaways, exclusive excerpts, coming releases, sales, free books, cover reveals and more.

Check out our complete list of authors, too!

No spam, no junk. That's a promise!

Sign Up Here

www.dragonbladepublishing.com

Additional Dragonblade books by Author Emily Royal

Headstrong Harts
What the Hart Wants, Book 1
Queen of my Hart, Book 2
Hidden Hart, Book 3

London Libertines
Henry's Bride, Book 1
Hawthorne's Wife, Book 2
Roderick's Widow, Book 3

Dedication

For Jasmine

Acknowledgements

Thanks go to my writing tribe the Beta Buddies, and my twitter tribe the UKRomChatters.

Thank you Sarah, for the wine, nibbles, hugs, café-writing sessions (particularly the one where you encouraged me, over tea and toast, to fire up the laptop and write the first scene of this book) and, more recently, for the socially-distanced walks and videochats.

And finally, I must thank the all the Scottish mountains I've climbed for the fresh air, breath-taking views, sore calves, blisters, midge bites, and, most importantly, the inspiration for Beinn Mo Chridhe.

Prologue

Perthshire, Scotland
1819

"I'M NOT JESTING, sir. You're now the thirteenth Duke Molineux."

Fraser drained his glass. The amber liquid burned his throat, and he choked and slammed the glass on the desk.

"Is the brandy not to your taste, Your Grace?"

The lawyer gave Fraser a look of smug disdain, no doubt considering whether a Highlander was fit to be called a duke rather than a savage.

"I prefer moonshine myself, Mr. Simpkins," he said.

"Fraser!"

Ma leaned forward; her brow furrowed with

disapproval. Despite her age, she was still a good-looking woman, but the presence of the black-clad cockroach of a lawyer, come to seek profit from the death of a distant relation, had tempered her good humor. Or was it the fact that Fraser had alluded to the illicit activities upon which their livelihood depended?

The woman sitting beside Ma bore a different look altogether. Though a beauty, with hair as golden as hay in the sunshine, and eyes the color of heather, her expression reeked of ambition. Jennifer—beautiful, lush Jennifer—who'd parted her thighs more times than he'd corked bottles of moonshine.

Ma's face had twisted with horror as the lawyer related the fate of the twelfth duke. But Jennifer's expression betrayed her greed. Jennifer used sex for her own ends. She'd taken many lovers, pitting one rival against another to heighten their desire. But, on hearing that her current lover had inherited a title, her expression had changed from the indifference of a woman who toyed with a man's heart, to the hunger of a woman seeking a prize.

And that prize was him. There was nothing like the prospect of being a duchess to renew a weary woman's vigor. Doubtless, she'd offer him the usual delights, which he'd sampled in her bedchamber, on this very desk and, if he recalled rightly, three times against the oak-paneled wall of the minstrels' gallery.

But never against the rock of his homeland, the hard granite which pulsed with the lifeblood of the highlands. He'd save that for the woman who won his heart if such a woman existed.

But now was not the time to think of rutting. Before him lay the unpleasant duty of seeing to an English estate crippled by debt, if the newspapers were to be believed, and clouded by scandal. According to Simpkins, the twelfth duke had possessed tastes rivaling the Marquis de Sade, had drunk and whored himself into near-bankruptcy, and finally met his maker after falling out of the top floor window of a brothel.

With a sigh, Fraser signed the document.

"Excellent," the lawyer said. "Perhaps we might schedule our next appointment at my offices in London once you're settled at Clayton House."

"Why would I want to go there?"

"To assume your responsibilities, of course," the lawyer said. "It's the Molineux London residence. You must be anxious to begin overseeing the estate, and my fees are very reasonable."

The lawyer licked his lips in a gesture, almost mirroring Jennifer's.

Another individual who viewed him as a prize.

"You imagine incorrectly, Simpkins," he said.

"But, sir," the lawyer said, his features now showing desperation, "these matters need to be settled."

"And they shall," Fraser said, "in a manner, and at a time, of *my* choosing. Not yours."

"But…"

"Be so good as to leave the papers with me, Simpkins," he said. "My mother will show you to the door."

Ma rose to her feet and ushered the cockroach out.

Jennifer's smile broadened, and she leaned forward and ran a fingertip along the edge of her gown, dipping it into the valley between her breasts.

"I think, my love, it's time for a celebration."

Did she think he'd offer for her now he was a duke? If she thought to use him, she'd discover he was a much better player at that particular game.

But for the present, her willing body would prove a pleasant diversion.

With a smile, he rose to his feet, not bothering to disguise the bulge in his breeches, and swept aside the contents of the desk.

Chapter One

Clayton House, London
1823

"HAVE YOU MISSED me?"

Lilah held out her hand, and the bird flew toward her and settled on her finger, dipping its head as if in welcome.

One of the few remaining souls in a crumbling ruin which had been abandoned for four years.

But that crumbling ruin provided Lilah with a haven from the incessant noise generated by her family who, now she'd embarked on her first season, insisted on trying to teach her propriety.

Especially Dexter. Though Lilah loved her brother dearly, the increase in his fortunes had come hand-in-hand with a disproportionate increase in his desire to elevate their status in society. Wishing to sweep aside their humble origins, Dex had paid a considerable sum to fund Lilah's debut, and he expected her to reward his investment with the dividend of a society marriage.

Which meant she'd have to surrender her liberty to a man who valued only three things in a woman:

Biddability, silence, and the ability to bear children.

But unlike her brother, she had no burning desire to marry a title—or marry at all.

The bird chirped, returning her to the present.

"I'm sorry, my friend," she said. "Here, I have a treat for you."

She held up a piece of bread, and the bird pecked at it, ruffling its feathers as if in thanks. Ripples of iridescence shimmered across the creature's back. The bird looked out of place in the aviary—a bright exotic prisoner among the dull, earthy colors of plants, which might once have conformed to aesthetics, but were now choked by ivy.

Four years of neglect had turned Clayton House into a ruin, as if the soul of its late owner, the twelfth Duke Molineux, had permeated into the fabric of the building and rotted it from within. And well, he might. Lilah shivered at her childhood memory of him—a beautiful youth whose exterior concealed a blackened heart. Soulless gray eyes, which glittered with mirth at the discomfort of others.

The whole line was rotten to the core. The first duke had earned his title from a grateful Henry Tudor after distinguishing himself in battle. But his successors had gained notoriety, which increased with each generation. The tenth duke had narrowly escaped the gallows after a spate of murders. The eleventh had been killed in a duel within a week of inheriting the title after compromising six young women in a single night. As for the twelfth—he'd debauched his way around London before ending his life in the manner by which he'd lived it—drunk, naked, and in the arms of a harlot—leaving a penniless widow who'd been turned out of the estate before he was cold in his grave.

Lilah lifted her hand, and the bird launched into the air and disappeared into the ivy. She would have freed it, but it would never survive in the wild. It had lost its independence, as she would lose hers if married.

Why was it that a woman was expected to marry in order to find fulfillment? Could she not thrive as an individual in her own right, rather than as half of a pair? If Dexter expected her to yield her liberty, it would have to be with a man who saw her as an equal.

And such a man did not exist, except, perhaps, Sir Thomas, who, for all that he was a baronet, at least appreciated the value of the lower classes.

She scattered the rest of the breadcrumbs on the ground and stepped back to let the more timid inhabitants of the aviary seek their bounty in peace. Closing the door behind her, she picked her way across the ground toward the main building.

Clayton House was a large mansion built during the Jacobean era, but through the years, each incumbent had added layers of ostentation, as if to establish their superiority of rank. To Lilah, the building served a purpose, for it was a reminder of the evils of society. It served to inspire her *Essays on Patriarchy*, and it provided her with respite from Dexter's admonishments and Dorothea's attempts to turn her into a lady.

She crossed the main hall and entered the library, where row upon row of books filled the shelves, their colors clouded with a thin film of dust, punctuated by occasional fingerprints, evidence of Lilah's trespass. Plucking a book from the shelf, she traced the title on the spine, running her fingertips across the smooth surface of the gold embossing. Byron's *Hours of Idleness*. Published when he was younger than her.

Might her poems be published one day?

What would it feel like to have her name embossed in gold on the spine of a book?

She smiled at the notion of realizing her dream.

A creak echoed outside, followed by a faint scratching. The sounds of London always filtered through the air—a voice from the street at the bottom of the drive, the cry of a bird, or the soft creaks as the fabric of the house expanded and contracted in the ever-changing temperature as day turned to night, summer turned to winter. Or perhaps it was one of the many rats which resided in the bowels of the building.

Lilah sat in an armchair beside the empty fireplace and opened the book.

Reading should be a means to further a moral and spiritual education. But Byron's words, written by a man renowned for debauchery, stirred unwelcome feelings in her body, and she closed the volume with a snap, coughing at the dust which tickled her nostrils.

To succumb to the body's desires was the first step to humiliation. And one only had to recall the fate of Lady Caroline Lamb or Augusta Leigh to understand the imbalance of society in favor of rakes such as Byron.

She had no desire to suffer humiliation at the hands of such a man. Her first ball of the Season had shown her the dangers of doing so, when, in search of the dance partner Dexter had taken great pains to secure for her, she'd come across him in flagrante delicto with another.

Which just went to prove that men of the aristocracy were not fit to rule the world.

She jumped at another crash—this time much closer.

Someone was in the house. A ripple of fear raised the hairs on the back of her neck. She stood from her seat and looked around the room.

Her gaze landed on a vase situated on a pedestal beside the window, decorated in bright, gaudy colors and embossed with gold leaf. It contained the ashes of the seventh duke. Perhaps, today, one of the cursed Molineuxs would prove himself useful in her hour of need.

She picked it up, drawing comfort from its cold hardness, as she tried to dispel images of ruffians and brigands ransacking their way through London and murdering the innocent.

She heard a curse right outside the door, which resembled a deep growl.

The door handle turned, metal winking in the fading sunlight, and she lifted the vase over her head, ready to defend herself as the door swung inward.

FRASER CROSSED THE front garden and stopped

when the house came into view.

It was worse than he feared. Clayton House was a bloody ruin. The cost of restoring it would reduce his funds to almost nothing.

He cursed himself for not coming to London sooner, though there had been little point while the Excise Act was still being debated. But now that the Act had been passed, he could openly attract investors and customers, and show these London fops, that compared to a MacGregor single malt, French brandy was nothing more than horse piss.

The building before him seemed to soak up the light, the windows, reproachful eyes staring blankly out. The light of the setting sun glittered on the glass, where some of the windows had been smashed.

Perhaps he should burn it to the ground and start again. Or let the dissidents do it for him. The newspapers had been full of stories of houses being ransacked. It seemed as if the Terrors in France had ignited bloodlust in the dispossessed, and a handful of riots had sprung up, resulting in the occasional nobleman finding himself standing outside a burning building in his breeches.

One paper, the *City Chronicle*, even encouraged such behavior. Not directly, of course, but a careful editor could use language to incite unrest. Only last week he'd heard someone complaining in Whites about a new series of articles entitled

Essays on Patriarchy. The author, a Mr. Jeremiah Smith, was nowhere to be found—most likely, too cowardly to write under his own name. The bastard had even made a reference to the Molineux lineage in his first piece.

Though Fraser might agree that the previous dukes had earned their reputation as wastrels, such notoriety risked his chances of using the title to further his business prospects.

A flicker of light caught his eye, then a shape moved across one of the ground-floor windows.

A trespasser. Or worse.

The front door was ajar, and he pushed through it, wincing as the hinges creaked. He paused but heard no movement from inside. Wrinkling his nose at the smell of dust, damp, and rotting vegetation, he crept across the hallway. Patches of mold adorned the walls, and the marble statues guarding the doors had a greenish hue.

As he moved deeper into the building, a noise came from behind a door to the right.

Someone was there. In his house.

The noise stopped, then he discerned faint footsteps. They were too light to be those of a man. Perhaps a child was playing hide-and-seek. With a stern word and a clip on the ear, Fraser could dispatch him with little trouble.

He pushed the door open. The walls of the room were lined with books, from floor to ceiling. A deep red rug lined the floor, its pattern illuminated by a thin ray of sunlight. Beyond, a pedestal stood by the window. It was empty. Presumably, someone had broken in and stolen whatever ornament had graced it.

A sound came from behind, but before he could move, pain exploded in the back of his head, and he crumpled to the floor.

THE UNCONSCIOUS MAN at Lilah's feet seemed to have shrunk in size compared to the ogre which had emerged through the door.

But nevertheless, he was a man, and a large one. Save the stubble on his chin, he looked every part the gentleman. A dark green jacket fitted his form like a glove, leaving little to the imagination regarding his athletic, broad-shouldered form. A wicked heat pulsed inside her body at the sight of his breeches through which muscular calves and thighs were visible to the point of wantonness. Polished black boots completed the ensemble, mud spatters evidence of his efforts to conquer the weeds and brambles surrounding the house.

A man of tenacity.

Thick, honey-colored locks framed a strong face with a high forehead, straight nose, and a square jaw, which could have been chiseled by

Michelangelo. Her lips parted involuntarily as her gaze traced the line of his mouth.

He let out a low groan and turned his head. The sunlight caught the strands of his hair, igniting a flare of red. Then he opened his eyes.

Her senses were assaulted by the most striking blue she'd ever seen. Two pools, the color of an ocean, stared back at her, and she took a step back.

Until now, she'd always believed her brother to be the most handsome man of her acquaintance. But he was nothing compared to the specimen before her. Had she not felled him by her own hands, assuring herself of his mortality, she would have believed him a gift from the gods.

He sat up, rubbing the back of his head and uttered an ungodlike curse.

"Fuck!"

Then he noticed her. A slow smile crept across his lips. An uncomfortable heat bloomed across her body as his gaze caressed her form, and he made no attempt to disguise his frank appraisal of her. Then his lips thinned as his expression hardened as he spotted the shard in her hand—a shard to match the remnants of the vase on the floor.

"What the devil do ye think you're doing, foolish lass?"

His voice, a low baritone, rumbled with a rich Scottish burr which resonated in her bones, and she drew breath, willing the cool air to temper the little pulse of longing.

How could a man have such an effect on her?

But the best way to fight fire was with fire—as she had learned years ago. He might be bigger and stronger than her, but he was only a man and, by the look of him, an arrogant one. There was nothing for it but to employ equal arrogance.

She dropped the shard and folded her arms.

"I might ask you the same thing," she said. "This is private property."

"Is that so?" He held out his hand. "Help me up, would you?"

"I'll do nothing of the sort."

"Frightened, eh?" A tone of amusement lightened his voice.

"I'm frightened of no man," she said.

"Then ye're a fool."

He rose to his feet and brushed the front of his jacket. A puff of dust swirled in the air, and he coughed.

No—not dust, but the contents of the shattered vase. Unable to suppress a giggle, Lilah let out a snort.

"What's so funny, lass?"

"The fact that the owner of Clayton House is blissfully unaware that a trespasser is currently breathing in his ancestor."

"I don't understand."

She gestured toward the shards. "The seventh duke has resided in that vase for almost two centuries. He weathered the great Fire of London, the riots against the gin taxes, a shooting inside his ancestral home—only to be felled at the hands of a woman defending his home."

"Not his home anymore, though, is it? The current owner would be within his rights to recoup the cost of that vase from the woman who broke it."

"I was defending myself against a trespasser!" she cried.

"Are you the owner?"

"I'm acquainted with the family."

It wasn't a complete lie. After all, the late duke's widow, Anna, was Lilah's friend.

The man folded his arms, mirroring Lilah's earlier gesture. "Then perhaps you'd care to tell me where the current duke resides."

"I have no idea," she said, "but I doubt he'd wish to see someone like you."

His expression hardened. "Ye mean a Scot?"

"No, a trespasser," she said. "The family has a reputation for chasing uninvited guests off the premises. Often with a big stick."

He let out a chuckle. "You're a feisty wee lass."

"I see no reason to laugh," she retorted.

"On the contrary, I find myself highly entertained," he said, a maddening mix of amusement and over-confidence in his voice. "Perhaps I'll tarry awhile. I'm in need of company and a good book."

Infuriating boor! Did he think to invade her solitude with his overly large frame and particular brand of arrogance?

"You'll find nothing to entertain you here," Lilah said. "I claim rights of possession by virtue of having arrived here first."

"Then, you're here with the owner's blessing?"

Unwilling to voice the lie, she nodded.

"If he's generous enough to admit you, I'm sure he'd have no objection to my presence here." He nodded toward the broken vase. "It would, at least, remove the need to defend your person—and a very delectable person it is, too—if you're accompanied by a gentleman."

"You're no gentleman," she said.

He laughed. "Are you a lady?" he asked. "Ladies don't prowl around abandoned houses they've no business in. Shouldn't you be taking tea in a parlor somewhere, practicing whatever accomplishments you need to snare a husband?"

A ripple of indignation rolled over her. "How do you know I'm unmarried?"

"Because, lass, no man worth his salt would permit his woman to roam around London unaccompanied."

"Perhaps my husband gives me more freedom than society dictates."

He moved toward her, his body blocking out the sunlight, and took her shoulder. Barely suppressed male strength vibrated through his fingers.

"If I were your husband, lass, I'd turn you over my knee and spank ye raw for being such a hellcat."

She let out a squeak of protest, but couldn't stop the raw pulse of primal need.

"You've no right to speak so!" she protested.

"I have every right."

He squeezed her shoulder again and released her. Suppressing a whimper at the sense of loss, she pushed him away.

"Y-you have no right to be here!"

He moved toward the chair she'd vacated and sat. Then he picked up the book of poems and flicked through it.

"Byron," he said, a bored tone in his voice. "A mere beginner in the art of seduction."

"Byron's one of the finest poets there is."

"You've not lived 'til you've read the words of Burns," he said. "Byron dresses up his emotions with pretty speeches, but Burns understood the raw sensuality of a coupling. I could teach you, lass. I'm sure ye'd be a willing pupil."

Her breath caught at the flare of lust in his eyes. Anger and indignation warred with her own need, and she pointed at the door.

"Get out," she said. "Leave me in peace. At the very least, you should stand. It's ungentlemanly for a man to remain sitting when a lady is standing in his presence."

"Then come and sit beside me."

"Why can't you just go?" she asked. "I don't believe the owner would care for your presence here."

He closed the book with a snap and dropped it on the floor.

"That's where you're wrong," he said.

"How so?"

He crossed one leg over the other with casual, easy grace. "To whom do you think you've been speaking?"

"To a boorish, uncouth Scotsman!"

He threw back his head and laughed. "I've been called worse by many a woman," he said. He rose to his feet and bowed, clicking his heels together with a snap.

"Permit me to introduce myself," he said. "Fraser Malcolm Alistair MacGregor, thirteenth Duke Molineux, and owner of the property in which you are standing."

Chapter Two

FRASER FOUGHT TO suppress a laugh as the expression on the lass's face turned from righteous indignation to horror.

She concealed her shame well; he'd give her that—and she showed more spirit than most. Did she display as much spirit in the bedchamber?

His body hardened at the thought of grappling with her beneath his bedsheets—the thrill of the chase while they battled for supremacy until she finally yielded.

She regained her composure and straightened her stance, as if to appear taller. He smiled inwardly at her courage. She was small, even for a woman, and had dealt a lucky blow with that vase. The back of his neck still throbbed.

"How do I know you're who you say you are?" she said. "You could be a robber."

"I could ask you the same," he replied. "Shall I summon my lawyer to settle the matter? Or, perhaps the Runners could determine which of us is the criminal."

"The criminal?" Her voice lifted a notch.

"I'm alone, lass," he said, "if that's what you fear."

"I'm not afraid of you."

He moved toward her and caught the faint aroma of French lavender.

"Perhaps, ye're more afraid of yourself," he said.

She tipped her head up to meet his gaze.

She might, to the untrained eye, be described as unremarkable, with hair the color of peat. She had a heart-shaped face and an upturned nose with a determined little mouth, which spoke of an interior forged from steel. But her most arresting quality was her almond-shaped eyes, which were the color of whisky.

And whether she knew it or not, they glittered with arousal.

"If you really are the duke," she said, "then *you're* the criminal for letting this house fall to ruin."

"Bricks and mortar," he said. "Is that all you care about?"

A spark of anger flashed in her eyes. "Of course not!" she said. "I care nothing for mausoleums. It's the living souls that depend upon an idle aristocrat that I care for!"

"Such as?"

"The birds trapped in the aviary," she said, gesturing toward the window. "Nobody has tended to them for four years! Should they be left to rot as consequence for the misfortune of being in the power of your cursed family?"

"Birds?" he said. "Is that all?"

"Men like you live to shoot them out of the sky!" she snorted. "And what about the servants and tenants who rely on you for a living? Four years is plenty of time for dismissed servants without a reference to sink into the gutter and die."

"So, you're laying deaths at my door, now?" he asked.

"Your hand might as well have dealt the blow which killed them," she said. "But you'll continue to hide behind your title and abuse the underprivileged."

"Why in the name of the devil would I do that?"

"Because it's in your blood! The Molineux line is rotten to the core."

"You know nothing about me."

"I don't need to."

"Then you're a madwoman."

She raised her hand, and he caught her wrist and drew her hard against his chest.

"Take your hands off me!"

"Ye gods, lass, you're like a terrier!" He laughed. "All teeth and claws, yapping at a man's ankles. You need taking in hand!"

He circled an arm round her waist, and she drew in a sharp breath as her body molded against his as if it belonged there. A spark of desire flared in her eyes, and her cheeks bloomed that delicious pink which a woman in need could never conceal. He dipped his head until their mouths almost met. She grew still, and her breath caressed his skin. He lowered his gaze to the smooth, porcelain skin of her neck, where a faint pulse rippled at the base of her throat.

His mouth watered in anticipation. The men of his ancestry would mark such fresh, virgin skin as their own, to lay claim to their women.

There was something to be said for the old ways.

He flicked his tongue out and ran it along the seam of her lips. She let out a soft sigh, and he caught the faint taste of warm honey. He withdrew his tongue, and a whimper escaped her. She tilted her head, almost imperceptibly, to bring their mouths closer again, an involuntary act driven by need.

"Tell me what ye want, lass..."

Face flushed, she parted her lips, and he slipped his tongue inside her warm, welcoming mouth. She curled her fingers round his arms and held him close. A groan reverberated through her body as he took ownership of her mouth, devouring her, savoring the sweet taste of fire and honey.

He broke the kiss, and she pressed herself against him, a low groan bubbling in her throat. She pressed her lips against his mouth, and the tip of her tongue grew insistent as she sought entrance. But he withdrew, and a frown creased her forehead.

Clearly, this was a lass who was used to getting what she wanted, a lass who had no use for words when it came to conveying such raw need. He placed his lips against the corner of her mouth, then peppered her chin with a line of feather-light kisses, teasing her mouth with his tongue. She parted her lips again and let out a frustrated little mewl when he did not oblige her demand.

He smiled against her lips. "I'll wager you want my hands on ye now, lass, now ye've had a taste of pleasure."

She stiffened. Her hands, which had clung to him, urging him on, now pushed him away.

He blinked to clear his vision and saw a blur in the corner of his eye before a sharp sting exploded on his face.

"How dare you!" she cried. Hair disheveled, she still bore the look of a woman in need, though she fought to hide it.

"Ye want me, lass," he said. "I know when a

woman's ready for coupling."

The indignation at his crude language rippled through her expression, but not before a wild longing glittered in her eyes. What would it be like to bed her properly—to take her against the hard granite of the highlands, among the heather!

She wrenched herself from his grasp.

"You crude creature!"

"You weren't unwilling, lass."

"You're worse than your predecessor. His only desire was to add to his long list of conquests. But I shall *not* be added to yours. I aspire to better things, and have no time for the baser needs of the savage."

"Oh, a savage, am I?" he said, suppressing the laugh at the struggle so evident in her expression. "Why deny yourself pleasure when you've been fashioned for it?"

"There's more to life than pleasure."

"That's not what you were telling me earlier, lass."

"I said no such thing!"

"Not with your words..." he lowered his voice to a whisper, "...but with your body ye were begging, were ye not?"

She flushed and looked away, instinctively crossing her arms to conceal the twin peaks which had been poking at the muslin of her gown.

"I'll not dignify that question with an answer."

He let out a laugh. "You have no need to, lass. I've already discovered how to turn that sharp little bark into a purr of pleasure."

"I see no point in continuing this conversation," she said. "Rest assured, I'll never darken the doors of this house again, now I've had the misfortune of meeting its owner."

She turned her back and retreated through the door.

"Farewell, my sweet little terrier!"

She increased the pace, uttering a curse as she disappeared through the main doors.

As soon as he established himself in lodgings, he'd make inquiries as to the identity of the hellion. The quality of her gown indicated she had money, but her manner was not that of a lady.

A courtesan, perhaps? And one with an intellect beyond that of the usual predatory female.

With such a quarry to be had, perhaps living in London wouldn't be a hardship after all.

Chapter Three

"I MUST SAY, Delilah, dear, you seem out of sorts today."

Lilah's friend nodded toward the cup in her hand, which had remained untouched.

"Is the tea not to your liking?"

"No, it's delicious, as usual," Lilah said, sipping her drink. Overly sweet, but Anne always indulged her, arguing that Lilah needed to enjoy the luxuries her family could now afford, with little or no guilt.

Which is what *he* had said—the infuriating rogue who possessed the unnerving skill of ascertaining what unsettled Lilah the most. The rogue who understood her basest desires, even more than she did.

"Has something happened?" Anne persisted.

Yes, something had happened. Lilah had almost

given herself to a stranger.

Worse than a stranger. Molineux. The successor to Anne's first husband.

But the last thing Anne needed was a reminder of her first marriage.

Lilah changed the subject.

"Have you visited Mrs. Forbes recently?"

Anne nodded. "She works too hard," she said. "Much like you, Lilah, dear, she seems determined to ignore the pleasures in life. I often tell her she should never have established her sanctuary."

"But if she hadn't," Lilah said, "then not only would disadvantaged women have one less place in which to find shelter, but we'd never have met."

"For which I'm grateful, dearest Delilah."

"As am I," Lilah said. "You're one of the few women who doesn't give me the cut whenever I walk into a ballroom. I can't understand why my brother insists on spending a fortune parading me around prospective suitors when I'd rather earn my fortune writing."

"Have you had any success with your poetry?" Anne asked.

"Not yet," Lilah said, "but Mr. Stock paid me an advance for my latest installment of *Essays on Patriarchy*."

"Should you be writing such material?"

"I don't see why not. Apart from Mr. Stock

and yourself, nobody knows the identity of Jeremiah Smith.

"I found your last essay rather inflammatory," Anne said. "No good can come of making such an overt attack on the aristocracy."

"If it encourages people to think, then I am content."

"What if it encourages them to *act*?" Anne asked. "It takes only a small spark to ignite a flame. The discontent of the masses is the oil that douses the wood of an uprising. Imagine how dreadful the Terrors in France must have been! What if that happened in London?"

Lilah swallowed a mouthful of tea, wrinkling her nose at the taste. "You exaggerate, Anne."

"Wars are won and lost at the command of the written word, not the sword or the pistol," Anne said. "You should stick to poetry."

"Nobody's interested in my poems," Lilah said. "It took me long enough to persuade Mr. Stock to publish my essays. If I were a man, he'd have agreed immediately. I daresay your husband would have no trouble finding someone willing to publish if he wrote poetry."

Anne let out a laugh. "Much as I love my dear Harold, I have to confess, he lacks the talent."

"How is he?" Lilah asked.

"In perfect health," Anne said. "I swear he works almost as hard as your brother. He's in the process of concluding a deal with a distillery owner to sell and distribute whisky, of all things."

"Whisky?"

"He expects demand to increase given the new freedoms in production and distribution," Anne said, "though I understand little of it myself. The owner's an excellent man, though a little— *rugged*." She hesitated as if to continue, then shook her head and gestured toward the teapot. "Another cup?"

"No, thank you."

"But you must stay for supper. Harold will be joining us."

"In which case, I'd be glad to accept."

"Excellent!" Anne said. "Mrs. Bowles has been marinating the pork all day, and the smell coming from the kitchen is enough to make a stone statue salivate."

"It sounds too good to miss."

"It's Harold's favorite," Anne said. "Ah! Here he comes."

The parlor door opened, and Mr. Pelham appeared.

"Harold!" Anne jumped to her feet and crossed the room. Her husband drew her to him for a brief kiss.

"My love," he said. He turned to Lilah. "Miss Hart. A pleasure, as always."

"Delilah is joining us for supper," Anne said.

"Excellent!" he said. "It'll make a four. We

have another guest." He turned and called out. "Come in, old chap. Don't stand on ceremony."

Another man appeared at the doorway, and Lilah caught her breath. Mr. Pelham was a tall man, but his companion towered over him. Clear blue eyes met her gaze, and a smile curled across the lush, sensual mouth. He raised his hand in greeting, a strong hand with long, lean fingers, which two days ago had set her skin on fire with the promise of pleasure.

He rubbed his cheek, the very same cheek she'd slapped, and a twinkle of mischief glittered in his eyes.

"Molineux, old chap," Mr. Pelham said, "permit me to introduce my wife's friend, Miss Delilah Hart. Miss Hart, may I introduce Fraser MacGregor, Duke Molineux."

"Delilah Hart," the newcomer's tongue curled round her name, and he held out his hand. She took it, and he lifted her hand to his lips.

"A beautiful name," he whispered. "Delilah— the woman who brought the strongest of men to his knees."

His breath sent a rush of heat over her skin. She tried to pull free, but he tightened his hold, flicked his tongue out, and traced a line across her hand. His nostrils flared, and a low rumble reverberated in his chest.

"What a delectable perfume," he said, his voice a low whisper. "It reminds me of pleasure shared."

She snatched her hand free, her skin on fire where his lips had been. A wicked smile curled across his lips.

Curse him!

"Miss Hart, is something the matter?" Mr. Pelham asked.

The newcomer winked at her. Curse him, he actually *winked*! As if they shared a dirty secret!

Unable to fight the anger which burned inside, she rounded on Anne's husband.

"Mr. Pelham, do you know what manner of man you've brought here?"

"Of course," Pelham said. "He's my new business partner. And a very fine chap he is."

"He's a Molineux!" Lilah protested. "The latest in a long line of rakes. Who knows how many women he's debauched?"

Rather than show discomposure, the huge Scotsman folded his arms, leaned against the doorframe, and smiled. "You impugn my skills, Miss Hart, if you infer my conquests were unwilling."

"Perhaps you ignored their protests," she retorted.

He let out a chuckle. "I've never known a woman to object," he said. "I've only known her to beg."

"Mr. Pelham," she said. "I will not spend another moment in this man's company. I insist you turn him out."

"Don't be a fool," Pelham said. "You can't dictate to me with your feminist sensibilities. Be reasonable, please."

Lilah turned to her friend. "Anne, you agree with me, don't you? Surely you object to an acquaintance with such a man!"

Anne shook her head. "Delilah, you shouldn't judge him because of his lineage."

"You of all people should understand how rotten that family is. Or perhaps you wish to ingratiate yourself with a duke in order to elevate your social status from being the wife of a commoner?"

"That's enough!" Pelham cried. "Only you could manage to insult three people in a single sentence. If I were your brother, I'd thrash you for such incivility. You're exhibiting just the sort of behavior that will prevent your family from being accepted in society. If your brother knew what a hellion you are…"

"Och, Pelham, leave the lass be."

Lilah jabbed a finger at the huge Scot. "I can defend myself," she said. "I need no help from a rogue."

His lips curled into a smile. "I'm a rogue, am I? I suppose that's better than being a savage."

"You should be taught the error of your ways," Lilah said.

"Likewise," he replied, his smile broadening.

"As I said when we met, you need to be turned over a man's knee."

Swallowing her indignation, Lilah grasped her reticule and almost ran out of the house, his words echoing in her ears.

FRASER COULD HARDLY suppress his laughter as the red-faced lass exited the parlor. A spitfire, certainly, but she had spirit, even if it came hand in hand with a dose of loathing toward his ancestors.

Mrs. Pelham let out a sigh. An attractive, delicately built woman, he'd learned from Pelham that she was the widow of the previous duke and, by all accounts, had suffered at his hands. Miss Hart had an excuse for her dislike of him, but the violence of her reaction spoke of something else.

She wanted him—her body had told him that, loud and clear. And she didn't like it.

And, by the gods, he wanted her.

Delilah…

The name suited her, each syllable rolling off the tongue as he savored his name on her lips.

"Molineux, I must apologize," Pelham said.

Fraser shook his head. "No matter. I believe I rattled her the other day when I caught her prowling around Clayton House."

Mrs. Pelham sighed. "She visits there regularly to tend to the birds in the aviary." She shook her head. "Forgive me, I should have realized…"

"Nevertheless, she had no cause for such incivility," Pelham interrupted. "She may be your friend, my love, but she's foul-tempered with it and harbors an unnatural prejudice against the *ton*. She fancies herself something of a warrior."

"In what way?" Fraser asked.

"Justice for the put-upon, equal rights for women. Probably sick puppies, as well."

"Harold, don't mock my friend," Mrs. Pelham said. "Her heart is in the right place, and she has good reason for her prejudice."

"That may be," Pelham said, "but if her brother knew about today, he'd give her a damned good thrashing."

"Her brother?" Fraser asked.

"She's Dexter Hart's sister," Pelham said. "Or, I should say, *one* of his sisters."

"The banker?"

"The very same."

Dexter Hart, the proprietor of Hart Bank, was rumored to be the most ruthless businessmen in England. Fraser could well believe it, for how else could a man rise from almost nothing to being one of the wealthiest bankers in London, in less than five years?

But because of his humble origins, Hart was

snubbed by half of the ton. According to Pelham, most of the older families refused to bank with Hart, even though he offered competitive lending rates—rates that had tempted Fraser to secure an appointment with the man.

Fraser shook his head. "I imagine even Hart would have trouble controlling that little hellion."

"She wasn't brought up within the confines of society," Mrs. Pelham said, "and therefore doesn't understand why she must abide by its rules."

"I wish Hart luck in his endeavors with her," Pelham said. "It's the worst kept secret in Whites that he's trying to marry his siblings off to titles."

"Perhaps that explains Miss Hart's dislike of the aristocracy," Fraser said. "I imagine if she were instructed to do anything, she'd resolve to do the exact opposite."

"It's not only that," Mrs. Pelham said. "My late husband was not a kind man, as I can testify."

"Anne, my love, there's no need…" A look passed between Pelham and his wife—care and concern on his part, and reassurance on hers.

"There was an incident when Delilah was younger," she continued. "When he was a boy, the late duke used to visit the estate on which the Harts were tenants. He was at Harrow with the eldest son. I don't know the particulars of what happened, for Delilah has not divulged them."

"Dear God!" Fraser said. "Was she harmed?"

"Not in the way you mean," she said, "but it resulted in her brother confronting them, which earned him a thrashing, and the family was evicted shortly after."

Fraser shook his head. "It's no wonder she hates the *ton*," he said, "but it doesn't explain why Hart wishes to ingratiate himself with them."

"He doesn't," she said. "He wants to conquer them. As to my friend, I only tell you so you can understand her. She may be uncivil toward you, but she has good reason."

"Anne, my love…" Pelham warned.

"No, it's all right," Fraser said. "I appreciate your honesty.

She glanced at Fraser, then back to her husband. "Harold, I think I'll retire until dinner is served. I'm rather tired, and I'm sure the two of you have business to discuss."

"Please don't leave on my account, ma'am," Fraser said.

She dipped into a curtsey and smiled, then, after giving her husband a brief kiss, slid out of the room. Pelham crossed the floor and picked up a decanter.

"Drink? It's a rather fine Madeira I imported last year."

Fraser nodded, and Pelham poured two glasses, then sat, motioning Fraser to do likewise. He raised his glass.

"To a successful business venture!"

Fraser lifted his glass. "I'll drink to that."

"So," Pelham said, his gaze fixed on Fraser. "You met Miss Hart at Clayton House?"

"Not two days ago," Fraser said. "She's full of fire. I'll give her that."

Pelham laughed. "She's a hellcat! I'll never understand why women are so different from each other. She's the exact opposite of my Anne."

"I don't know, Pelham," Fraser said. "Women may appear to be different disguises, but beneath the surface, they are all drawn from the same keg—driven by the same needs and desires.

"Perhaps you've yet to encounter the woman to satisfy your needs," Pelham said. "I believe that for every man, there exists the perfect mate—unique to him. The trick, of course, is in identifying your mate and bagging her before she slips away."

"My needs are well satisfied, I assure you," Fraser said.

"Ah, yes," A slow smile stretched across Pelham's mouth. "I hear Mrs. Emma Whitford's *accomplishments* are legendary.

Good lord, could a man not take a mistress without the whole of London gossiping about it?

"Accomplishment in a mistress I can deal with," Fraser said, "but incarceration in the parson's cage I can do well without. I have no intention of being *bagged*."

"But you must marry if you want an heir."

Fraser shook his head. "I wouldn't wish the responsibility of that godforsaken dukedom on anyone. The common man doesn't view the aristocracy with any favor, I assure you. Just look at the French and what they did in the name of equality."

"The French are hotheaded and impetuous," Pelham said. "Not words I'd use to describe the English. If an Englishman had his limbs ripped off by an elephant, he'd find it hard to muster anything more than a small tut of annoyance."

Fraser sighed. "I wish I could believe you, my friend, but the masses have always been ruled by the whims and desires of the powerful. A word to the unwise can do a lot of damage, particularly when portrayed in the popular press. Have you read the *City Chronicle?*"

Pelham nodded. "You refer to the infamous Jeremiah Smith and his *Essays on Patriarchy?*"

"The very same. While I may agree with the refreshing outlook a member of our sex displays, the tone of his article bears an undercurrent of malevolence. Such inflammatory language, in the wrong hands, could incite the mob. We shouldn't fear the swords of the uneducated generals, but the pens of the educated anarchists."

Pelham sipped his drink. "You worry unnecessarily. Besides, being a Scot, you should know a thing or two about mob mentality, given that your countrymen declare wars of independence against our nation on a regular basis.

"What use is war," Fraser said, "when disagreements can more easily be settled if the two sparring figureheads actually talked to each other rather than sent their subjects to engage in mass murder?"

"Have a care," Pelham laughed, "or I might believe you to be Mister Smith, given your anarchic leanings."

"On the contrary," Fraser replied. "Society is built on a backbone of tradition, establishment, and hard work. But it doesn't mean we shouldn't indulge in pleasure, otherwise what's the point in living?"

"Then," Pelham said, "by your philosophy, you should look to producing a son and heir to further the establishment, of which you are a part, whether you like it or not. And you should find yourself a wife. But I'd advise you not to follow the path Dexter Hart intends to tread. Marriage should be more than a business deal to snare a dowry. It should be for love."

"Love can be purchased," Fraser said. "That's what a mistress is for."

"No," Pelham said. "Love bought for hire is temporary. When you fail to pay the rent, you'll find yourself evicted. A courtesan secures her income by persuading her protector that she loves him. A wife should need no persuasion to love you."

"Then, if you were advising me, Pelham, how would you suggest I go about prospecting for a wife?"

"Your title will render your task easy, my friend. At the first ball you attend, you'll find yourself surrounded by young ladies and their overbearing mamas, all vying to outdo each other and secure the hand of the newest duke in town."

"Then remind me to refuse every invitation forthwith," Fraser said. "I have no wish to surround myself with young ladies."

A wicked smile curled across Pelham's mouth.

"What about hellcats?"

A small spike of lust pricked at Fraser's body, and his breeches became too tight. He crossed his legs in an attempt to hide the evidence of his arousal. But his companion's laugh told him he'd failed.

"Our little hellcat is determined not to indulge in any form of luxury," Pelham said. "She says it only serves to affirm the distinction between the rich and the poor."

"Hardly the worst crime a young woman can commit," Fraser said.

"I could forgive her that," Pelham said, "were it not for her determination to spoil everyone else's pleasure."

Pleasure…

Fraser's skin tightened at the memory her body squirming under his hands, those lush, pink lips, parted in surprise and wonder as he gave her a taste of pleasure.

"She's determined to hate all men—single men, at least," Pelham continued. "But perhaps given how her season started, she can be forgiven."

"How her season started?"

"She caught her suitor in an uncompromising position with another woman," Pelham said. "Let's just say that the delectable Mrs. Whitford is a very—popular—woman."

"Good lord!"

"Had she been in possession of a knife, I daresay the man's ancestral line would have ended with him," Pelham said, "and, knowing Miss Hart, she'd have fashioned his balls into a pair of earrings." Pelham rose from his seat. "But I believe it's time to change the subject and discuss whisky rather than wildcats. I'm anxious to hear about your plans for using brandy casks to mature the liquor in."

Fraser nodded and held his glass out for Pelham to refill. At last, the real business of the evening could take place.

But as Pelham rattled on about his ledgers, Fraser's concentration slipped.

What would it be like to teach that hellcat about pleasure? Though he had a long way to go to convince his potential business partners that whisky was worth investing in, a greater challenge now tempted him.

To have Miss Hart beg to warm his bed.

As his Da had always said…

We MacGregors relish a challenge.

Oh, aye. He'd relish it very much.

Chapter Four

"SIT UP, DELILAH, dear. You want to make a good impression on Sir Thomas."

Lilah shifted in her seat, while Dorothea poured the tea.

Dexter remained still, his dark gaze focused on Lilah, disapproval in his eyes.

Having never known their parents who'd died shortly after she was born, Lilah viewed Dexter as a combination of father, brother, and, more recently, jailer. As head of the family, he expected obedience from the rest of his siblings. Dorothea considered herself the family matriarch, by virtue of her age. But in reality, Thea was a doormat, who deferred to Dexter on every occasion.

Even now, while undertaking a task as simple as pouring tea, Lilah's sister looked to their brother for approval.

Lilah rolled her eyes. "Don't worry," she said. "I can handle *Tommie Tiptoes*."

"Delilah!" Thea protested.

Dexter's expression hardened. "You'll show Sir Thomas the respect he's due."

When angry, Dexter lowered his voice rather than raised it. His detachment and control unnerved Lilah more than if he'd possessed a temper as hot as hers. A temper, driven by emotion, could be fought on equal terms. But to experience emotion, one must be in possession of a soul—something Dexter was sorely lacking.

"Sir Thomas is pleasant enough," Lilah said. "I'd go so far as to say he's the pleasantest specimen of our acquaintance in London. But, as you've said yourself, Dex, he's a man of middling rank, middling fortune, and middling character. Surely you'd aspire to something greater in your quest to sell me off to the nobility?"

"I had higher hopes for you," Dexter said, "but given that business with Lord Granville, you should count your blessings that Sir Thomas is willing to call on you."

"Is it my fault that I caught Granville with his breeches round his ankles, rutting some whore?"

Thea set her cup down with a clatter. "Delilah! Mind your language."

"Granville's morals may not be your responsibility," Dexter said, "but in wandering off on your own during that party to find him, you tarnished your reputation," he said. "Given that you both returned looking disheveled, it's no wonder the world believes you'd allowed him to anticipate the wedding night in a bid to snare his hand."

"As if I'd be so foolish," Lilah snorted. "He looked a mess because I'd slapped his face!"

"In London society, appearance is everything," Dexter said. "Truth is irrelevant."

"Then we should tear society down," Lilah said.

Dexter sighed and shook his head.

"Your brother wants what's best for you—for all of us," Thea said. "If you understood that, you wouldn't fight him at every turn. You know how hard it is for us to gain acceptance in society."

"Why should we ingratiate ourselves?" Lilah asked. "They hate us, and they always will, for we have no titles."

"Not at present," Thea said. "But your brother has been recommended for a knighthood. He's worked hard to better our fortunes, and the next step is to raise our position in society. He does it for us, Lilah. All you have to do is smile and be courteous. That's not much to ask, is it?"

"It's more than that," Lilah said. "You want me to relinquish my freedom. Neither of you understands my feelings. You think my dream of becoming a writer is a whim to be cast aside when a man decides he wants to own me."

"I do understand," Dexter said. "But in order to get what we want, we must first take responsibility and demonstrate that we deserve it. It's called growing up."

"Demonstrate to who, Dexter?" Lilah asked. "To you? Must I gratify you before I'm permitted to be happy? Is that why you drove Devon out of the house?"

"Our brother is a grown man," Dexter said. "He's free to make his own choices."

"Because he's a man?"

"Society doesn't frown upon a grown man lodging on his own."

"And you were glad to see him go," Lilah said. "A disfigured brother might risk your social standing."

Dexter's lips thinned, and his knuckles whitened as he curled his fingers round his teacup. Thea frowned at Lilah and shook her head in warning.

"Our brother is welcome here," he said. "He's a part of our family."

"Then what about Daisy?" Lilah asked.

The teacup shattered, and brown liquid splashed over Dexter's breeches. Thea leapt to her feet and let out a shriek.

"Jane! Jane! Come quickly, there's been an accident! The master's spilled his tea!"

Dexter lowered his gaze to his soaking

breeches. Liquid dripped off his lap, but he barely reacted.

Did nothing rattle him?

A maid rushed into the parlor, brandishing a cloth.

"Jane, help the master," Thea said.

Dexter raised his hand. "No, I'll deal with it." He fixed his gaze on Lilah. "And then, I'll deal with you."

He rose and exited the room.

"Jane, dear, could you clear up the mess, then bring in a fresh pot of tea?" Thea asked. "And some of Mrs. Brown's fruitcake, I think.

The maid bobbed a curtsey and set about picking up the shards of porcelain. After she left, Thea took Lilah's hand.

"You shouldn't vex your brother, so," she said. "You know he doesn't like to speak of Daisy."

"Why not?" Lilah asked. "Dex bores me to tears with lectures on how we must remain united as a family. Why, then, are there five of us, but one has been exiled into obscurity, and the other cannot bear to live here?"

"It's not that simple," Thea said. "Dexter may be harsh, but he has his reasons. While you played with dolls, he devoted his life to raising our fortunes. He blames himself for what happened to Daisy. But it's done, and there's no sense in dwelling on it. Not when Dexter's worked so hard to secure our future. He's not being unreasonable in expecting you to play your part."

"You even sound like him, Thea," Lilah said. "Can you not think for yourself?"

"I speak the truth," Thea replied.

"Then why don't *you* subject yourself to a Season?"

"I'm twenty-seven," Thea said. "I can best serve our cause by chaperoning you. You're the one with the best chance of securing a good match."

"And you consider Sir Thomas a good match?"

"He's very handsome," Thea said. "Imagine what it would be like to be on his arm at a ball!" She hesitated and lowered her gaze. For a moment, Lilah thought she saw disappointment in her sister's eyes—disappointment that the elevation of their fortunes had come too late for her to hope for anything other than a position as a chaperone—or a spinster aunt.

Then she looked up again and smiled. "He possesses a rare combination—a title, affability, and an interest in commerce. And he seems to like *you* a great deal, Delilah."

"We share the same views on society, that's all," Lilah said. "But despite what he says about reforming the aristocracy, he lacks the character to lead. He hangs on to Dex's coat-tails even more than you."

Thea rolled her eyes. "Why must you needle everyone you disagree with, Delilah? We cannot all be leaders. If Sir Thomas chooses to follow where others direct, then he'd make the perfect husband for a headstrong woman who wishes to control her destiny."

Lilah shook her head. "You mean…"

"I mean," Dorothea said, lowering her voice, "that if you want to pursue a career as a writer, while also satisfying our brother, then marriage to Sir Thomas may be the most effective means of achieving that. While you still have choices left open to you, Delilah, you must choose wisely. And that choice may be to accept his courtship."

"Assuming Sir Thomas would want to court a commoner."

"He's one of the few men of society to whom birth is not everything," Thea said. "But if you wish to secure him, you should refrain from cursing, at least until after you've signed the marriage register when the poor man has gone beyond the point of no return."

"I have no intention of *securing* anyone," Lilah said. "A man should want me for what I am, not what he wishes me to be."

Dorothea laughed. "In that, I agree with you. You'll need a husband prepared to put up with your rudeness."

No, she didn't. She needed a man with spirit,

who could meet her on equal terms. A man to spar with, a man who set boundaries, then challenged her to breach them, with the lure of danger in his eyes if she dared to defy him.

A man such as *him*—the infuriating Scot who'd sent a thrill through her bones as he threatened to take her over his knee.

She closed her eyes to relive the memory of their first encounter—the faint aroma of earth and mountain air, clear blue eyes before which her innermost desires were laid bare. Her breath hitched at the memory of his hands on her skin—warm, commanding hands.

"Delilah?"

Lilah opened her eyes.

"I do believe you're blushing!" Thea said. "Perhaps the prospect of Sir Thomas's company is not so distasteful after all?"

Before Lilah could respond, the door swung open. Dexter stood in the doorway with Sir Thomas Tipton.

With thick blonde hair fashionably cut, perfectly proportioned features, and pale blue eyes, Sir Thomas looked every bit the fairytale hero. He lifted his lips into a smile, and Thea rose to her feet, her cheeks blooming a delicate shade of rose.

"Sir Thomas, how pleasant!" she cried. "Delilah and I were just saying how we were looking forward to your visit."

Sir Thomas bowed and snapped his heels together.

"Miss Hart, a pleasure, as always," he said. "And Miss Delilah."

"Please, come in," Thea said. "Dexter, will you be joining us?"

"I don't think so," Lilah said. "You're too busy, aren't you, Dex? And you've already provided your valet with enough work." She turned to their guest. "Your suit is very elegant, Sir Thomas. The jacket goes very well with your breeches. It's terribly important to wear the right colored breeches when taking tea."

"Sir Thomas, if you'll excuse me," Dexter said, "I have some business to attend to. But my sisters will take the greatest care of you. Won't you, Delilah?"

Dexter shot Lilah a warning look, and she gave him her sweetest smile. "Of course, dear brother," she said. She gestured to the wing-back chair by the fireplace—the chair Dexter was always so very particular about being *his*. "Do sit down, Sir Thomas, and let me help you to tea."

Dexter exhaled sharply and took his leave.

"Sugar, Sir Thomas?" Lilah asked.

"Four, please."

She wrinkled her nose and dropped four lumps into a cup and handed it to him. Their hands touched, and he smiled and brushed his thumb against hers.

But try as she might, Lilah felt nothing from his touch. Not like…

"What news, Sir Thomas?" Thea asked.

"Nothing much," he said. "Yet another duke has arrived to strut around London and declare himself master of the world."

"And who might that be?" Thea asked.

"Molineux."

"Molineux!" Thea exclaimed. "Hadn't that line died out with the twelfth duke?"

"Apparently not, Miss Hart," he said. "Though perhaps it would have been better if it had. The present incumbent is not what I'd call a gentleman. He's a merchant. And a Scot."

"Don't you aspire to commerce yourself?" Lilah asked.

"Not at the expense of my estate, and not with illicit goods. Only a few decades ago, his countrymen were savages living in the wilderness. I swear I saw dirt under his fingernails. And he reeked of cheap perfume, most likely from frittering away the hours rolling around with harlots."

In that respect, Sir Thomas was probably right. No man as potent as *him* would live like a monk.

Lilah swallowed the stab of jealousy. Her hand shook, and she set her teacup aside.

"Is something the matter, Delilah?" Thea asked.

Lilah flushed and shook her head. "N-no," she said, avoiding her sister's gaze. "Sir Thomas, you said he deals in illicit goods?"

"Moonshine, Miss Delilah," Sir Thomas said.

"Moonshine?"

"Whisky. Disgusting stuff, by all accounts. The kind of liquor only good for etching into metal."

"I wouldn't know," Lilah said. "I've never tried it."

"I'd suggest you confine your tastes to a safer beverage," Sir Thomas said.

"Such as tea?" Lilah asked.

"Yes, Miss Delilah. A man's propensity to drink is his biggest failing. It renders him weak and incompetent. One can only imagine what it does to a woman."

Thea nodded. "I agree."

"Quite so," Sir Thomas replied. He glanced at Lilah. "When I marry, I'd want my wife to refrain from indulging in liquor."

Lilah rose to her feet, and Sir Thomas scrambled to do likewise. She crossed the floor to the bureau and picked up Dexter's decanter of port, then returned to her seat and poured a little into her teacup.

"Delilah!" Thea said. "You forget your manners."

"Oh, I'm sorry," Lilah said. "Would you like some port with your tea, Sir Thomas?"

He frowned, then smoothed his expression into a smile. "No, thank you, Miss Delilah."

"Do you object to my indulging in a little?"

"No, Miss Delilah," he said, "but I have no objection to anything you wish to do."

Yes—Sir Thomas would be the perfect husband to ensure Lilah maintained complete control of her life. Handsome, titled, and biddable.

In short, what most men wanted in a wife.

He'd give her everything she wanted, everything she asked of him.

But would he give her what she *needed*?

Chapter Five

"Y OU'LL LIKE DEXTER Hart, Molineux. Of course, the pertinent question is whether he likes *you.*"

Fraser turned from the window, which looked out over the Strand, and smiled at his friend. "You certainly have a high opinion of him, Pelham," he said. "Perhaps that's because he's funding your business."

"You could say I'm funding his," Pelham said. "Hart's a stickler over the repayments. And he's not one to lend money out of kindness."

"But he's a fair man, yes?"

"You'll find none fairer," Pelham said. "But kindness and fairness are not the same. If anyone's the living embodiment of that fact, it's Dexter Hart."

Pelham opened his pocket watch, then

snapped it shut.

"He'll be with us in exactly two minutes."

"What do you mean?" Fraser asked.

Pelham smiled. "Hart's a stickler for punctuality. He extols the virtues of arriving precisely on time. Lateness is to be abhorred, but an early arrival presents an equal lack of civility."

"An early arrival shows eagerness, which is to be applauded," Fraser said.

"Not if the other party is unready." Pelham gave Fraser a wicked smile. "Of course, an unexpected early arrival has its benefits. I once paid a visit to my wife's bedchamber a full half-hour before she was ready to leave for a soiree hosted by Countess Stiles."

"And was your eagerness applauded?"

Pelham let out a laugh. "Let me answer by saying that we arrived at the soiree almost two hours late. I believe my *eagerness* was viewed by my wife with pleasure."

"You're a fortunate man," Fraser said.

Pelham sighed, his expression akin to love-sickness. "Anne is the epitome of perfection."

For Pelham, perhaps—her sweet-tempered meekness would suit most men. But Fraser preferred a woman with a little backbone.

A feisty wee terrier to challenge him at every turn, until she yielded after a well-fought battle…

"Of course, Anne's friend is a charming creature," Pelham said, mischief in his eyes. "I'm sure

Miss Hart would also relish a little—*spontaneity*—in her intercourse with others."

Curse him! Even the mention of her excited Fraser.

"I daresay her brother would have something to say about that," Fraser said. "Unless Hart's one of those businessmen who exerts his prowess in the boardroom, then returns home and leaves his masculinity at the door to be ruled by the women inside."

"On the contrary, I assure you," a deep voice said.

Pelham crossed the floor, hand outstretched to greet the newcomer in the doorway, as a clock struck three. The man shook Pelham's hand, but his attention was on Fraser.

He was tall, though not as tall as Fraser, and he filled the doorframe with a commanding presence as if he'd long-since established that the world existed to serve him. His hair was cut shorter than fashionable, in a severe style that negated any softness that might be found in his features. Black as night, it seemed to absorb the light. Deep-set, clear blue eyes regarded Fraser with a cold expression. He lowered his gaze, then lifted it slowly, as if sizing Fraser up, inch by inch. Then he lifted a corner of his upper lip as if to convey that he'd scrutinized Fraser and found him wanting.

Hart's coloring might differ from his sister,

but Fraser recognized the same spirit, hidden beneath the man's cold exterior—and expression around the mouth which, in a man, would be considered resolute and determined, but in a woman, stubborn.

"Hart, old boy," Pelham said. "May I introduce you to Duke Molineux?"

The newcomer remained still, his eyes narrowing.

"A pleasure, Mr. Hart," Fraser said.

Hart raised an eyebrow. "I thought we were here to discuss business, not pleasure," he said. "And I wonder why a man of your rank would find it necessary to be accompanied by another. Or, indeed, why you'd not prefer to bank with Coutts, rather than me."

Ah, there it was, the trace of bitterness. Hart might disguise it well, but his lack of social status affected him.

"Mr. Hart, I'm here in my capacity as a businessman, not a duke," Fraser said.

Hart blinked. "In my experience, the two are one and the same when it comes to the need for a loan."

"Not necessarily," Fraser said. "Most businessmen will do everything in their power to honor the terms of the loan. A gentleman is more likely to declare his aversion to dealing with anything so vulgar as money, then use that as his justification for defaulting."

Hart's mouth twitched, and for a brief moment, Fraser saw the ghost of a smile before it vanished. Then he gestured toward a chair in front of the mahogany desk, which dominated the room.

"Please, sit. Both of you. Would you like some wine?"

Fraser shook his head. "I've no taste for it. I prefer whisky."

Hart rolled his eyes. "Is that not rather restricted, given the variety of wines that exist?" He poured a glass and handed it to Pelham.

"Not all whiskies taste the same," Fraser said. "I daresay there are more varieties in Scotland than there are wines in the whole of France.

"Forgive me," Hart said, "but I fail to understand how a simple grain in Scotland could exhibit as wide a variety in taste as the many different grapes to be found in France. You cannot expect me to lend to a business I don't understand."

"Then I must enhance your understanding," Fraser said. "There's a market ready and waiting, and with the new freedoms, I can now legitimately serve that market."

"The men of my acquaintance prefer port or brandy," Hart said. "You may believe you can sell your product to the moneyed of London, but first, you must sell the concept to me. What's so special about the grain?"

"The grain is only part of the process," Fraser said. "There are three further elements which can be used to render the taste unique."

"And they are?"

"Peat, water, and wood, Mr. Hart. The more peat, the smokier the flavor."

Hart wrinkled his nose. "I can't say that sounds appealing."

"The peat is an acquired taste," Fraser said. "A true Scot will always appreciate the taste of his homeland. The weak-bellied prefer a less peaty flavor, so, of course, I have adapted the quantities to ensure the liquor is better suited to an Englishman's tastes."

Hart set his mouth into a hard line. "So, you believe in compromising your integrity for material gain?"

Was the man deliberately trying to goad him?

Pelham lifted the wineglass to his lips, a smile in his eyes. Fraser wasn't going to get any help from his friend. If he wanted to win Hart over, he'd have to do it single-handed.

"I believe whisky the finest liquor in the world," Fraser said, "but if I'm to educate the world on its merits, I must first cater to their palates. I liken it to a governess who, when presented with a new charge, gives him the simplest mathematical conundrum, to avoid overtaxing his underdeveloped brain."

Pelham spluttered beside him, then set his

glass aside. Fraser smiled to himself.

First battle to me, Mr. Hart.

Hart folded his arms and leaned forward. "Why should I lend you money, Your Grace?"

"Your rates are competitive," Fraser said.

"Is that all?"

"You also understand business."

"You could say that of the partners at Coutts."

Fraser nodded. "But it's you I've come to see."

"You do realize my rates are competitive because I am more selective when it comes to lending," Hart said. "Most other bankers, when they see a high-risk investment, will add a premium to the interest they charge. But I'm not in the business of taking undue risks when it comes to a loan. Have you considered searching for a partner instead?"

Fraser shook his head. "MacGregor's is a family business."

"A partnership would reduce the risk," Hart said, "whereas a loan increases the risk, due to the fixed cost of servicing it."

"How so?"

"Let me explain the risk," Hart said, his mouth twitching into a smile, "in the manner of a governess teaching her charge about financing a business."

Despite his discomfort, Fraser found himself

holding begrudging respect for the man.

"Let's say you forecast a profit of two thousand pounds," Hart said, "and you're servicing a loan at the cost of eight hundred a year, your final return is twelve hundred. But what if you exaggerated your product's popularity, and your business profits are only half what you expect, at one thousand? You still need to service the loan of eight hundred, and you're left with only two hundred. That's one-sixth, Molineux. Your profits halve, but your return shrinks by a greater degree."

"And what if the profits are higher than forecasted?" Fraser challenged.

"Most businessmen overestimate their abilities," Hart said. He closed his eyes, then opened them and rose to his feet. "Forgive me, Your Grace, but I shall not be offering you finance. I wish you well in finding another backer."

"Hart, old boy, you'll not reconsider?" Pelham asked.

Hart frowned. "If I'm able to find a client willing to provide the funds, I can broker a deal," he said. "For a fee, naturally."

"Naturally," Fraser echoed. Hart glanced at the clock. "Forgive me, I have another appointment," he said.

Fraser reached inside his jacket pocket, pulled out a flask, and set it on the desk.

Hart made no move to pick it up. "What is

that?"

"It's a sample of my whisky," Fraser said. "Only three years old, but I believe it's of sufficient smoothness to be comparable to the liquor I intend to sell once the distillery is running at full capacity."

"Three years," Hart said. "I take it that means it was brewed outwith the law?"

"Before the Excise Act came into force, yes," Fraser replied. "Therefore, not only is it a symbol of goodwill, it's also a mark of my trust."

"What do you intend me to do with it?"

"I'd prefer you to drink it," Fraser said. "I won't take offense if you give it to your cook for use in a syllabub. Though, grant me leave to feel somewhat peeved if you gave it to your butler to clean your brass with."

Hart uncorked the flask and sniffed the contents. "Not altogether unpleasant," he said. It smells too good to be used on my brass." He smiled. "Perhaps I'll reserve it for the silverware."

He held his hand out. Fraser took it, and for a moment, the two men stared at each other as Hart increased the pressure. Then he released Fraser's hand and called for the footman who ushered them out of the building.

As they stepped out onto the Strand, Fraser let out a curse.

"Damn the man!"

Pelham laughed. "He likes you, Molineux."

"How can you tell?"

"Because you're still standing. Come on, I think we deserve a drink."

Halfway down the street, Fraser turned to look at the building they'd just exited, and he discerned the silhouette of a man in the window of the office.

If that was how Dexter Hart treated the people he liked, then God help his enemies.

Chapter Six

LILAH TOSSED A piece of bread into the water. A line of birds veered toward her in the manner of a marching army—one large, white general leading the patrol, followed by four soldiers.

A terrier appeared and yapped at the birds. The adult swan hissed and reared out of the water, flapping its wings.

A voice called out, and the dog scampered toward a rotund lady dressed in dark purple silk, and Lilah recognized Lady de Bron.

She had, since Lilah's arrival in London, taken delight in snubbing her entire family. Now that Lilah was embarking on her first Season, she'd given her the cut direct at three parties. To women like Lady de Bron, birth was everything, no matter how wealthy Dexter might be.

But from what Dexter had said only last week, Lord de Bron was in financial straits, with multiple creditors foreclosing. The man had come to Dex cap in hand, begging for a loan, at which point, her brother had said he'd taken as much delight in evicting the lord from his offices as the lady had taken in insulting Lilah.

Dex may be stern and unforgiving, but at times he proved he wasn't a complete arse. His desire for retribution for wrongdoing toward all members of his family, at least, meant that the *ton's* bullies were reluctant to insult him publicly.

Lilah smiled to herself. Dex was right in his view of the world. The aristocracy was losing its grip on power, and in the not too distant future, a new age would dawn—an age of commerce and industry where a man's ability to earn a living for himself and foster occupations among the working class would garner greater respect than his ability to recite his ancestral line back more than ten generations.

Which was why Dex and Sir Thomas were friends. Sir Thomas was the first member of society to publicly welcome an acquaintance with Lilah and her family. And he shared her views on the need for the system of the aristocracy to be replaced by a world based on merit.

Dexter would welcome Sir Thomas as a brother-in-law. And he was the least repugnant of all the young men she'd been obliged to spend time with at all these tedious parties and soirees Dex had taken her to.

He'd be a safe husband. Safe and respectable.

But was a life worth living if there were no risks to be taken? Passion could only be achieved through risk and adventure, and Sir Thomas would never ignite the kind of passion that shatters hearts and moves the heavens. Not like…

As she watched the swans disappear along the Serpentine, the skin on the back of her neck prickled with anticipation, and the scent of wood and spices filled the air.

"They're not unlike the eagles at home," a deep voice spoke from behind. Ignoring the thrill which rippled across her skin, she turned around.

He towered over her, framed by the light of the setting sun, and for a moment, his hair formed a golden halo around his face.

He gestured toward the retreating swans. "Beautiful creatures, but their beauty hides such savagery."

"Swans are nothing like eagles, Your Grace," Lilah said. "An eagle hunts its prey. The swan was protecting herself and her young from a terrier."

"And, as we both know, the terrier can be a feisty wee soul, who strikes fear into the heart of even the strongest opponent…" he smiled, his eyes glittering with amusement, "…even if she's a head smaller than the man she spars with."

She opened her mouth to reply, and he raised

a hand.

"Shall we declare a truce, Miss Hart?" he asked. "I've no wish to fight you, stimulating though that may be. I am in need of friends."

"A duke should have no trouble in securing friendship here," she said.

"That rather depends on how discerning he is in his choice of friends," he replied. "Perhaps you adopt a similar level of discernment, lass, for you seem to be alone this morning."

"I'm here with my family," she said.

"Then why can't I see them?"

"Sometimes, I'm in need of solitude. I often find the company of others a little overwhelming."

"Then, I shall take my leave."

"No!" she cried. He raised his eyebrows, and she swallowed her embarrassment. "At least, don't go on my account," she said. "I was about to leave. I've been standing here too long, and it's getting cold."

He held out his arm. "I would be honored to accompany you until you rejoin your family. And you have my word that I will take no offense if you find my company overly oppressive or overly *stimulating*."

Unable to fight the compulsion to touch him again, she took his arm.

"That's better," he said. "Tell me, Miss Hart, what's a young woman such as yourself doing in a public place unchaperoned?"

"I care little for such matters," she said.

"You should care," he said. "Think of your reputation."

He might pretend to be different, but deep down, he was like the rest of them, obsessed with reputation and social status. But at least it lessened her guilt over the defamatory statements she made about the Molineux family in her *Essays in Patriarchy.*

"Why must a woman be made to value her reputation so much?" she asked.

"Because, like it or not, and I happen to like it not, in order to survive in the world, we must abide by its rules to some extent. A ruined reputation can destroy a woman's life."

She snorted. "I don't care what the preening peahens of society think of me."

He let out a laugh. "That much is clear, lass. But consider those around you. It's a sad fact that a woman's ruination damages the lives of her loved ones, especially her sisters. No doubt, your brother would agree."

"Dorothea's reputation is quite safe, I assure you," Lilah said.

"And your other sister?"

Her stomach tightened. *How did he know about Daisy?* She turned away, her cheeks warming.

"Forgive me," he said. "I see I've broached an

unwelcome topic of conversation."

"But it's clearly a topic which others are content to speak of. Might I ask who you were discussing my family with?"

Now it was his turn to look uncomfortable. "I heard mention of it at Lady de Bron's card party."

"Why on earth would you spend time with that woman?"

"I had no idea how disagreeable she was until I spent an evening in her company."

"And what did she say about us?"

"I'm not one to repeat gossip, Miss Hart."

"But you'll allude to it and leave me wanting."

He smiled. "Very well, she said that your parents displayed a singular lack of imagination when naming you all. And she referred to a sister who disappeared in suspicious circumstances and a brother who is never seen and refuses to speak to his family."

"Devon prefers to live alone," she said. "He dislikes company other than his closest acquaintances, but he does have friends. More than Dexter, at least."

"Then, perhaps Mr. Hart should widen his circle of friends."

"You'll struggle to secure a friendship with Dex," she said. "Even the best of men would find it difficult, for he trusts no one."

He placed his hand on his chest in a gesture of mock hurt. "You wound me, Miss Hart, if you think me not a good man."

"I said the *best* of men, Your Grace, not a good man."

"Then I'll take comfort in knowing that while you do not consider me the best of men, at least you consider me to be a good one."

"I have yet to see evidence of that," she retorted.

His body shook with laughter. "I must say the ladies of my acquaintance in London are proving more of an intellectual challenge than I'd anticipated," he said. "Mrs. Pelham, for example, has a little more character than the—what did you call them?—ah yes! *Preening peahens*."

"Anne is an exception," Lilah said. "I'm astonished at how level-headed she is given what she endured at the hands of your predecessor."

"My predecessor?"

"The twelfth duke was not kind. But given his ancestry, it was not unexpected."

He stiffened and lowered his arm.

"I must strive to overcome your prejudice."

"Prejudice?" she snorted. "You're a man with money and a title. What can you know of prejudice compared to a woman?"

"Like yourself?" he asked. "My dear Miss Hart, consider your privileges. You'll never want for food, warmth, or shelter from the elements.

When the time comes, your brother will choose a husband for you, and you'll settle into the comfortable life of a society lady with a litter of children to occupy yourself with. What can you have to complain about regarding prejudice?"

Indignation swelled within her at his assumption that her primary objective was to secure a husband.

"I've no intention of shackling myself to the whims of a man for some time yet," she said. "I'm interested in far more than the securing of a home and the procreation of children!"

A passing couple stopped and stared.

"Well, *really!*" the woman cried. The man with her steered her off the path as if afraid Lilah's presence might taint her.

Lilah glanced at her companion. Though he looked straight ahead, his eyes shone with mirth, and his lips were curled into a lop-sided smile.

"So, Miss Hart, what do you wish to do, if procreation has no appeal?"

"I shan't tell you," she said. "You'll only laugh."

He stopped and turned to face her, and her body jolted at the intensity of his eyes.

"You have my word. I won't laugh."

"I want to write," she said. "Poetry—words from the heart which express the soul. But nobody will read my poems, let alone publish them. It seems as if fiction is the province of men."

"I beg to differ," he said. "What about Mrs. Radcliffe? I understand she's a favorite among young ladies who dream of being rescued from abomination by a dashing hero."

"I have yet to find even one editor willing to consider my poems."

"Perhaps I can assist."

"How so?" she asked.

"The trick in any business is to ascertain what the other party wants or needs. If they believe you can service that need, then they'll do business with you. It's a matter of discovering what that need is and finding a cost-efficient way to provide it."

"You mean bribery?"

"Depending on your outlook, all business transactions are a form of bribery, Miss Hart. But I'd be happy to help in any way that I can."

"Why?"

He shrugged. "I'm fond of poetry, and though I consider Burns the only poet worth reading, I'll make an exception for you, Miss Hart. The sponsorship of a duke cannot harm your chances of success."

"I've no wish to gain recognition by foul means."

"I can help you to secure an audience," he said. "Recognition would arise from the quality of your work. You could always choose a male *nom de plume* if you feel your sex is a barrier."

"I don't know…"

"At least consider it, Miss Hart," he said. "The offer is there and will stand indefinitely, but I shall take no offense if you decline." He smiled. "I must admit, I'd relish reading poetry as light relief from the effluent, which fills some of the newspapers."

"Such as?"

"Have you heard of Jeremiah Smith?" he asked.

"N-no."

Realistically, Lilah was telling the truth. How could she have heard of Jeremiah Smith if he and she were the same person?

"He writes for the *City Chronicle*," he said. "His last article was a shallow attempt at wit, likening the line of Molineuxs to the ancient Pharaohs who inbred their way into insanity. What I first thought was going to be a series of remarkable critiques on our patriarchal society has turned into cheap sensationalism. You should read his work. It's a prime example of how *not* to write."

Before Lilah could answer, a couple approached them. The Honorable Sarah Francis was on her sixth Season, an impressive record, but not one to be proud of. Her father, Viscount Francis, was rumored to have exhausted his funds in his attempts to get her off his hands.

"Molineux! How pleasant to see you!"

Lilah's companion stopped. "I don't believe I've had the pleasure, Mr...."

"*Viscount* Francis," the man said. "We were introduced at Whites. May I present my daughter, the Honorable Sarah Francis?"

The lady inclined her head and held out her hand. Fraser took it and bowed.

"Charmed."

"As am I," she replied.

"Forgive me, Miss Francis, I have an appointment," he said, "but perhaps we may meet again."

"I do hope so." Her voice bore a note of desperation identical to her father's.

Fraser released her hand and steered Lilah back along the path. After about ten paces, she heard a snort of laughter.

"What's the matter?" she asked.

"It never ceases to amuse me to observe how certain individuals simper over the hands of those they believe will be useful to them," he said. "The pleasure is magnified one hundredfold when I find myself the direct recipient of a desperate viscount's simpering, and that of his horse-faced daughter."

"Viscount Francis has some influence," Lilah said. "You'd find his friendship to your advantage."

He chuckled. "You're as ridiculous as they

are, lass, if you believe me foolish enough to fall for such insincerity. What do the people of London see when they look at me? Half of them would spit in the face of the Scotsman, and the other half would prostrate themselves at the feet of the duke."

"And which do you prefer?"

He stopped walking and lifted her hand to his lips. A thrill coursed through her as his hot breath caressed her skin.

"Neither," he said. "I'd rather endure the frank rudeness of a wee terrier."

"You think to insult me?"

His mouth curled into a smile, and a spark of danger shone in his eyes.

"Of course not, lass," he said. "But I'll wager you'd prefer the raw honesty of a Highlander over the insincerity of a fop."

He took her wrist and caressed her skin with his thumb in a light, tender gesture, which sent a firebolt of need through her.

"Shall I be honest, Miss Hart?" He lowered his voice. "I think ye're a woman in need of pleasure."

"Nonsense!" she said, her voice tight. "The pursuit of pleasure is the origin of the evils of society."

"Strange words for a young woman," he said. "Do you really think that life is there to be denied? Why should we merely *exist* when we can *live* instead?"

"What do you mean?"

"I think ye know what I mean, lass."

He drew her close, and his eyes darkened. Her heart fluttered at the hunger in his expression.

She parted her lips in anticipation and tipped her head up. She only had to move a little closer...

"Delilah!"

Dorothea's voice broke the spell, and she withdrew from his grasp.

Her brother and sister stood before them. Dexter's brow was furrowed as his gaze passed from Lilah to her companion. Thea's appraisal, though just as searching, was considerably less critical.

"Delilah, perhaps you'd care to explain yourself," Dexter said. His voice held an edge of steel, and he moved closer, his body casting a shadow across the path.

Lilah turned to her companion. "Your Grace, may I present my brother and sister, Mr. Dexter Hart and Miss Dorothea Hart? Dexter, Dorothea, this is Fraser MacGregor, thirteenth Duke Molineux."

"Yes, I know who he is," Dexter said, "and I *want* to know why you're in his company, unchaperoned."

"Forgive me, Mr. Hart," Fraser said. "I happened upon your sister a short while ago and offered to accompany her until she rejoined her family."

"You know him, Dex?" Lilah asked.

Dexter's eyes narrowed.

Fraser exchanged a glance with Dexter, then smiled. "Mr. Pelham was kind enough to introduce us shortly after I arrived in London."

"Have you been long in London, Your Grace?" Thea asked.

"Almost a month."

"And what do you think of it? How does it fare in comparison to Edinburgh? Your accent is Scottish, yes?"

"I've never been to Edinburgh, Miss Hart. I'm afraid I'd be considered something of the savage, for I prefer the wildness of the Highlands to the confines of a city."

Thea smiled. "Do you dislike London?"

"Not all of it," he replied. "I have found much to admire here."

His gaze settled on Lilah, and warmth bloomed in her cheeks. His mouth twitched, and her lips tingled with the thought of his kiss. As if he read her thoughts, his tongue flicked out and caressed his lower lip.

"I've heard much of the friendships you've been making while in London, Your Grace," Dexter said, "some of them considerably more—*intimate*—than others."

"Dexter!" Thea admonished, before casting a glance at Lilah.

"Forgive me, Molineux," Dexter said. "I was intimately acquainted with Mrs. Whitford at one time. When you see her next, do give her my best wishes."

Dexter's words doused the warmth in Lilah's heart.

Mrs. Whitford. The harlot who Lord Granville had humiliated her with.

"Dexter, please!" Thea rolled her eyes. "It's not seemly to talk of a harlot, not when the duke may be looking for a wife.

Fraser laughed good-naturedly. "I assure you, Miss Hart, I have no desire to find a wife in London."

Stricken with shame for desires which were not returned, Lilah pulled her arm free.

"A man must enjoy himself," Dexter said.

"True, but the whole sorry business of courtship is not an activity which holds any interest for me," Fraser replied. "I have a considerable amount of work to do to restore Clayton House to make it habitable."

"You intend to settle in London?" Dorothea asked.

"My heart is in the Highlands, Miss Hart," he replied, "but while I'm expanding my business, I must accept that London is the center of the commercial world."

"Is there much work needed?"

"I believe so," he said. "The structure of the main house is not altogether sound, and the furnishings have succumbed to the elements. Some of the outbuildings are in want of attention."

"I hear the aviary is in need of repair," Thea said, glancing at Lilah.

"Work is already underway," he said.

"And what of the inmates?" Despite herself, Lilah couldn't help asking.

His gaze settled on her. "Rest assured, Miss Delilah, the birds are being tended to. I've been informed that to simply free them would be to sign their death warrant."

"Of course."

"But," he continued, "if they have been enjoying the company of a visitor these past two years, I would not wish to see them deprived of further visits."

He winked at Lilah, and she looked away. Not only did he delight in relating tales of his conquests of doxies, now he wished to ridicule her in front of her family!

"Would you mock me, sir?" she asked.

"On the contrary, Miss Hart," he replied. "You've done well to tend to the birds these past months, and I'd consider it an honor if you continued. I'm sure they'd be pleased to see a friendly face."

Dexter snorted. "You're not seriously saying that birds are intelligent enough to possess a working memory or that they have feelings?"

Lilah sighed. Dexter may be a shrewd businessman, but he sometimes displayed a shocking lack of insight.

"I wouldn't dismiss such a theory so readily, Mr. Hart," Fraser said. "Every sentient being has the ability to form a genuine attachment with another. Take swans—they mate for life, do they not? Such loyalty to another creature shows they have risen above the sentiments of the savage."

"Unlike a bachelor," Dexter said. He pulled out his pocket watch. "Forgive us, Molineux. Much as I'd relish the continuation of this conversation, we have a dinner appointment. Delilah, it's time to go home."

Lilah frowned at her brother. Why did a man always seek to give a woman instruction? But perhaps it was for the best that she leave. Fraser's presence was beginning to unsettle her. In a few short moments, her feelings had gone from the thrill of having him near her to indignation in the knowledge that he'd taken a mistress in London—and finally settling on disappointment, that, at most, he viewed Lilah as nothing more than a diversion.

Chapter Seven

FRASER WATCHED MISS Hart walk away on her brother's arm.

An intriguing young woman, but he couldn't make her out. At first, she'd seemed determined to hate him due to his lineage, but he'd recognized the signs of female attraction. And now, once more, the evidence was before him, in her reaction to the mention of Emma Whitford.

Was she jealous? She had no need. Fraser had parted with his mistress shortly after encountering Miss Hart. But he smiled at the notion that she believed she had a rival.

Her eyes had flashed when her sister mentioned marriage!

Fraser might have declared he had no intention of marrying, but that was out of a desire to be excluded from the circus that was the marriage mart. There was little joy in parading a young woman around London under the watchful eyes of chaperones and ambitious parents. And the rituals didn't stop with a proposal. In most cases, both parties were forced to sign a contract detailing the full exchange of goods, as if the bride and the groom were mere commodities.

If Fraser were to cleave himself to a woman, he would *take* her—claim her as his ancestors did, and to hell with the niceties. And no simpering miss would do. He needed a feisty hellion capable of handling herself and to provide him with stimulation, not to mention excellent bed sport. It wouldn't do to shackle himself to a debutante whose mama had instructed her to lay back, spread her legs, and close her eyes until the ordeal was over. His perfect mate would be a willing participant, with her eyes and body open and ready for him, eager to learn how to pleasure him as thoroughly as he pleasured her.

"Your Grace?"

He started in guilt at the voice, as if he were a wayward adolescent caught fisting himself in the woods, and he moved his hands instinctively to conceal the bulge in his breeches.

Ahead of him, a woman sat on a bench, a sketchbook on her lap. The sunlight illuminated blonde tresses, which her bonnet could not completely conceal, and her eyes shone like pale sapphires.

"I thought I recognized you," she said.

"Mrs. Pelham." He approached her and bowed and waved away her attempt to stand. "No, don't trouble yourself. I've no wish to interrupt you."

"The interruption of a good friend is not unwelcome."

"You're too kind."

She swept a line across the page with her pencil. "On the contrary," she said, "I've experienced enough of the world to distinguish a good man from an evil one."

"It's not always easy in a society dominated by artifice."

"It's true that a poor character can have the appearance of goodness," she said. "All of us wish to portray ourselves in a flattering light. Take this drawing, for instance." She gestured toward her sketchbook. On the page were a number of drawings of the men and women who frequented Hyde Park. One figure stood out from the rest— an oversized woman with an ostentatiously decorated hat. The line of her dress was accentuated by curves implying great rolls of flesh. A bulbous nose completed the caricature. Beside her was a small, rotund terrier. On closer inspection, the dog's face bore an uncanny resemblance to its mistress.

Fraser suppressed a laugh. "You've not given Lady de Bron the appearance of goodness."

"I draw likenesses as I see them." She smiled and flicked through the pages until she settled on one.

It was a simple portrait which had captured the essence of the subject in a few strokes. Wide, expressive eyes stared out from the page, challenging the observer into daring to criticize her. The brow was furrowed in concentration as if the subject wondered why the artist deemed her worthy of having her likeness drawn. The lips were parted slightly, and he closed his eyes at the memory of their sweet taste. Would they part for him again? The eyes spoke of a determined sadness as if she bore the troubles of the world on her shoulders.

The portrait spoke of a woman doomed to perpetual dissatisfaction.

Would she ever know contentment? Or pleasure?

"I've never seen a truer likeness," Fraser said. "You've captured her spirit perfectly."

"Delilah was an unwilling subject," she replied, "but she agreed to sit for me, nonetheless."

"If I know Miss Hart, she'd be determined to deny herself the pleasure but would be willing at the blink of an eye to sit for *your* sake."

"You know my friend well." She fixed him with a direct gaze. "She refused to accept the portrait as a gift, saying it would encourage vanity. I do wish she'd enjoy life more. She seems to believe pleasure is sinful."

"There's nothing wrong with indulging in a little sin," Fraser said.

She laughed. "You're a rogue, sir. No wonder Miss Hart finds you infuriating."

"She said as much?"

"You must forgive her temper," she said. "And forgive her aversion to your family name. The twelfth duke was an unkind husband, but I have forgiven him because he left me alone to indulge in his excesses, and his death brought about my freedom. His cruelty as a child is something Delilah cannot forgive or forget. I dare say she will, one day, but until then, I'd ask you to understand her. She's the most formidable champion for those she esteems highly."

"That she may be," he said, "but she shouldn't feel the need to fight all the time."

"Perhaps she needs to be taught the meaning of pleasure."

She spoke the truth. Miss Delilah Hart needed a lesson in pleasure.

And who better to instruct her than himself?

Chapter Eight

"I'M SORRY, MISS Hart, I cannot publish these."

The editor of the *City Chronicle* held up a sheaf of papers, and Delilah snatched them from his hand.

"Are they no good, Mr. Stock?"

"The words flow well, but there's no passion, no feeling. A poem is not an essay, my dear."

"It's all writing, isn't it?"

"I'll admit that they require the action of putting pen to paper, but they are totally different. You wouldn't compare the daubs of a child to a Gainsborough portrait, merely because they both use brushes and paint, would you?"

"Are you likening my poems to a child's daubs?"

"Of course not."

She folded the papers and placed them in her reticule.

"Is it because I'm a woman?" she asked.

"If that were so, I wouldn't be publishing your essays, would I? Many of our readers tell us how much they agree with Jeremiah Smith's sentiments. He's getting quite a following, and our agreement is that you write twelve essays in total. Perhaps you should maintain your focus on that."

"Jeremiah Smith can continue to write his essays," she said. "I could use a different name for the poems."

"It's out of the question, Miss Hart. Now, as my time is short, I wish to discuss your current essay. That is, after all, what I'm paying you to write."

She snapped her reticule shut. There was little point in advancing into a battle that was lost before it began.

Mr. Stock picked up another sheet of paper and handed it to her.

"The final version," he said. "It goes to print tonight."

She glanced at the words on the page. The original words may have been hers, but the essay had been peppered with revisions, subtle alterations at strategic intervals to change the tone of the piece.

"You've altered it more than I expected," she

said. "I'm not sure I'm happy with that."

"I'm not asking your opinion, Miss Hart, I'm showing you as a courtesy."

"But the language is somewhat inflammatory, Mr. Stock." She gestured toward the middle of the page. "Take this line, for example, where you refer to tearing down the livelihoods of the downtrodden." She pointed to the bottom of the page. "And here, you liken the aristocracy to the gods of old, languishing in the heavens while the world suffers. I made no reference to gods in my original work. And as for the final line—*a true god would rise from the ashes of his home should it be destroyed.* Those are not my words, Mr. Stock."

"It's what our readers want."

"But it reads like a call to rise up against the aristocracy! And I don't like the reference to the Molineux family."

"That reference was in your original, if I recall, Miss Hart," he said. "You've always been eager to use the Molineuxs as an example of the corruption which must be stamped out. And you have told me several times that the aristocracy is an outdated concept which must be replaced."

"Yes, but I wouldn't condone a revolution," she said. "Just look at what happened in France!"

He gave her an indulgent smile. "Miss Hart, your imagination is running wild. You should give my readers a little more credit. They're intelligent enough to understand the true message of your articles. All I've done is make your work a little more exciting to maintain their interest."

Lilah read the article again, then set it aside and nodded. "Very well."

As Anne had often reminded her, she needed to consider her overall objective and not the detail. Not only did her essays help to raise awareness, but the income she received from Mr. Stock helped to fund Mrs. Forbes's shelter for disadvantaged women. A little integrity could be compromised if it suited a higher purpose.

She glanced at the clock in Mr. Stock's office. It was nearly four o'clock, and Sir Thomas had promised to call and take tea. An hour delay at Devon's lodgings should enable Lilah to escape an afternoon of insincere congeniality while she weathered Dorothea's criticisms and Dexter's admonishments about her behavior.

Devon may be many things, but there was little chance of the youngest Hart brother ever being described as insincere.

Or congenial.

"I SUPPOSE YOU'RE expecting tea."

Lilah rolled her eyes at her younger brother as he gestured toward a threadbare chair. He turned to the footman who'd ushered her into the drawing room.

"Fetch a pot of the stuff, would you?"

"Very good, sir."

"And another bottle of my usual."

The footman bowed and left.

Lilah sat beside her brother. "Devon, should you be indulging at this hour?"

"It's half-past four," he said. "By now, the dandies at Whites will have drunk themselves into varying degrees of mental incompetence while boasting about their conquests."

"But you're not a dandy," Lilah said, "neither are you mentally incompetent."

"I think half of London would disagree with you," he said.

Delilah took his hand. "That's because they don't know you as I do, Dev. Perhaps if you ventured out more…"

"I do go out," he interjected.

"I meant during the day, Dev, attending functions, not prowling round the streets at night. What about the Stiles's ball? We've all been invited. You should come with us."

"Looking as I do?" He grimaced, puckering his scarred cheek. "I desire no man's pity, nor his ridicule. I'm done with being stared and laughed at."

"Your face is more likely to elicit honesty than one that's pleasing to look at," Lilah said.

"At least you won't be subjected to the insincerity of a flatterer. Besides, it's a masked ball, so nobody has to look at you."

"If you're trying to make me feel better, Delilah, you're failing," he growled. "Do you know what it's like to have someone stare at you in morbid fascination, then avert his eyes as if in fear that my disfigurement is contagious?"

"No, I don't, I'm sorry, Dev," Lilah said. "But you can't hide away forever. Your spirits have been so low since your—accident. A wider acquaintance will restore them."

Devon sighed. "You sound like bloody Fossett. He's always trying to drag me outside."

"Your friend cares for you, Dev," Lilah said. "If he didn't, he'd have given up on you months ago."

"Whereas you persist in seeing me out of family obligation."

Why did Devon have to be so infuriating? He'd always been the fun-loving brother to offset Dexter's brooding seriousness—the brave soldier who'd been breaking hearts since reaching adulthood and who, most likely, had enjoyed a different woman at every camp.

Until the night that had destroyed his life.

"Why are you here?" he asked. "Don't tell me it's to inquire after my health or to persuade me to go to that damned ball. You're avoiding Dexter again, aren't you? Or avoiding the latest suitor he's lined up for you."

Lilah's cheeks warmed, and she looked away.

"I knew it!" He let out a bark of laughter. "Dex will have a hard task on his hands, finding a man to control *you*, Lilah. But he never loses, you know that. You'll have a fight if you defy him. In which case, your time is best served managing your own life, rather than interfering in mine."

"I interfere because I love you, Dev," she said. "Don't you want to be happy?"

"You don't understand, Delilah."

"Then explain it to me," she said. "I don't care what you look like, and neither does Dexter."

"That's where you're wrong, little sister. Appearance is everything to Dexter because society cares about it, and Dexter cares about society."

He took her hand, his fingers, calloused from soldiering, rough against her skin. "Forgive me, Lilah. I know you meant well by coming here. You deserve to be happy more than I. Take my advice and enjoy your life and its privileges while you can. You never know when it'll be taken from you."

"You want me to be happy?"

He nodded.

"Then come with us to the ball."

The footman arrived, brandishing a tray of tea things and a decanter.

"If you promise to come, I'll take tea with you and read you my latest poem," Lilah said.

Devon rolled his eyes. "That settles it, little sister. I'll come if you promise not to hound me with your shrewish nagging, nor torture me with your attempts at verse."

For a moment, she detected a glint of humor in her brother's eyes.

Dexter might have given up on him, but there was hope for Devon yet.

As Lilah returned home, she heard Thea call out.

"Delilah, is that you? Sir Thomas and I were wondering where you'd got to."

She pushed open the door. Sir Thomas was sitting on the sofa, flanked on either side by Dexter and Thea. The men stood as she entered the room.

"Will you join us for tea?" Thea asked.

"I was going to rest," Lilah said. "I'm rather tired. I've been visiting Devon."

Dexter drew in a sharp breath but said nothing.

"Is our brother well?" Thea asked.

"As well as can be expected. I believe I've managed to persuade him to attend the Stiles's ball."

"Which reminds me," Sir Thomas said. "With your brother's permission, there's something I'd like to ask you." He glanced at Dexter, who nodded encouragement.

Her heart sank. Surely Dexter wasn't going to put her through the indignation of suffering a proposal from Sir Thomas in front of witnesses? Was this her brother's way of manipulating her into accepting?

"I would very much like to secure your hand for the first two dances."

Lilah could almost taste her relief, and before she could stop herself, she nodded.

Sir Thomas reached for her hand. "Capital!" he cried. He lifted her hand to his lips and kissed it.

Dexter gave her a brilliant smile, and she could swear she saw cold triumph in her brother's eyes.

Chapter Nine

"His Grace, the thirteenth Duke Molineux!"

A ripple of interest threaded through the ballroom.

Fraser had hoped for a discreet entrance, but he'd not accounted for Earl Stiles's overenthusiastic footman.

He adjusted the mask over his eyes and approached his hosts.

The countess held out her hand and smiled, her green eyes resonating against the scarlet silk of her n mask.

"It's a pleasure to see you here tonight, Your Grace," she said. "I've heard much of your enterprise. My husband is eager to taste your whisky once you're in a position to distribute it."

"Then I shall ensure you're sent one of the

first bottles," Fraser said.

"You're too kind," she said. "Rest assured, we shall treat it with respect and refrain from using it to clean the chamber pots."

She winked, then resumed her attention on her husband.

A masked ball was a great leveler. It removed the disadvantage of a limited acquaintance because the guests hid behind anonymity. Not knowing the name of one's dance partner could not be branded a mortal sin. And, of course, any insult or faux pas could go unpunished if the perpetrator's identity remained unproven.

But concealed identities had their disadvantages for a man on the hunt. And Fraser was in search of a very particular quarry indeed. His hosts were renowned for their eccentricity in inviting guests who distinguished themselves by means other than the possession of a title. Given that Earl Stiles was one of the few aristocrats to bank with Hart, Fraser had high hopes of snaring his quarry for a dance, if nothing else, tonight.

A couple standing near the terrace doors caught his eye. The man raised his glass to Fraser in salute, and the woman with him, her delicate frame dressed in a pale lilac silk dress with a mask to match, dipped into a curtsey.

"Molineux!" she said. "I'd know that red hair anywhere."

Fraser bowed. "Mrs. Pelham, are you not

dancing?"

"I will if you ask me."

"Wouldn't rather partner your husband?"

"That depends on whether I wish to survive the evening unscathed," she said. "I'm afraid Harald's prowess in the boardroom is matched by a corresponding lack of it in the ballroom."

"I'm guilty as charged," Pelham said. "The last ball we attended, I trod on Anne's shoe and ripped her dress. If you return her to me with all four limbs intact, you'll have greatly exceeded her expectations for the evening."

"Then it would be my honor," Fraser said.

He led her onto the dancefloor, where the couples had lined up behind Earl Stiles and his wife.

The dance began, and Fraser's partner steered him across the floor, gently correcting his errors with a gracious smile.

"Are you enjoying the dance?" she asked.

He gave her an awkward smile. "I find myself unfamiliar with the steps."

"Then perhaps my limbs are in danger, after all," she laughed. "Would you prefer a reel?"

"I suspect the company would find a reel somewhat savage."

"Then we must teach them," she said.

Fraser's gaze settled on another couple further down the line. The gentleman's jacket was a little too bright a shade of red to be considered tasteful. But the man's partner caught Fraser's attention. Shorter than most, her wiry figure bristled with unkempt energy. Her gown was gray as if she sought to blend into the shadows so as not to attract notice.

Yet, how could she not be noticed? Her vitality vibrated all around her, crackling like a storm about to break.

Their eyes met, and she lost her footing and stumbled. Her partner pulled her to him, and her mouth twisted as if she issued a sharp riposte.

The dance concluded, and Fraser steered his partner across the floor.

"Will you dance again?" she asked.

"I doubt many ladies would relish being trodden on," he replied with a smile.

"Nonsense!" she cried. "There are plenty of ladies here tonight with dance cards yet to be filled. You'll be much in demand."

"Then I must do all I can to remain anonymous," he said. "I can't imagine anything worse than being subjected to idle chatter about the inanities which ladies—present company excluded—concern themselves with."

"You are, of course, at liberty to enjoy the evening as you see fit," she said. "There are many men who prefer to sit in the corner and watch rather than participate in the dancing."

Fraser glanced across the room to where a solitary man sat, his face almost completely concealed beneath a black mask. Even from a distance, he could see the man's eyes glowered with distaste as he observed the couples. A glass of brown liquid in one hand, the other curled in a fist, resting on his knee.

"I see only one such man," Fraser said. "Who is he?"

"That's Major Hart."

"Hart?" Fraser asked. "Then he's related to…"

Mrs. Pelham nodded. "He's Delilah's other brother and something of a recluse. He lives alone and rarely ventures out. In fact, I'd not met him before tonight."

"Did he arrive alone?"

"Yes," she said. "He seemed very civil when Delilah introduced us, but she advised I leave him be, for he dislikes company."

"Perhaps he has something to hide."

"We all have something to hide, Your Grace."

Most people did. Except one. The delectable Miss Hart exuded raw honesty. Sharp-tongued, argumentative women had no need for deception.

After Fraser returned Mrs. Pelham to her husband, he turned and strode across the dance floor, ignoring the hopeful glances of the young ladies in his path. His focus was on one woman only. Ballroom etiquette be damned, the urge to claim her was too strong to resist.

She stood at the far end, her back to him, engaged in conversation with the dandy she'd been dancing with earlier.

Her body stiffened as Fraser approached as if she sensed him. Before he could reach out and touch her, she spun round and tipped her head up. Her mouth was set in a hard line of hostility, but she could not conceal the feverish excitement in her eyes, which glittered through her mask.

"Would you do me the honor of dancing the next set with me?" he asked.

Her companion placed a possessive hand on her arm, but she shook it off, her gaze fixed on Fraser.

"I regret I am unable to, sir."

"Are you engaged for the next dance?"

"Yes, she is," the dandy said.

She flashed a look of irritation at her partner. "No, I'm not."

Fraser moved closer. "Permit me to remind you, Miss Hart, for I believe you are promised to *me* for this dance, at least."

He took her hand, and her lips parted, and she drew in a sharp breath. Her nostrils flared, and her eyes shone with need.

"There!" he coaxed gently. "You remember your promise, Miss Hart, I see it in your eyes. And you wouldn't wish to deny me the *pleasure*, would you?"

She nodded. "Of course, I quite forgot," she said. "Shall we?"

LILAH TOOK THE huge Highlander's arm and tried to lead him onto the dance floor, but he resisted. Instead, he grasped her hand and pulled her toward him.

"You'll find, lass, it's the man who takes the lead."

"You're a savage," she hissed.

He chuckled. "Your outlook has been tainted because you've been dancing with boys. It's time ye danced with a man."

His grip was strong, commanding, and though she wanted to fight against it, the thrill which coursed through her body at his touch conquered her resolve.

"I dislike being in the center of a room," she said.

"I find it the perfect position for us."

"Why?"

"Because it announces to the room that you are mine."

Her body pulsed at his words, and her cheeks warmed until she felt her face was on fire. She daren't look round the room—she imagined everyone's eyes on her.

"I'm not fond of the attention," she said.

"I thought a lady craved attention."

"Not I," she said. "Too much attention tempts a person to flaunt oneself. I'd rather carry out my life in private."

"And remain hidden from the world?" he asked. "If I had a body like yours, I would not hide it from appreciative eyes."

"You wish me to dress like a harlot and reveal my flesh to the world?"

"Of course not, Miss Hart." He leaned over and dropped his voice to a whisper, his breath tickling her ear. "But, perhaps, your flesh may be revealed in private, for the eyes of a single admirer."

His words sent a wicked pulse through her, and she shifted her legs to ease the unfathomable ache.

A number of other couples joined them, and the music began. Though he lacked prowess at dancing, he moved across the room with the self-assurance which came hand in hand with raw male power. Almost every unattached lady's gaze was upon them, looking at Lilah with envy, and her partner with longing.

"I suppose you relish the adoration of the room," she said.

"I should be offended."

"I doubt a man such as yourself would take offense to anything I say or do," she said tartly.

"You seek to indulge in pleasure without one thought for those less fortunate."

"And you seek to deny yourself and the rest of the world the joy of pleasure."

She tried to withdraw her hand, but he held firm.

"No, Miss Hart," he said. "You're mine for the duration of this dance, and I expect you to honor your promise to me."

"A dance is not a marriage, sir," she said. "And I believe you voiced your opinion on marriage very clearly the other day."

His lip curled into a smile. "Only because I find that every unmarried woman of my acquaintance is driven by a single purpose."

"Which is?"

"To snare a husband," he said. "By declaring my aversion to marriage, I ward off predators. I am no different from any hunted creature."

"I've no wish to marry either," she said.

"Doesn't every woman want a home of her own, a family?"

"So says the voice of patriarchy."

"Ah!" he exclaimed. "I should have known it. Jeremiah Smith!"

Her stomach turned to ice at his words. How could she have been so foolish! Had she unwittingly revealed her identity? She lost her footing and stumbled against him.

"Miss Hart, are you all right?" The arrogant

mirth in his expression had disappeared—
replaced by concern.

"I-I became a little overheated," she said.

"Let me take you onto the terrace."

"No," she said, "there's no need."

A wicked glint shone in his eyes. "You're right not to trust me, lass. At this moment, I'd struggle to trust myself."

At that moment, they were separated in the dance, and Lilah found herself linking arms with the elderly Lord Whitshire. A rather dull man, but she welcomed the respite from the assault on her senses brought about by the huge beast who had the power to render her as helpless as the swooning misses she despised.

As she moved from partner to partner, she watched him. Each lady he partnered seemed to fall under his spell as soon as he took her by the hand, her body melting into his arms before he moved onto the next. By the time Lilah rejoined him, her jaw ached from gritting her teeth.

Jealousy was an ugly emotion, particularly in a woman, and to be reduced to such a state was not to be borne. But he showed little sign of noticing the maelstrom of emotions that boiled inside her.

"It seems you're familiar with Mr. Smith's work," he said. "Though I shouldn't be surprised by it."

This time she was prepared for his inquisition.

"How so?" she asked, keeping her voice level.

"Because you share the same sentiments. But I must admit to being disappointed in you."

She swallowed her fear, waiting for the recrimination. Would he expose her in front of the whole company? He had every right to, given the defamatory comments about the Molineux family, which had filled her latest essay.

"I'll settle with your disappointment," she said. "Better that, than be one of the numerous women dependent on your approval."

To her astonishment, he laughed. "If I understand you correctly, Miss Hart, you believe I'm patron to a long string of mistresses, and that I'm an object of desire for half the women in the room tonight."

"Well, aren't you?"

"I shall leave *you* to decide whether I'm an object of desire, Miss Hart."

"If I'm such a disappointment, you'll not care for my opinion," she said.

"Forgive me, I meant no disrespect," he said. "My disappointment comes from knowing that the pretty words you use to declare your opinions are, in fact, those of another. Do you admire Mr. Smith's talents?"

Why could he not think of something else to discuss? His interest in Jeremiah Smith needed to be diverted.

"I haven't really considered it."

"Even though I admire the passion in his words, I despise the man."

"You do?"

"But you're an admirer of the man as well," he said, his smile slipping. "Does he know you're such a devotee of his work as to quote it yourself without citation? Do you use his words when penning your poems?"

"Of course not."

"Good," he said. "If you wish to succeed as a writer, you must use *your* words, not someone else's."

Were the situation not so distressing, Lilah would have laughed at the irony of it. He expressed nothing but admiration for her work, though he did not know it to be hers. But were she to reveal her identity as Jeremiah Smith, he would despise her.

"Miss Hart, are you all right?"

"Yes, thank you."

He shook his head. "Forgive me, perhaps I was a little harsh. There's no shame in using the words of another. Often, we do it without realizing, particularly if those words resonate with us. But though you share Mr. Smith's sentiment, I hope you don't despise the Molineux line—or at least the newest ascendant—as much as he."

"I assure you that I do not despise you, Your

Grace."

He smiled. "I shall be content with that, Miss Hart. In one aspect, I do admire you."

"Which is?"

"Your honesty," he said. "Most women seek to flatter. But you give your opinions freely and without deception or intent to tell me what you think I wish to hear. It's a quality I value most of all."

The dance concluded, and the couples drifted toward the edge of the room.

He took her hand and kissed it. "For your frankness alone, I honor you, Miss Hart. To atone for my earlier rudeness, I'll offer my services once more in seeking a publisher for your poetry, if you'd be so kind as to let me read them."

His eyes shone with sincerity, and she acquiesced. Beneath the boorish exterior and the Molineux name lay the heart of a good man.

"Very well," she said. "I'll ask Dexter to invite you to his next card party. You may read them then."

"Excellent!" he said. "Perhaps I might even ask Smith's publisher to look at them."

"Please don't."

"Why not?"

She hesitated. "I don't think the *City Chronicle* would publish poetry written by a woman."

"Use a pseudonym," he said. "I have the perfect name for you."

"Which is?"

"Terence West."

"It sounds rather silly."

"But perfect for you," he said. "You're my West Highland terrier, which snaps at a man's ankles."

"I don't know whether to be flattered or insulted."

"I've no intention of doing either," he replied. "As you are honest with me, I wish to be honest with you."

He gave her a deep bow, brushed his lips over her hand, and withdrew. He may be a savage, but his sincerity had the potential to disarm her. Ignoring the stab of guilt at her own deception, she curtseyed and rejoined her party.

For the remainder of the evening, she accepted Sir Thomas's gallantry. He was pleasant enough.

But what might it be like to relinquish control, if only for a moment, and yield to pleasure at the hands of a man capable of awakening such need within her?

Chapter Ten

LILAH FOLLOWED HER sister and their guests into the drawing room, where the card tables had been set up. Sir Thomas sat at a table and placed a stack of coins in front of him. He beckoned to Lilah, but she ignored him. He was a little too competitive at cards. Fortunately, Dorothea had already offered to partner with him.

The tables filled up, and the players placed their bets and shuffled cards. Soon, the air filled with the clink of coins and the exclamations of joy or sighs of frustration as the players settled into the evening.

Lilah reached for a glass of wine and settled in a side chair to observe the players.

"Do you not play cards, Miss Hart?"

The rich Scottish burr sent a thrill through

her.

"I've read one of your poems," he said.

"I only gave them to you this evening."

"I must confess being ungracious toward my hosts as to have spent part of the evening reading the first one. You have some talent."

She sipped her drink. "Are you flattering me?"

"Not at all."

"Then you're being gallant."

"I'm not a gallant man, Miss Hart. I prefer frank honesty over flattery. Were your poem the worst I'd ever read, I would tell you. As it is…" he hesitated, "…the words show accomplishment, but they lack something."

"Which is?"

"Passion, Miss Hart," he said. He shifted his knee until it touched hers, and she could feel his body heat through the fabric of her gown. She lowered her glass, and he leaned toward her.

"Shall I fill you?" he asked, his voice a low whisper. She gave an involuntary cry, and he nodded toward her glass. "You've finished your wine." He reached for the glass, and a shock of need coursed through her as his fingers slid over hers.

"Are ye thirsty?"

Her skin tingled with the anticipation of his touch. He dipped his finger into the glass, then ran the tip around the rim, until a single note rang out.

"Hush!" she hissed. "People will hear."

"Your brother's guests are too occupied in losing their money," he said, "and the danger of being watched heightens the pleasure."

Circling his hand round her wrist, he placed his fingertip on her skin, where her pulse raced.

"Ahh," he whispered. "I can feel the thrill inside you." He traced a path around her wrist, then followed a line along her arm until his fingertip disappeared under her sleeve.

How could such a simple act be so...intimate?

"All you need, lass, is a little indulgence in the pleasures of life, to unleash the passion which lies hidden beneath this..." The tip of his tongue flicked out and moistened his lower lip, "...this *deliciously* smooth skin."

Lilah withdrew her hand. "Are you seducing me while criticizing my poems?" she asked.

"I'm giving you my honest opinion," he said. "But I promised I'd help you. I'm most anxious to assist you in finding a publisher. Or, I'd be happy to assist you in publishing them yourself."

"I don't want charity, Your Grace."

"You'd profit from them on your own merit, I assure you," he said.

"I'm not interested in a profit for myself," she said. "My writing pays for..." He lifted a brow, and she hesitated, "...my writing *will*, I hope, help to support Mrs. Forbes's establishment for disadvantaged women."

"Ah, Mrs. Forbes," he said. "I've heard Mrs. Pelham mention her. Are disadvantaged women your passion, Miss Hart?"

"Do you mock me, sir?"

"Of course not," he said. "I'm merely curious."

"Mrs. Forbes has devoted herself to bettering the lives of women fallen on hard times," Lilah said, "mostly widowed mothers unable to support themselves. She's trying to help them learn the skills required to seek gainful employment."

"Employment?"

"Her aim is for them to gain financial independence."

"And you wish to help her?" he asked.

"I visit regularly to help around the house. But she's also in need of funds. Mrs. Pelham provides her with a regular stipend, and I wish to do my part."

"What do you do for them?"

"I help teach them some of the basic skills needed to manage their income," she said.

"You mean you're teaching them mathematics?

"Do you ridicule the notion of teaching arithmetic to women, Your Grace? Or is it the thought of teaching the lower classes you find repugnant?"

"On the contrary, Miss Hart. Education should be available to all, regardless of their age, sex, or social status."

"I wouldn't have thought a man capable of such beliefs," she said.

"Then, as I've said before, lass, that's because you're unused to being acquainted with a *real* man."

His voice sent a thrill through her, but before she could respond, Thea clapped her hands.

"Time for a little dancing before supper!" she cried. "Mrs. Pelham, would you oblige us on the pianoforte?"

"Of course, Miss Hart." Anne Pelham rose to her feet, while Dexter directed some of the men to move the card tables.

Lilah's companion plucked her glass out of her hands and set it aside. "I thought tonight was a card party."

"Dexter despises gambling," she replied. "He prefers to play against his enemies rather than his friends. He says gambling leads to ruination."

"Not for those of us with self-control."

"Sadly, not everyone exhibits such care," she said. "The temptation of easy money can ruin any man when he's pitted against a foe beyond his skill. Dex is a master at it."

"Then remind me never to make an enemy of him."

The music began as Anne practiced a few

scales, and a number of couples formed a line. Lilah jumped as a hand was placed on her shoulder. She looked up into the eyes of Sir Thomas and brushed his hand aside. His face creased into a scowl, then he smiled.

"I believe you're engaged to me for this dance, Miss Hart," he said.

"No," she replied. "I'm sitting this one out."

"I'm sure your companion would release you into my care, Delilah, my dear. He mustn't possess you all evening."

The duke stiffened at Sir Thomas's familiar address but said nothing.

"I'm my own person," she said.

"Very well," he replied. "I'm sure Miss Vine would oblige me. I hear she's an excellent dance partner."

He sauntered off, toward a young lady sitting beside Countess Stiles.

Fraser stretched in his seat, then crossed his long legs. "That young whelp is trying to make you jealous by wooing Miss Vine."

"He's unlikely to succeed," Lilah said. "The countess is a formidable chaperone."

Sir Thomas bowed to Miss Vine. Her face creased into a frown, and the countess gave him a dismissive wave. He retreated, taking a full glass of wine from a footman as he passed, settled into a chair, and he drained his glass in a single gulp.

"It looks as if Sir Thomas has suffered the

indignation of a rejection," Fraser said. "Shall we further his discomfort by joining the dancers?"

"That would be cruel," Lilah said.

"Then perhaps *I* should invite Miss Vine to dance."

Lilah rolled her eyes. "Now *you're* seeking to make me jealous."

"Then dance with me."

She shook her head. "While I don't intend to dance with Sir Thomas, I have no wish to further his humiliation by dancing with another."

"Then you are his for the evening, Miss Hart, if you are forbidden from partnering with another. I thought you were your own woman."

"I am, but that doesn't prevent me from being sensible to the feelings of others."

He let out a laugh. "It seems as if your friend's feelings are not so wounded after all."

Lilah looked across the room to see Sir Thomas joining the dancers with Thea on his arm.

"Your sister has done both Sir Thomas and me a favor," Fraser said. "You are now free to be claimed."

"But…"

He took her hand, and they joined the bottom of the set. Sir Thomas's eyes widened when he saw Lilah, but before he could speak, the music began.

Anne had chosen to play a lively reel, and

Fraser seemed to come alive with the music of his homeland. His firm grip, when it came to their turn to lead the dance, was possessive in nature, yet she found herself delighting in being claimed as he guided her across the floor. When the dance concluded, the couples dispersed, fanning themselves. Thea instructed a footman to open the terrace doors, then called for supper.

"Come, Miss Hart," he said. "Let me escort you to supper."

"I'm a little overheated, sir, and not hungry."

"Then shall we venture into the garden?" He steered her through the doors and out into the night. Voices echoed in the air as some of the guests followed. He led her across the terrace toward a bench concealed in the shadows, and he sat and drew her beside him.

"Your presumption could be deemed impertinent," she said.

"I like to take what I want," he said, "and I believe you enjoy being taken."

She tried to free her hand, but his grip was too strong.

"Unhand me."

He dipped his head until his mouth was close to her ear, then he spoke in a low growl. "If that's what you wish, lass," he said, "but I am giving you what you need."

"No," she said. "You're taking what you want."

"If I see something I want, Miss Hart, I'll claim it," he said, "but only where there is a genuine desire to yield."

He ran his thumb across her wrist, and her skin tightened. He grinned. She opened her mouth to protest, but a whimper escaped her lips as he brushed his hand across her body, the movement touching her breast, as if by accident.

But his actions were never inadvertent. Her nipple hardened at the touch. His eyes sparkled, and he gave a gentle squeeze, sending a pulse of longing to the secret place between her thighs. She shifted to chase the sensation away.

"So responsive," he whispered.

"I am my own woman, sir," she panted.

"Aye, that you are. But deep down, even the feistiest filly yearns to be mastered."

"I do not yearn… oh!" she cried out as he cupped her breast again. Unlike the light touch of before, his hands squeezed her flesh, and his expert fingers massaged and caressed while her body pulsed in response.

"Your body cannot lie, lass," he said. "I want ye. Badly. My whole body aches with the need of it, the need to be inside you."

"How can you say such crude things!"

"I speak the truth, lass, and you know it," he said. "Would you prefer the pretty speeches of a boy, or the raw honesty of a man who promises unbridled, earth-shattering pleasure?"

A firebolt of lust shot through her body, and she swallowed to hide the small cry which threatened to burst from her.

"Are all Scotsmen as uncouth as you?"

"We're wild, lass," he admitted. "We seek pleasure where we can. We live on the raw landscape of the Highlands, where we take our women against the rocks and among the heather."

His words sent a wicked thrill through her, and an unfathomable ache begged to be eased.

"Allow me," he whispered.

He placed a hand on her thigh and waited. The ember of pleasure dulled, and she shifted her legs apart.

"Shall ye feel pleasure at my touch?"

She drew in a sharp breath at the anticipation of sweet release, and he dipped his head and brushed his lips against hers.

"Have I shocked you?"

"Yes," she whispered, "but I find it not un-welcome."

"I will not ruin you," he said. "I value you too highly. But I can promise pleasure you've never known before. If you ask it."

He lifted the hem of her gown. His fingers caressed the skin of her thigh, and she drew in a sharp breath.

"You're so responsive to my touch, lass," he whispered. "It's as if nature fashioned you just for me."

Her blood warmed at his gentle words of praise, intensifying the need which almost burned.

"Shall I kiss you?" he whispered. "I warn ye, my kisses won't be gentle."

She tipped her face up, offering her lips, and he claimed her mouth. Hot, hungry lips devoured her. She circled her tongue around his, and he growled in approval. Then he broke the kiss, and the brief shock of disappointment was met by a surge of need as he placed open-mouthed kisses across her chin, following a line along her throat. He continued to caress her thigh, moving toward the heat at her center, then his fingertips met the sensitive flesh where her thighs met, and her body shuddered.

"Do you want me?" he whispered.

She nodded.

"No, lass," he said, his voice rough. "I must hear it. Say ye want pleasure at my hands."

"Yes," she panted. "I want you to...to give me pleasure."

A deep groan rattled in his chest, and his mouth crashed over hers. His hand, which had been teasing her flesh, now caressed her, moving back and forth across her folds until a surge of need swelled from within.

He plunged his finger inside her, and a myriad of color burst in her mind as intense, pure pleasure tore through her. He silenced her cries with his mouth, claiming her with his tongue, mirroring the gesture of his expert fingers, which thrust in and out, intensifying the pleasure. He took her in his arms and held her while the wave receded, uttering gentle words of praise until she fell into a delicious languor, relishing the joy of yielding herself to another.

FRASER OUGHT TO feel guilty, but need had shone in Miss Hart's eyes the moment he'd touched her. Beneath the veneer of the bluestocking lay a sensual creature with passions not unlike his, needing to be sated.

And she'd been so responsive to his touch! Imagine what it would be like to be truly inside her!

She moved against him, and his manhood, which had hardened the moment he'd touched her damp curls, surged against his breeches. The need to bury himself inside her screamed at his every nerve, but he had no right to ruin her. She was worth more than a sordid fuck in a Mayfair garden.

She stirred and opened her eyes. Dark with desire, they glittered in the moonlight, and she smiled.

"Thank you."

"Are we indulging in idle pleasantries so soon?" he teased.

She reached up and placed a hand against his cheek. He closed his hand over it, rubbing his fingertips along her skin. She looked like a goddess in his arms, face flushed, lips swollen from his kisses.

"That was..." she shook her head as if struggling to express herself "...wonderful."

"No man can pleasure you like a Highlander," he said. "Our ancestors were lusty, virile, and passionate."

She blinked, and a bead of moisture formed on her lashes.

"Oh," she whispered, "I..."

"Don't speak," he said. "These things are best left unsaid. As much as I enjoy the thrill of a coupling outside, I have no wish to scandalize you."

"Then you should have thought of that before," a voice said.

He looked toward the direction of the voice. Their hostess stood before them, arms folded, as if in challenge.

"What the devil have you been doing to my sister!"

Chapter Eleven

"THEA!" MISS HART cried. "How long have you been standing there?"

"Long enough."

Fraser scrambled to his feet. "Miss Dorothea," he said, "I can explain."

"There's no need," she snapped. "I can see what you were doing."

"We've done nothing wrong," Lilah said.

"I beg to differ, Delilah," came the reply. "Count yourself fortunate nobody other than I saw or heard what you were doing. You sounded like a rutting sow."

"I say," Fraser said, "there's no need..."

"There's every need!" she cried. "Delilah's not one of your harlots to debauch on a whim. I cannot understand why my brother invited you tonight. If it were up to me..."

"But it wasn't up to you, was it, Thea?" Lilah said. She stood and folded her arms, ready for battle. Though Dorothea towered over her younger sister, Delilah snapped with all the tenacity of a terrier. Her spirit warmed Fraser's blood, and he found himself hardening again.

"I'm a free woman, Thea," she continued, "I should be permitted to make my own choices and take responsibility for the consequences."

"If Dexter caught you, he'd have whipped you raw with his own hands," Dorothea warned. "And as for *you*," she jabbed Fraser in the chest, "he'd have you shot like a dog."

"Thea, please," Lilah said. "Don't tell Dexter, I beg you!"

"Why shouldn't I?"

"Because I'm your sister, and you love me and want me to be happy. Haven't we always said we must stick together, that happiness ranks above all?"

"But Dexter wants…"

"What about what *I* want, Thea?" she pleaded. "Didn't you complain to me only yesterday that our happiness was overshadowed by Dex's ambition? The role of the society debutante sits ill on my shoulders, just as much as the state of permanent spinsterhood sits on yours."

Dorothea drew in a sharp breath, and for a moment, she looked like she might explode with rage. Then she blinked and lowered her head.

"Tidy yourself up, Lilah, before Dex sees you." Then, she resumed her attention on Fraser, and the cold anger returned to her expression.

"Be thankful my sister pleads your case, *Your Grace*. You have five minutes to return to the house, after which I'll return with my brother's pistol."

Before he could reply, she turned her back and retreated into the house.

Lilah let out a sigh. "I'm sorry about that."

"Don't be," he replied. "Your sister is looking out for you. Love can turn even the meekest woman into a lioness. But in one aspect, she's right. I thought little of your reputation, in my desire to give you pleasure."

She blushed and smoothed her hair. "I'd be uttering a falsehood if I said I didn't enjoy it. Why are women vilified by society for enjoying such—pleasures—yet a man is applauded, even expected to debauch himself."

"I wouldn't say we're *expected*, Miss Hart."

"No?" Her voice took on an edge of fire. "What about *your* activities since you came to London? The infamous Emma Whitford would, I'm sure, testify to the degree to which you enjoy the pleasures of the flesh."

A stab of shame needled at him, followed by a wicked sense of triumph. So—Miss Hart was jealous of the attention he'd given another. Little did she know that from the day he'd met Miss

Hart and almost taken her against the wall in the crumbling remains of Clayton House, he had lost his appetite for any other woman.

"If you must know the truth, Miss Hart, I've not encountered Miss Whitford's company since the day you and I met, nor am I likely to again."

The look of relief in her eyes lasted for a moment before she changed her expression into indifference. "I care not," she said. "I've no intention of giving my heart or body to anyone. Tonight was an experiment. I wanted to understand the pleasure which you seem to think is the key to my literary prowess."

"And was the experiment satisfactory?" he asked. "Did I perform as expected?"

A smile curled along her mouth, and she looked away. "My appraisal of your skills has been favorable so far."

"I'm glad to hear it," he said. "Of course, in order to test a hypothesis appropriately, one must take a sufficient sample size."

He reached out and touched her neckline, and she drew in a sharp breath. He could almost imagine those needy little peaks beading against the material of her gown. He only had to lower her bodice, and they would be his, ripe and ready for him to taste.

"The discerning diner must sample the meal at least five times," he said. "Anything less, and he'd fail to reach a credible conclusion as to whether it's the finest thing he's ever tasted."

"Five times?" her voice came out in a squeak.

"Aye, lass," he breathed. "At least five times."

"I applaud the thoroughness of your research."

"And would you consider adopting a similar degree of diligence?"

"Perhaps."

He traced a line across the front of her gown until he reached the valley between her breasts. Their gazes locked, and he hooked his finger round the material and pulled her toward him. He lowered his head and brushed his lips against hers, suppressing the need to tear her dress off. Then he withdrew his hand, and a low whimper escaped her lips.

Were he to throw her to the ground and rut her, she'd be willing and ready. But his little terrier deserved to be worshipped like a queen.

Or a duchess.

"Miss Hart," he said, his voice tight, "I must return you before your sister comes out and shoots me."

Disappointment glowered in her expression, but she nodded.

"Perhaps, if it's not too forward of me to suggest it," he said, "you may wish to continue your research? Without pleasure, you're in danger of becoming staid and dull."

She bristled at his words. "And you, sir, are

too frivolous. Your objective in the world is to make money and seek physical gratification. You should care more about the world in which we live."

"Very well," he said. "Shall we make a deal? How about I promise to do more to further the cause of good in the world if you promise to indulge in the pleasures it has to offer. There's much we can teach each other."

"And how might we achieve that?" she asked.

"Come to Scotland with me," he said. "Come and see what the beauty of the Highlands has to offer."

A smile crept across her face, and she nodded. "I'll agree, but on two conditions."

"Which are?"

"The first is you must persuade Dexter to permit it, without sustaining a bullet to the chest."

"Fair enough," he laughed. "And the second?"

"You must volunteer your services for my charitable activities. Mrs. Forbes is always in need of resources."

"I'll make a donation if that's what you mean."

"Oh no," she said, a wicked glint in her eyes. "You must attend the shelter and provide your services."

"That seems easy."

She shook her head. "Mrs. Forbes has very strict rules about men. No man is allowed abovestairs. You'd be confined to the scullery, though if she's feeling generous, you might be permitted in the coal cellar. I daresay a day of being under the direct order of a woman, confined to the servant's quarters, will either prove your mettle or break you."

"Very well," he said. "Consider your challenge accepted. In fact, if you are free, shall we call on Mrs. Forbes tomorrow?"

She hesitated as if she'd expected him to decline.

Teaching his little terrier about pleasure?

This was going to be fun.

Chapter Twelve

A S LILAH ENTERED the breakfast room the next morning, Dexter was already there. His dark gaze followed her as she approached the buffet. The hour was late for Dexter, who was usually at his business premises by now.

She spooned scrambled eggs onto her plate, then sat at the table.

"Brother, do you have a particular reason for being here at this hour?" she asked.

"I wish to speak to you regarding Molineux."

Her cheeks warmed under his scrutiny.

"Why?"

"I think you know," he said. "Why else do you bear the expression of a child with its fingers caught in the sweetmeats?"

Her heart sank. Had someone heard her last night? Or had Thea betrayed her?

She pushed her plate aside. The fork clattered onto the table, splattering eggs onto the tablecloth. A footman rushed forward and removed the offending items.

Dexter frowned. "You do believe in making life hard for the servants, don't you? Mrs. Harris will now have to waste her time removing that stain when she has better things to do with her day."

"I can clean it myself," Lilah said.

"That's not the point."

"No, Dex, the point is that Thea's been spying on me."

"What on earth has your sister got to do with this?" Dexter asked.

So, Thea hadn't ratted her out. Then, who?

"Who've you been speaking to?" she asked.

"The man himself," Dexter said. "He came to ask my permission for you to visit his estate in Scotland. He said you'd already agreed to go."

"Did someone mention Scotland?" a voice asked. Thea entered the room, helped herself to eggs, and sat at the end of the table opposite Dexter.

"Molineux has invited our sister to Scotland next month," Dexter said.

Thea froze. "Oh, *has* he? I trust you refused."

"Thea, why don't you keep your pointy little nose out of my affairs," Lilah said.

"Delilah Hart, there's no call for such incivility," Dexter growled. "We have a difficult enough time being accepted in society without you and your wild tongue."

"We know nothing about him," Thea said. "He has the look of a debaucher. Dexter, you must refuse."

"I've already given my permission," Dexter said. "He's not one to accept denial easily. I agreed, provided he observed propriety. Sarah will, of course, attend you on the journey, Delilah, and Molineux's promised that his mother will act as chaperone during your visit."

"I don't need a maid," Lilah said. "I can look after myself."

"Either you take Sarah, or I'll hire the most cantankerous dowager I can find to accompany you from the moment you leave the house until you return," Dexter said. "I've already told Molineux I'll cut his balls off with a butter knife if he compromises you, but don't think I won't punish you either."

"And what did he say?" Lilah asked.

The corner of Dexter's mouth twitched into a smile before the stern expression returned. "He promised that if he returned you with a hair out of place, he'd offer his..." he hesitated, "...his full complement of manly parts on a silver platter for me to hang in the garden for the titmice to peck at."

Lilah spluttered her tea, contorting her face

with the effort not to laugh.

"In return for granting my permission, you must do me a favor," Dexter said.

"Which is what?"

"I want you to visit his distillery," he said. "I'd like to know if it exists and whether it's as productive as he's told me."

"You're interested in whisky?"

"Perhaps," Dexter said. "He's looking to consolidate his loans, and I'd like to know if he'd make a sound investment."

"You want me to snoop?" She shook her head. "I can't do that."

"Delilah, I'm placing a lot of trust in you by giving my permission for this trip," he said. "I'm asking very little in return."

"Very well, I'll tell you what I see," she said, "but I won't be dishonest about it. If he asks me why, I'll tell him."

"It's not dishonesty," he said. "It's due diligence. And it may be a means by which I can help him."

"Help yourself, you mean," Lilah said. "I've never known you to indulge in acts of philanthropy."

"I still don't trust the man," Thea said. "Why should he issue an invitation to *you*, Delilah?"

"Is my company so abhorrent that I ought never to be issued an invitation?" Lilah asked.

"Of course not," Thea replied. "I only asked if

he had a particular reason."

Lilah blushed. "When I accused him of being too frivolous, he said I should enjoy life more. He's agreed to help me with Mrs. Forbes at her establishment, and in return, I agreed to visit Scotland."

"He's trying to ingratiate himself," Thea said.

"I don't think so," Lilah replied. "I believe he's genuine. He's attending Mrs. Forbes today."

Thea let out a laugh. "He won't be there, Delilah," she said. "You've been played for a fool."

Lilah stood and pushed her chair back. "We shall see."

"Stay where you are, Delilah."

Lilah stopped at Dexter's voice, which resonated with the tone he used when about to admonish or dismiss a servant.

"What is it, Dex?"

"There's another condition of your going."

"Let me guess," she said. "You want me to have as dull a time as possible?"

He sighed, and for a moment, she caught a glimpse of tenderness in his eyes before the usual stern expression returned.

"No," he said. "I want you to take care. Though he seems an honorable man, he is a Molineux. And I, for one, will never forget what his predecessor did when you were a child. Make sure you are chaperoned at all times."

"Of course." She rolled her eyes. "This is about propriety again, isn't it?"

"No," Dexter said. "It's about the concern of a loving brother."

Perhaps Dexter was in possession of a heart, after all.

"MIGHT I HAVE a word, Your Grace?"

Fraser looked up from the pile of silverware he was polishing with Miss Hart, to the woman standing at the kitchen door, the owner of the establishment Miss Hart had brought him to. She wore a plain dark blue gown and an apron covered in stains. Her iron-gray hair was tucked into a cap. Dark brown eyes watched him, suspicion in their expression.

"Mrs. Forbes," Miss Hart said, "I've already vouched for..."

"Delilah," the woman interrupted, "I must hear it from his own lips and make up my own mind. I've learned, to my cost, the folly of taking something on trust. Perhaps you could tend to Rose's children while I have a word with him?"

"But..."

"Mrs. Forbes is quite right, Miss Hart," Fraser said. "She wishes to trust me for herself and ensure that I have not duped you. And I would not have it any other way."

"Are you seeking to ingratiate yourself, sir?" Mrs. Forbes asked.

"I wouldn't dare be so impertinent," Fraser said. "Any form of subterfuge is to be abhorred. I believe in complete honesty and revile those who conceal the truth."

Miss Hart flinched, and a slight bloom crossed her cheeks. She rose from her seat, excused herself, and exited the kitchen.

"Miss Hart seems discomposed," Fraser said.

"Perhaps she has something to conceal."

"What can she have to hide?" Fraser asked.

"We all have secrets," Mrs. Forbes said. "It's how we protect ourselves." She leaned forward. "Why are you here?"

He picked up a fork and rubbed the cloth against it, running his fingertips along the tines.

"I'm here to help," he said. "It seems s you are in need of resources—time and funds—both of which I can give you."

"Miss Hart told me a different story," Mrs. Forbes said. "She said you'd made a wager with her. That she'd teach you to look at the world from the eyes of the less fortunate and, in turn, you'd teach her to enjoy the pleasures the world can give her."

She fixed him with her direct gaze, and his cheeks warmed with shame, as if he were a young lad being admonished by his nanny.

"You make me sound like a cad, Mrs. Forbes."

"I speak as I find."

He smiled. Despite her hostility, her directness was a refreshing change from society ladies who fawned over him for having a title.

"Very well," he said. "I agreed to come here because Miss Hart wishes to open my eyes to the plight of others. And I can assure you, Mrs. Forbes, that once my eyes are fully opened, I've no intention of closing them again."

"Mere words, sir, honorable though your sentiment may be."

"Aye, they are," he said, "but perhaps some actions will assure you of my sincerity. I understand you seek to provide introductions into employment for your inmates once they're ready to leave your premises and seek independence. I can help in that regard. I have an expanding business in need of employees, and my house in London will soon need staff."

"What about Miss Hart?" she asked. "Are your intentions toward her just as honorable?"

"That depends on your definition of honor," he said. "I have no intention of deceiving, hurting, or disappointing Miss Hart. Neither will I treat her as inferior because of her sex. I shall respect her wishes and desires and strive to understand her sentiments."

He leaned closer and lowered his voice. "But,

as I have pledged to open Miss Hart's eyes to the delights of such pleasures which can be experienced in order for her to enjoy life to the full, I cannot promise that some of the more *conservative* members of society would consider my intentions to be honorable."

Mr. Forbes's mouth twitched into a smile.

"I believe my friend may have met her match," she said. "She needs someone to challenge her in order to keep her stimulated."

"I intend to stimulate her at every turn."

A cough made him look up. Miss Hart stood in the doorway, holding a baby in one arm and a child aged about four or five, clinging to her free hand. Her hair had come loose, and tendrils surrounded her face. The sight was not unwelcome, as it reminded him of her disheveled state when she had come undone at the touch of his fingers. He drew in a sharp breath as his breeches became too tight.

Mrs. Forbes exchanged a look with Miss Hart, then rose from her seat. "I trust the silver won't be too taxing for you, sir," she said. "If you perform satisfactorily, then next time you visit, I may permit you to serve tea in the parlor."

She approached Lilah, and the two exchanged a quiet word, then she kissed the baby on the cheek, patted the toddler's head, and left the kitchen, closing the door behind her.

Lilah joined him at the table, and the child

fidgeted in her hand.

"Let me help," Fraser said.

"Take Will. He'll be less trouble."

Fraser reached for the child, but the boy shrank back and buried his head in her skirts.

"I can think of better places to hide than a lady's dress, young man," Fraser said. "There's barely enough room for her legs. And when she moves, you must move with her to avoid discovery. I prefer to hide somewhere much more exciting, such as the coal cellar. You could remain there for hours undetected."

The child turned to face him, curiosity in his expression.

"Of course," Fraser continued, "I wouldn't hide in the coal cellar during winter. Imagine what would happen if you were shoveled into the fire by mistake?"

He lowered himself onto the floor until his eyes were level with the child's. "What say you, young sir? Would you relish the prospect of being roasted on an open fire? I daresay if we surround you with a few potatoes and a carrot or two, you'd make a tasty meal."

The child giggled, and Fraser lifted him into the air.

"So, young man, what would you like to do when you're older?" he asked. "Are you an adventurer? Perhaps a privateer who'll make his fortune on the seas?"

The child's eyes lit up. "Would I get to fight pirates and brigands?"

"I daresay ye would. A captain must lead by example and show he's stronger than the rest of his crew."

"I should like to fight," the boy said.

"Really!" Miss Hart said, disapproval in her expression. "He's too young to be discussing such things."

"It is never too soon for a boy to learn how to be a man," Fraser said.

"He's a child," she chided.

"And he lives in a man's world. You wouldn't want him to hide in his mother's skirts all his life, would you?"

Fraser turned to the child. "Of course, a man, even a seafaring captain, must be gallant." He winked at Miss Hart, and she rolled her eyes in exasperation.

"In order to truly become a man," he said, "you must learn to protect those around you, as well as think for yourself."

"I should like that," the child said. "Then, I can look after Mama and my sister."

"Shall we learn the skills of a man together?" Fraser asked. "See this silverware here? A gallant knight must learn to take care of his sword by cleaning and polishing it."

He pointed to a butter knife. "This," he said, "is a similar shape to a scimitar, used by the

Moors during the crusades. Imagine how silly the warriors would have looked if their blades were dull and lifeless on the battlefield. Now picture the blade shining in the sunlight, flashing with light, fire, and determination."

The child picked up the knife and inspected it.

"Shall you tend to your sword, Sir Will?" Fraser asked.

The boy picked up a cloth and began rubbing the knife with it.

Lilah smiled. "I've never heard such a ridiculous speech be employed in order to acquire free labor from a child," she said. "You are to be commended, sir, for you seem to have a natural talent when it comes to children."

"Careful, Miss Hart," he said. "That is dangerously close to a compliment."

He addressed the child, though he fixed his gaze on Miss Hart. "I do believe, Sir Will, that I've just won a victory. I have earned praise from my harshest critic."

She let out a laugh. "I doubt I'm your harshest critic when there must be so many to choose from."

"Perhaps not my harshest," he said. "I'll leave that thorny crown for the despicable Jeremiah Smith and his confounded essays."

She flinched and looked away.

"Perhaps," he said, "a more fitting label for

you, is that of the critic whose opinion I most value."

She colored and dropped her gaze to the baby in her arms.

"Of course," he continued, "I could say the same for your talent with children. That wee bairn has hardly stirred and seems quite at home with you."

She looked up and smiled. For a brief moment, a connection sparked between them, and he pictured her sitting upright in bed, cradling a baby with brown eyes and a shock of red hair…

The moment passed, and she looked away. She might profess not to aspire to motherhood, but the need radiated through her body until he could almost taste it. The need to be loved, unconditionally, and to love in return.

They spent the rest of the afternoon in companionable silence, Fraser polishing the silver, aided by Will, and she tending to the baby. As Fraser was placing the last of the knives into the box, Mrs. Forbes entered the kitchen.

"I see you've completed your task," she said. "Delilah, dear, your tea's waiting in the parlor."

Fraser pulled out his pocket watch. It was almost four o'clock. "It's time for me to leave," he said. "Mrs. Forbes, I thank you for your hospitality and trust I may be of service to you again. In the meantime, I have a token of my appreciation for you."

He reached inside his jacket pocket and pulled out a small flask.

"What's this?" Mrs. Forbes asked.

Fraser lowered his voice to a conspiratorial whisper. "I trust you won't turn me into the authorities, Mrs. Forbes," he said. "This is if I say so myself, a rather fine malt."

"And it's not legal?"

"It is now the Excise Act has been passed," Fraser said, "but this particular whisky was, as we say, distilled under the light of the moon."

She opened the flask and sniffed at the contents. Then she lifted it to her lips and took a sip. Almost immediately, she spluttered and set the flask down.

"Ye gods! It's burning my throat!"

"It is a little warming, to be sure," Fraser said.

A snort came from his left.

"Miss Hart, are you well?" he asked. "Perhaps you'd care to join Mrs. Forbes in a taste? Unless you think it would be too much for you."

She fixed him with a stern look, reached for the flask, and took a gulp. Her cheeks reddened, and her eyes glistened as she returned the flask to Mrs. Forbes.

"Well?" he asked.

"An acquired taste indeed." Her voice came out in a hoarse whisper. "Might I suggest, Mrs. Forbes, that you reserve it for your apostle spoons? If you dipped them into this, it would remove any tarnish at a stroke. Though be careful, it might dissolve the metal if left in for too long."

He clutched his hand to his chest in a gesture of mock hurt. "You impugn my product, madam. But I will confess this particular whisky is a little smoky on the palate. The whisky we're currently producing will be a little sweeter, to cater to the English palate.

Miss Hart wrinkled her nose. "I doubt my palate will ever see fit to enjoy whisky."

"But you were willing to taste it," he said.

"I'll try anything new, Your Grace."

He rose to his feet and gave Mrs. Forbes a bow. "Today has been an education," he said. "I hope you'll permit me to visit you again."

"Of course," she said. "And no, Miss Hart will see you out. Delilah, dear, make sure he leaves by the back door." She turned to Fraser. "I mean no disrespect, but I trust you understand our need for discretion."

Miss Hart handed the baby to Mrs. Forbes, then led Fraser to the back door.

"May I accompany you home?" he asked.

She shook her head. "Thank you, no. I promised Mrs. Forbes I'd help prepare supper." She opened the door, and he breathed in the rush of fresh, evening air.

"Do you have safe passage home?" he asked.

"Dexter is sending his carriage later." Her

face softened, and she lifted her lips into a smile.

"Your brother is a little stern," Fraser said, "but he seems a good man."

"Despite his appearances, he loves us all and wants what's best for me, even if we disagree on what that is."

"There's no shame in being loved by another."

"And..." she hesitated... "are you loved by another?"

"A man has no need to be loved."

"We all need love," she said. "A soul without love would wither and die. I believe the root cause of the evils of the world is the absence of love."

"And on what do you base your argument?"

"One only has to look at those whom we despise."

"Such as?"

"Your predecessor is the most obvious example," she said. "The twelfth duke lacked a mother's love because she died giving birth to him. As for his father, he was the epitome of evil."

"You seem to know a lot about the Molineuxs."

She looked away. "They're notorious," she said. "Their history is a lesson to society. The very worst of men."

"And is there no evil to be found among your

own sex?" he asked.

"There are plenty of examples. The Honorable Sarah Francis is one of the most unpleasant creatures I've had the misfortune to meet."

"But her father seems to love her," Fraser said.

"He indulges her," she replied. "But indulgence isn't love, and neither is showering a daughter, wife, or mistress, with gowns, trinkets, and money. It's merely a form of bribery to absolve oneself from having to show affection or love. I'd rather be loved any day."

"And that you shall be," he said. He took her hand, and she curled her fingers round his. Her skin was cool and smooth.

Her breath caught, and she bit her lip and tilted her face to his.

"So, Miss Hart," he said. "Did you speak the truth earlier?"

She lifted her eyebrows in question.

"When you said you were willing to try anything," he continued. "Is it now time to begin your education in the pleasures the world can give you?"

"You make it sound unsavory."

"On the contrary," he said. "I refer to the pleasure bestowed on us by Mother Nature. The clear air of the Highlands, the soft heather, the majestic mountains. A land rugged and wild."

"I'm ready," she whispered. He lowered his

head until their mouths almost met. She parted her lips, and her breath, warm and sweet, caressed his mouth. He lifted his hand and caressed her neck. He only needed to move a little closer, and he could claim her.

"Miss Hart!" A voice called out from within the house, and she pulled away.

"I must go," she said. "Until we next meet."

He lifted her hand to his lips. "Until then."

Chapter Thirteen

T HE CARRIAGE ROCKED sideways, and Lilah woke up. She yawned and stretched. Beside her, Sarah slept comfortably, but the man sitting opposite watched her, a thoughtful expression in his clear blue eyes.

"How long have I been asleep?" she asked.

"About an hour. We're almost there—take a look."

Lilah lowered the window and was met by a rush of cool air. The landscape was a vibrant green, which turned purplish toward the horizon, where a mountain stretched toward the sky. Slopes, dotted with trees, grew higher with jagged snow-topped peaks, which glistened in the sunlight.

"It's beautiful," she breathed.

"It's my home."

His words resonated with love. Almost as soon as they'd left London, his transformation had begun. Fraser was quite different compared to the brash Scotsman she'd sparred with on their first encounter.

The mail coach had been full when it left London, but by the time they reached the Scottish border, the other passengers had disembarked. At each inn they'd stopped at during their journey, he acted the perfect gentleman, only touching Lilah to help her in and out of the carriage. Though he'd observed propriety, she was disappointed.

Now they were in his private carriage, which had been waiting for them at Edinburgh. He'd grown even more distant as if the intimacy of his own coach had heightened the barrier of respectability.

What had happened to his promise that he would teach her pleasure?

Perhaps he'd taken Dexter's warning seriously. As Lilah's brother had waved them off at the Saracen's Head in Holborn, he asked Sarah whether she'd packed her mistress's butter knife, then pointedly asked the ostler how easy it might be to geld a stallion with it.

"The mountain looks very high," Lilah said.

"It is," he replied, "but not insurmountable."

"Have you climbed it?"

"Aye, but it's a strenuous walk. There's a

drover's road to the pass, just there." He pointed toward a dip in the mountain. "From then on, one must tackle the rocks to reach the summit."

"Will you take me there?"

A lazy smile crept across his face. "If I had my way, I would *take* ye anywhere, lass."

Her blood warmed at the wicked sensations his words elicited. She glanced toward Sarah, but her maid slept on. Not even the motion of the carriage over the bumps in the road roused her.

"You will see my home soon," he said. "Once we've passed the forest, the road begins to rise. Glendarron Castle is at the top."

Almost as soon as he spoke, the carriage entered a forest. Lilah leaned out of the window and looked up. The sun peeked through the trees in specks of light, which flickered as the carriage raced on.

"Are you sure I won't be inconveniencing your mother?" Lilah asked.

"Of course not." He grinned. "Ma always said I'd grow too big to be handled. She'll be delighted to meet the woman who's proven her wrong."

"In my opinion, mothers of dukes don't take kindly to being contradicted in matters regarding their sons."

"But I was not raised to be a duke," he said. "I was raised to be a *man*."

He took her hand. "There," he said. "Look!"

The trees thinned, and she caught a glimpse

of a tall, square building. Without adornments, the building looked purely functional, a marked contrast to the ostentation of the castles she had seen in picture books as a child.

"It's rather plain," she said, then immediately gasped in shame. "Oh! Forgive me."

"There's nothing to forgive," he said. "Your honesty is what I value most about you."

She turned her face away, unwilling to let him see the expression in her eyes. Mr. Stock had been demanding her next essay, and Lilah had spent some of the evenings during the journey penning the final details in the safety of her chamber.

But she could not reveal her activities to the man who sat opposite her, the man who intrigued her more than any other she'd met. She had determined to hate him for being a Molineux but, just as she refused to be defined by her sex, he refused to be defined by his lineage and title.

And she found herself struggling not to fall in love with him.

At all costs, he must never discover the identity of Jeremiah Smith.

"My home may be plain," he said, "but I wouldn't have it any other way. I cannot abide decoration purely for the sake of appearance. And I believe, Miss Hart, that's something you and I have in common."

"I believe it is."

He smiled. "A man incapable of accepting criticism is no man at all."

She shifted uncomfortably in her seat. "I meant no disrespect to your home, sir. I like its regularity of form. It has been built with practicality and security in mind."

"True," he said. "My ancestors were diligent in their determination to protect themselves from marauding English invaders. I trust I can rely on you, Miss Hart, to enter my estate with no intention to subjugate its people."

"I am unarmed, sir."

"Not all weapons strike a blow to the body," he said. "Hearts and minds can also be breached. An army might lay siege to a fortress for days, surveying the cracks in the walls, and the hinges on the doors. But a clever general will assess the softer target. The people within."

"And you think me a clever general?" she asked.

"You could conquer the strongest fortress, Miss Hart, if you set your mind to it," he said. "And this particular fortress would relish being conquered."

He rubbed his thumb over the back of her hand, and her skin tightened with need. Before she could react, the carriage drew to a halt. Voices spoke outside, and he withdrew his hand.

The carriage door opened to reveal a liveried servant.

"Welcome home, sir."

He stepped out of the carriage, then took Lilah's hand in a firm grip, and helped her out.

"Come," he said. "Let me introduce you to Ma."

At close range, the castle looked more imposing than it had from a distance. The stone was dark gray, mottled with deeper flecks of black and red. The entrance, a large, deep archway, housed two solid, wooden doors, built to withstand the centuries. Thick, iron hinges were embedded in the wood at either side of the doors, and wide, heavy-looking rings formed the handles.

A woman stood in the forefront. There was no doubting her identity. Tall and graceful, her hair was silver with flecks of red. Though simply clothed in a black gown trimmed with lace, she bore the demeanor of a queen. Clear blue eyes regarded Lilah thoughtfully, and her mouth was set into a firm line.

A ripple of apprehension shuddered through Lilah. As a child, she'd read history books about the wars of independence between the Scots and the English. One book had depicted the Scottish women as even fiercer warriors than the men. Without a doubt, one such warrior stood before her now.

Lilah's companion placed a hand in the small of her back. His touch bore a note of protection and possession as he gently propelled her forward.

The woman exchanged a brief look with her son, then her lips lifted into a smile.

"Ma," he said. "May I introduce Miss Delilah Hart. Miss Hart, my mother, Mrs. Finola MacGregor."

Lilah dipped into a curtsey. "A pleasure, ma'am."

"Och, we'll have none of that, young lady." The woman took Lilah's hands and pulled her into an embrace. "I'm pleased to welcome you to my home," she said. "I despaired my boy would ever bring a young woman to visit me."

"Ma!" he exclaimed, and when Lilah turned to look at him, pink spots had grown on his cheeks.

The woman laughed—a deep, hearty chuckle which belied her elegant exterior, and she gestured toward the door.

"Let's get you inside out of the cold, my dear. You must find our weather unpleasant after the warmth of London."

"London can be just as chilly," Lilah said. "I'm looking forward to reacquainting myself with Mother Nature, having been confined in a city for so long."

"A woman after my own heart," Mrs. Mac-Gregor said. "I think you'll enjoy the land here."

"I'm keen to explore everything during my visit," Lilah said. "His Grace has been telling me about the mountain, and I'd like to climb it."

"What, *Beinn mo Chridhe?*" the woman exclaimed. "Fraser, you don't intend to drag the poor lass up there?"

"Of course not!" he protested. "Though I was hoping to give her a tour of the distillery before supper."

"Have you asked your guest what she wishes to do, Fraser?" She gestured to Lilah. "Do you want to spend your time in a factory building, and up a freezing mountain, lass?"

"Oh, yes!" Lilah said.

Fraser raised his eyebrows at her enthusiasm.

"I relish the prospect of being on top of a mountain," she said, "looking out over the world, undisturbed. As for the distillery, I'm eager to learn how whisky is made. I've seen the passion His Grace has for it and wish to understand it for myself."

"His Grace!" The woman shook her head. "I'll never get used to your title, Fraser. But it seems as if my wee boy has finally found that which I never believed existed. A Sassenach worthy of his acquaintance."

"Ma!"

Lilah suppressed a laugh at the image of the tall, brawny Scot, a duke who commanded respect anywhere in the world by virtue of his sex, wealth, and title, being cowed by his mother as if he were an embarrassed child being asked to perform for the adults at a family gathering.

Mrs. MacGregor took Lilah's arm. "Let me show you to your chamber, my dear," she said. "Fraser, Miss MacKenzie will be joining us for supper. Perhaps you can ensure you've returned from the distillery in time to welcome her? She's missed you dreadfully and has spoken of little else since she heard you were coming home. I know you'll have missed her. I expect her at seven."

He shifted uncomfortably on his feet, then nodded.

Lilah let herself be led inside, but a sliver of apprehension rippled through her.

Who was Miss MacKenzie?

Chapter Fourteen

LILAH'S MAID HAD just finished unpacking her trunk when a servant arrived to show her downstairs. With a sigh, she donned her pelisse and followed him. She'd hoped to have time to explore her chamber. The view out of the window, dominated by the mountain with its unpronounceable name, was breathtaking. But the light was fading, and by the time she returned, it would be dark.

Fraser waited at the main doors and held out his arm. She took it, and he led her outside to the carriage.

"Is your distillery far?" she asked.

"It's situated by the burn, just three miles away."

"Is your mother coming?"

"Whatever for?" he asked.

"She's supposed to be my chaperone. Or should I send for Sarah?"

"Don't you trust me?"

Her cheeks warmed despite the cool air. She might trust him, but she wasn't sure whether she could trust herself.

"Of course I do," she said.

The carriage set off with a jolt. He began to describe the features of the estate—the outbuildings once used for illicit distilling, the croft housing the ghillie, and the moors where the cattle roamed until the drovers came to take them to market. His voice grew earthier, and his brogue came to the fore.

She closed her eyes, wanting him never to stop, but the carriage halted outside a large, stone building with a tall chimney.

"Here we are," he said, pride in his voice. "The MacGregor distillery."

A short man dressed in a plain black coat and breeches met them at the entrance. He glanced at Lilah, then gave a deep bow.

"Welcome home, Master Fraser."

"It's good to be back, Hamish. How goes production?"

"We have over fifty gallons maturing in the new casks, sir. The excise officer no longer fears for his life, and we've already received an inquiry from a London merchant as to when he can expect delivery."

"You've been productive," Fraser said. "Are the employees settling in?"

"It's never easy with such a rapid expansion, but folks are grateful for the work."

"Good," Fraser said. "I'd like to meet them today when I show Miss Hart round."

The man's eyes widened. "Ye'd show a lady round the factory?"

"You forget your manners, Hamish. Some ladies, even English ones, do more than sit indoors and embroider cushions. Now, lead the way."

The building was humming with activity. Everywhere Lilah looked, she saw men and women working together. As they passed, the employees hailed Fraser as if he were a long-lost friend. He stopped and spoke to each one, praising them for their industry and promising they'd be rewarded for their dedication.

"You employ women?" Lilah asked.

"As you see."

"That's unusual."

"But not unfair," he replied. "A woman toils as hard as a man. Most of them are widows with no source of income, or wives of men incapable of working through illness or injury. I would not see them destitute by virtue of their sex."

"What about the ones with children?" Lilah asked.

"Family needs are provided for," he replied.

"We grant them a stipend for life when they're too old to work, and a nursemaid to take care of their children until they're old enough to attend the local school."

"A school?"

"We fund a school on the estate," he said. "The surest way to lift a man out of poverty is to give him the means to do that himself. And the best way to achieve that is through education, wouldn't you agree, Miss Hart?"

"I find myself agreeing with you more than I'd expected."

"Excellent!" he said. "I have a mind to discuss it with your Mrs. Forbes when I next see her."

"You think she could advise you on how to run a school?"

"No, but some of her women seeking a fresh start, particularly those with children, may wish to come here. I've already suggested it to her."

"You think a woman would wish to travel so far from home?"

"I'm certain of it," he said. "There are many women looking for a new beginning, away from their pasts. Why not come here? Despite what you hear about my countrymen, we welcome newcomers. Fresh ideas, new people... It's how we grow."

"Then it seems as if *your* education is complete," Lilah said.

"My education?"

"The plight of the disadvantaged, a greater understanding of the world. You recall our bargain?"

"Ah, yes, our bargain." He met her gaze, hunger in his eyes. "But I must still complete *your* education, must I not? I believe we'd agreed on five lessons in pleasure. Four yet remain."

She dropped her gaze to his lips—those full, sensual lips. She had only to move forward a little, and she could taste them.

He smiled and drew back. "I believe we must add another lesson."

"Which is?"

"To show you that I am more than an uncouth Scot or a libertine lord."

She had judged him unfairly.

"I believe my education with regard to you has already begun," she said, "but I'm eager to learn about your whisky, even if I don't like the taste."

"Then you have set a challenge, Miss Hart," he said. "I must persuade you to taste it again."

"I can't see myself enjoying it a second time."

"There are many different forms of whisky," he said. "The taste depends on many factors."

"Such as?"

"The water is an important part," he said. "Our water is collected from the burn, which comes straight from the mountain—fresh and clear, almost sweet to the palate. One must also consider the barrels in which the whisky is aged. We're experimenting with different barrels, including sherry casks. The sherry should infuse a level of sweetness. But I'm also eager to experiment with different barrels to impart a variety of flavors. However, I must stay my enthusiasm until we can reap the rewards of our efforts. And for that, I have Hamish to thank. He acts as a steady hand to prevent me from sinking too much of my assets into the venture."

"Hamish seems a sensible fellow," Lilah said.

The man in question gave her a stiff bow. "I do my best for the master."

"Come," Fraser said. "Let me show you the whole process from start to finish."

He ushered her into the main part of the building.

A dry, acrid smell caught at the back of her throat, and she coughed. "What the devil is that?"

"The peat smoke," he said, laughing. "Only a Sassenach would choke at the most beautiful aroma in the world! I once heard tell that, to an Englishman, the smell of peat smoke is akin to his grandmother's week-old undergarments roasting on a coal fire."

"Why use something so disgusting?"

"The smoke is used to dry the grain," he said. "The longer we smoke the grain, the stronger the taste of peat. Every Highlander has peat in his blood. It's the fuel which keeps us warm in winter. It gives our land the richness on which our plants and animals thrive."

He escorted her into another room that contained a number of wide, fat wooden barrels. The smell was not unpleasant, at least not compared to the peat smoke she'd inhaled a few moments ago.

"This is where we add the yeast to the mash," he said.

"How long does it take?"

"It differs depending on the strength of taste, miss," Hamish said. "It can be ready in two days, but we leave it for four. The extra two days imparts a deeper flavor. Though the master intends to sell to the English, who are unlikely to appreciate the complexities of a good whisky, he's unwilling to compromise on quality merely to cater to their unsophisticated palates."

"Your master is a man of integrity," Lilah said. "I cannot abide a man willing to trade his principles for profit."

"Or a woman," Fraser said. "I want to yield a profit, of course, but my primary objective is to share my passion for good whisky with the rest of the world and leave a legacy for the people who depend on me."

Once again, guilt pricked at Lilah's conscience. This man, who she'd admonished for being a profligate, had done more to help others than she ever could. He had every right to indulge in the pleasures of life.

What had *she* done, other than stitch a few torn sheets for Mrs. Forbes, yell abuse at the aristocracy, and write naïve political pieces?

Her motivations, which she'd believed to be honorable, were driven by nothing more than vanity—an attempt to use the notion of social inequality to further her writing career. She had convinced herself it was for the greater good, but in reality, the only person it served was herself.

A warm hand took hers.

"Miss Hart?"

She looked up into a pair of kind blue eyes. Now that her own eyes had been opened to the truth about herself, she could not meet his gaze. She blinked to clear the moisture pricking at her eyelids.

"The smoke…" she said.

"Of course." Gentle hands steered her out of the room. "Hamish, perhaps you could find Miss Hart a glass of water."

"Of course, sir." The man disappeared.

"Is there more to see?" she asked. "I wish to continue."

"Good," he said. "I've left the best until last."

The next room contained four large copper vats with a bulbous shape at the bottom, tapering to funnels at the top.

"This is where the fermented mash is distilled, concentrating the liquor," he said. "A wood fire heats up the liquid inside the vat, and because the liquor boils before the water does, we can catch it and separate it from the water and impurities in the mash."

Lilah placed her hand on one of the vats and ran her hand along the smooth contours of the metal.

"It's cold," she said.

He placed his hand over hers. "My da told me the vats were fashioned in the shape of a pagan goddess," he said. "Smooth, ripe curves for a man to claim, and a delectably firm, round bottom."

He moved beside her, and his body heat seeped through the material of her pelisse. A light cough came from behind, and he moved away.

"Your water, miss." Hamish stood in the doorway, a glass in his hand. She took it and sipped the water.

"Thank you," she said.

"It's from the burn," he said, pride in his voice. "Perhaps, if you find our water to your liking, you'll appreciate our whisky one day."

"I find myself appreciating much of what I see here," she said. She turned to her companion. He took the glass from her and lifted it to his lips, turning it deliberately so his mouth met the spot where she'd sipped it.

"Delicious," he said. "A taste like no other, and one I hope to indulge in many more times." He returned the glass to Hamish. "You may leave us now," he said. "I'm sure you've plenty to do."

"Very good, sir."

"There's one more thing I have to show you, Miss Hart," he said after the foreman left. "The cellar."

He took her to the back of the building, where a flight of steps descended into the darkness. He reached for a lamp which hung from a nail in the wall, struck a flint, and lit it.

"Follow me."

At the bottom of the steps, he raised the lamp.

"Look."

A row of barrels was stacked neatly against the far wall. Letters had been stamped on the end of each barrel, and as she moved closer, Lilah could discern the writing.

MacGregor 1823

Underneath were other, fainter letters.

H. Pelham & Co.

"These are Mr. Pelham's barrels!" she exclaimed.

"I purchased his sherry casks," he said. "But don't worry, I gave him a good price."

He approached a barrel and traced the line of the letters with his finger. "I hope it's worth it," he said. "The waiting will be the worst part."

"When will you distribute them?" she asked. "Your foreman said you'd already received an order."

"Not for three years, at least," he said. "The whisky needs to mature properly. Ideally, I'd lay them down for at least five years, but I've sunk more than I can afford into the business and must generate a return as soon as possible. Not every buyer is willing to pay three years in advance."

"Three years! Won't it go bad?"

His laugh echoed around the cellar.

"No, lass," he said. "It could go untouched for twenty years and taste all the better for it. We only need to worry about the angels."

"The angels?"

"For each year of maturation, some of the spirit is lost, and legend says it's the angels taking their due. But we can forgive them, for over the years, the taste deepens and mellows. The longer the maturation, the better the taste. And, of course, the higher the price we can command."

"And how would you know," she said, "if the production of whisky has been illegal until now?"

"Whisky has been produced hereabouts under the light of the moon for centuries," he replied.

"Then, the Excise Act must be an unnecessary burden for you."

"On the contrary," he said, "I've always been an advocate for the Act, for it has legitimized production, which will ensure that whisky can, at last, enter the drawing rooms of London."

"And you believe society's taste will run to whisky?" she asked.

"I've staked everything I have on it."

"Then I applaud your bravery," she said.

He pulled out a pocket watch and opened it. "We must be leaving," he said. "Ma will wonder whether I've abducted you."

Lilah smiled. "Does your mother take her duties as chaperone seriously?"

"She's taken a liking to you, lass. She sees the same qualities in you that I do."

"You're too generous."

"I think not," he replied. "You're the most honest person I know."

His eyes shone with faith in her, and his smile warmed her bones.

What would it be like to be loved by him?

Chapter Fifteen

B Y THE TIME they returned, night had fallen, and Lilah was unable to see the mountain. After Sarah finished pinning her hair, she made her way to the drawing room.

Fraser stood by the fireplace, a glass in his hand. Sitting by the window was his mother, and beside her, a young woman.

Mrs. MacGregor rose to her feet. "Miss Hart, I trust you enjoyed your excursion?"

"Very much," Lilah replied.

"May I introduce you to Miss MacKenzie, a close family friend?"

The young woman stood and dipped into a curtsey. She was exquisite. Flame-red hair had been arranged in a cascade of curls to frame a heart-shaped face. She had perfectly-proportioned features—a small nose, high cheekbones, and a rosebud mouth. Her eyes, a clear green, narrowed as she looked at Lilah, as if sizing her up to determine whether she posed a threat.

"Charmed, I'm sure, Miss Hart," she said.

Lilah mirrored the curtsey. "A pleasure to meet you, Miss MacKenzie."

Despite the fire, a frost had descended in the room.

Mrs. MacGregor gestured toward the dining room. "Shall we go in?"

"Of course," Miss MacKenzie said. "We've been kept waiting, and dinner will be getting cold."

"It's just an informal family supper," Fraser said.

"Nevertheless, traditions should be respected," she replied. "Come, Fraser, take my arm. You've been away from home too long. London has claimed far too much of you already."

She glided across the room to Fraser, who held his arm out, and she curled her hand around it and leaned close. "We've missed you," she said in a loud whisper. "I trust we'll see plenty of you now you're back, where you belong."

He displayed no emotion, but Miss MacKenzie's face glowed with satisfaction.

"Miss Delilah," Mrs. MacGregor said. "Would you accompany me?"

Lilah took the proffered arm and walked with her hostess into the dining room. She had never seen a room so *Scottish*. Dark oak panels lined the walls, decorated with candle sconces. On one wall hung a woolen plaid with a red background, decorated with blue and green stripes, the contrasting colors shimmering in the candlelight. Beside it, hung a tapestry depicting a hunting scene—a stag in the forefront being speared by a band of men who looked like savages with shaggy red hair, heavy swords, wearing plaids in a pattern to match the wall hanging. A huge mountain dominated the background, above which a pair of eagles circled.

In the forefront, where the deer had been speared, blood ran from the wound, staining the rocks red.

Unlike the delicately embroidered screens of the parlors in Mayfair, the tapestry depicted life without embellishments. Nature in its raw fashion, together with the brutality and savagery of Highland life.

"Do you like what you see, Miss Hart?" her host asked.

"It's like nothing I've seen in my life."

"Look behind you," he said.

She turned toward the opposite wall. A stag's head mounted on a large, polished block of wood greeted her.

"Perhaps our guest finds our country a little too much for her," a female voice said. Miss MacKenzie watched Lilah with a slight smile on her lips, though her gaze was hard and cold.

"Not at all," Lilah said, "but I'll admit you wouldn't find quite such an honest depiction of a hunt in London's drawing rooms."

"Is that because the English are unwilling to face the truth?" Miss MacKenzie asked.

Lilah gestured toward the tapestry. "Were you to display such a raw picture of brutality in a Mayfair dining room, I doubt the diners would enjoy their venison as much."

Miss MacKenzie gave a snort and reached for her wine.

"Do you find our honesty unsettling, Miss Hart?" Mrs. Macgregor asked.

"On the contrary, I admire it," Lilah said. "I take it your ancestors are in the picture?"

"Aye," Fraser said, pride in his voice. "That's my great-grandfather leading the hunt. Auld Willie led him a fine chase."

"Auld Willie?"

"The stag."

"And your great-grandfather had him stuffed and mounted?"

"He ate him. But to honor their battle of wits, he had him mounted, so we would remember him. I think you would have liked him."

"Your grandfather or the stag?"

He let out a laugh. "My grandfather, Miss Hart. He was a fellow countryman of yours."

"He was an Englishman?"

"Aye. It's due to him that I suffer the misfortune of being a duke. His older brother was the ninth duke. But my ancestor was, if I understand, something of a rebel. He left to marry the daughter of a Highlander who fought against the English in several battles, and his father disowned him."

"Then you could argue that justice has finally been served, now that the title has fallen to you," Lilah said.

He shook his head. "It comes with responsibilities and expectations I neither need nor want."

"Ah, but your particular title comes with the least expectation," Lilah said. "Your predecessor was hardly a paragon of honor."

"You sound just like Mr. Smith," he said. "Do you sympathize with his attempts to discredit me in print?"

"Of course not." She resumed her attention on the dish in front of her, a creamy broth of smoked fish. "The soup is delicious, Mrs. MacGregor."

"Thank you, Miss Hart. It's a variant of a traditional Scottish recipe, which has been in our family for generations. Most families will have their own particular version."

The conversation turned toward food for the rest of the meal. When supper was concluded, Fraser escorted them into the drawing room where he poured them each a glass of whisky.

"I thought you said Miss Hart loathed the stuff," Miss MacKenzie said.

Lilah's cheeks warmed at the notion that he'd been discussing her with his…

His what?

Family friend? Lover?

Or betrothed?

"I'm willing to try it again," Lilah said.

Miss MacKenzie sipped her whisky and smiled. "I find first impressions tend to be the most accurate."

Fraser handed Lilah a glass. "I've mixed it with a little water. It improves the flavor."

She took it, ignoring the warmth of his hand as her fingers brushed against his, and sipped it. The flavor burst on her tongue, a smoky, earthy richness, which warmed her throat as she swallowed.

"That's delicious," she said. "Somehow not as harsh as the liquor I tasted in London. Are you sure it's the same?"

"Perhaps your taste is improving," he said.

Miss MacKenzie let out a snort. "It's rather fickle to change one's mind at the persuasion of others."

"But necessary, if one is to grow," Lilah said. "I admire a steady character, but an unwillingness to change one's opinion can be a sign of weakness. I have the utmost respect for a man or woman who admits when they've been at fault."

"What would become of the world where opinions continually changed?" Miss MacKenzie asked.

"It would be a better world, Jen," Fraser said.

Lilah flinched at his familiar address. Miss MacKenzie smiled and placed a possessive hand on his arm.

"Of course, dear Fraser, you're always so understanding. But I would counsel you against the folly of inconstancy."

"Jennifer, my dear, I trust you'll never find me inconstant."

"I do hope not," she said, caressing his arm. Then she released him, took a seat on the couch beside the fireplace, and patted the space beside her.

"Do join me, Miss Hart," she said. "I'm anxious to know you better."

"Are you?"

The smile slipped. "Of course," she said. "My Fraser mentioned you so often when he wrote, I almost believe we're friends already."

"Friends, Miss MacKenzie?"

"Oh, yes!" she said. "Please, if it's not too forward, you must call me Jennifer, if I might be permitted to call you... What would I call you?"

Forward, indeed, but with three pairs of eyes on her, Lilah could hardly object. Dexter would have had a fit at such familiarity. But Dexter was not here. And something told Lilah it was better not to make an enemy of Miss MacKenzie.

"Of course," she said. "You must call me Delilah."

Miss MacKenzie linked her arm through Lilah's. "How wonderful!" she said. "Fraser, my love, did you not hear that? Delilah and I are friends. Perhaps you might tell me about London, for I hear society is somewhat fierce there."

"No fiercer than in Scotland," Lilah said.

The smile slipped again, and Miss MacKenzie took another sip of whisky. "Ah, but at least the infamous Mr. Smith doesn't reside here," she said. "Now there's a scoundrel if ever one existed."

"Mr. Smith?" Lilah asked.

"Jeremiah Smith," Mrs. MacGregor said. "Have you read any of his articles in the *City Chronicle*?"

"I-I may have read some," Lilah replied, tightening her grip on her glass.

"Are you an admirer?"

"Certainly not."

"I am glad of it," Mrs. MacGregor said. "He must be a detestable man to write what he does, to say such horrible things about us."

"Aren't his remarks directed at the aristocracy in general?" Lilah asked.

"Then why does he always refer to the Molineuxs? Fraser has sent me every one of that man's articles. I find them most distressing."

"Then, perhaps he shouldn't send them," Lilah said.

"Would you have me conceal the truth from my mother?"

"No," Lilah replied, "but those articles will make no difference to the world. They'll soon be forgotten, and the paper on which they're printed will line London's fireplaces."

"It's always best to know what your enemy is thinking about you," Mrs. MacGregor said. She smiled and raised her glass. "Perhaps we should talk about the writing of a pleasanter nature. Fraser tells me you're something of a poet."

Lilah shook her head. "I enjoy writing verse, that is all."

"I hear you're quite the proficient. My son praises your work highly and says you're in the process of having a volume published."

"That is my dream," Lilah said, "but I fear your son has grossly exaggerated my talents."

"I doubt that, my dear." Mrs. MacGregor said. "My son is the most honest, truthful person I know. Of course, a mother's love will render me biased."

Mother and son exchanged glances, and Lilah's heart tightened at the expression of love in his eyes.

"Your opinion is justified," Lilah said. "From what I've seen today, he's a man of integrity and is destined for success."

"Quite so," Miss MacKenzie interjected, her voice carrying an undertone of desperation as if she were unwilling to let the conversation flow without her input. "I've always said so, have I not, Fraser? I like to think that my unwavering support, together with your mother's, of course, has encouraged you to pursue your venture outside of our homeland."

Fraser nodded. Miss MacKenzie shot a glance toward Lilah and continued. "Of course, every successful man needs continued support. Where better to find it than in his homeland?"

Could the woman be any more obvious? If she ventured to London, she'd find a twin soul in the Honorable Sarah Francis. She possessed all the animosity that Sarah felt toward any woman she saw as a rival, together with the desperation which exuded from her every time an unmarried, titled man ventured within ten feet of her.

"To achieve success," Miss MacKenzie continued, "a man must focus on his business interests whole-heartedly. He can only do that in confidence if he is assured that his home, family, are looked after by another."

"Such as a wife?" Lilah asked.

"A wife lives for her husband," Miss MacKenzie said. "My life will be complete when I can support someone I've pledged to honor and obey."

"You believe a woman should be defined by her husband?" Lilah asked. "Can't she have interests or pursuits of her own?"

"Only insofar as they do not hinder the husband's ambitions."

"She may wish to earn a living of her own," Lilah said.

Miss Mackenzie curled her lip. "Only if she wishes to emasculate her husband."

"Miss MacKenzie!" Mrs. MacGregor exclaimed. "I hardly think…"

"No, no," Lilah said, laughing. "It's a reasonable question which any woman in pursuit of equality must be prepared to answer. There are many women in the city of London, earning respectable incomes to support themselves."

"Are they married?" Miss MacKenzie asked.

"Married women often help their husbands in running a business."

"Perhaps you wish to earn a living from your writing," Miss MacKenzie said. "An impossible task, given that you must first convince a man to publish your work."

Lilah opened her mouth to respond but thought better of it. Though she wished to set this spiteful young woman straight by relating the success of her *Essays on Patriarchy*, she had no wish to reveal her identity as the author.

Fraser came to her rescue. "Commercial success does not always go hand in hand with the quality of the product, Jennifer. I've had the privilege of reading a number of Miss Hart's poems and have found them to be excellent."

Lilah looked up, and their eyes met. His glittered with warmth, reflecting the orange glow of the fire, and his lips curled into a smile.

"How wonderful!" Mrs. MacGregor said. "Would it be too forward of me to ask you to read one aloud for us? I am very fond of poetry, am I not, Fraser?"

He gave his mother an indulgent smile. "Ma was once privileged enough to meet the Bard," he said.

"Perhaps our guest is unaware of the Bard," Miss MacKenzie said, her tone sullen.

"I'm well acquainted with the work of Robert Burns," Lilah said. "His Grace was kind enough to introduce me to the *pleasures* of Burns's poetry the first day we met." She gave him a saucy smile. "I'm sure you remember that day well."

"How could I forget?"

Was it her imagination or had his voice taken on a gravelly tone?

"Are you working on a poem now, Miss Hart?" Mrs. MacGregor asked.

"I am."

"I'd love to read some of your work if it's not an imposition."

"Miss Hart is never without her writing materials," Fraser said. "She spent every evening writing during the journey here."

Guilt stabbed at Lilah at the pride in his voice. For the past few days, she'd abandoned her poetry in favor of completing her final essay as Jeremiah Smith.

"I'm not sure..." she hesitated. Her hostess interrupted her.

"I promise not to compare you too unfavorably with Burns, my dear. I would encourage every woman, married or not, to cultivate her passion, to ensure she maintains her independent identity."

Lilah had an ally in Mrs. MacGregor, which only made her subterfuge even more treasonous.

"Perhaps another time," Lilah said. "I'm rather tired."

"Is our Highland air too much for you?" Miss MacKenzie asked.

Ignoring the young woman, Mrs. MacGregor took Lilah's hand. "You poor dear," she said. "Not only have you been subjected to such a long journey, my son saw fit to drag you round his factory without a single thought for your comfort. Fraser, you should take better care of your lovely guest."

"I assure you, ma'am, he's taken the utmost care of me," Lilah said, "but I am very tired, and would beg to be excused."

"Then I'll bid you goodnight," her hostess said, "and see you tomorrow morning, where I trust a hearty breakfast will revive you."

Lilah rose to her feet, curtseyed, then exited the room, but not before she caught a look of triumph in Miss MacKenzie's eyes.

Tonight she'd learned two things. Her host was a man beyond compare, a man she could grow to love.

And, she had a rival for his affections.

Chapter Sixteen

A N OWL SCREECHED outside, and Lilah sat upright, heart pounding.

Voices chattered in the distance—servants clearing up after dinner and laying the fires in preparation for the morning. How was it that the men and women who tended to the rich retired much later than the people they served and were obliged to rise earlier?

She wiggled her toes, which had grown numb with cold. The owl screeched again, and she slipped out of bed. A shaft of moonlight streamed through the window, and she crossed the floor to look outside.

The moon sat directly above the mountain, illuminating the jagged peaks and the patches of snow. In the peace of the night, she could watch the mountain unobserved. Tall and silent, it guarded the land like a sentinel or a pagan god of old. Perhaps it was from the mountains where the people of this land drew their strength.

Footsteps approached. Someone was outside.

She crossed the floor and pulled the door open.

He stood before her, his large frame filling the doorway. A candle flickered in his hand, illuminating his face, which bore a frown of concern.

"Is there anything wrong?" she asked.

"I came to see if you were all right," he said. "You seemed out of sorts tonight. Was the meal not to your taste?"

"It was delicious."

"The company, perhaps?"

She looked away.

"You must forgive Jennifer," he said. "We grew up together, and she expects me to offer for her."

"And will you?"

"No."

"Does she know you intend never to marry?"

He shook his head.

"You should tell her," she said. "It's not fair to let a woman believe you feel something that you don't. It's dishonest."

"That's why I admire you, Miss Hart," he said. "Jennifer displayed such incivility, yet you champion her cause and admonish me for my lack of honesty."

Her mind wandered to the article she'd just finished.

"I'm not honest," she said. "You don't know me."

"I know you better than you think, lass," he said. "From the moment we met, I knew you were different. Other women bend back and forth, weaving themselves around the people they seek to manipulate to gain what they want. Like water, they follow the easy path. But you…" He sighed, his chest rising and falling in a shuddering motion as if he struggled to contain himself. "You're like the mountain. Straight and true, you never deviate from your path, no matter the temptation."

Guilt pricked at her conscience, and she spoke harshly to conceal it. "You came to my chamber, risking my reputation, to tell me that?"

"I'm here out of genuine concern for your welfare," he said.

"I'm well, as you see."

"Why are you awake?" he asked. "Is there anything you need?"

"No," she said. "I have been admiring the view from my window. The mountain is so beautiful. Will you take me there tomorrow?"

He smiled. "I promised, didn't I? I agreed to show you pleasure five times to complete your education, and I have only done so once. You have four more."

She reached up and touched his face, unable to fight the need to feel his skin against hers.

His nostrils flared, and he closed his eyes.

"Miss Hart, you know not what you are doing."

She tipped her face up. "I'm asking you to honor your promise," she whispered.

He lowered his mouth and brushed his lips against hers, then peppered her face with light kisses. His breath tickled her ear.

"I want ye—badly," he said, his voice hoarse, "but I would never scandalize ye."

Her body hummed as his brogue became more prominent. He moved against her, and she felt his maleness, hard and hot against her stomach through her nightrail.

"Would you show me pleasure?" she asked. "Like before?"

"Ma is sleeping on this floor at the other end of the passageway."

"I have no wish for your mother to join us," she said.

A low growl rumbled in his chest. His knuckle brushed against her breast, and a small gasp left her lips as her nipple beaded.

"So responsive," he breathed. "You're a natural, Miss Hart. Your body was made for seduction."

"No, Your Grace, it was made for you." She

reached for his arms. "Are you to continue my education, sir?"

"I see I have an eager pupil." He entered the chamber and closed the door behind him.

"Am I to be your prisoner, Your Grace?"

"I'd like nothing more, lass, than to tie ye to the bed and have my way with you."

She shivered with anticipation at his deliciously wicked suggestion.

"Ah!" he said. "I see you're not averse to the notion of being at my mercy. But I merely wish us not to be disturbed."

"Surely we'd hear anyone coming?"

"Lass," he said, "ye'll be too busy screaming my name to notice any passersby."

He took her hand and led her toward the bed, then he lowered his gaze to her chest where her nipples poked insistently against the fabric of her nightrail.

She sat on the bed, and he pushed her back, his hands gentle yet firm.

"Do ye trust me, lass?"

"Yes."

She yielded and let her body relax. He gave a low rumble of approval and lifted her clothing. Strong, warm hands caressed her legs, moving slowly toward the juncture of her thighs, where she felt wet.

"Oh, lass, you need me as much as I need ye."

"H-how can you tell?" she stammered.

He inhaled deeply. "I can smell it, lass. You're ready for me."

She blushed at his wanton language and her body's reaction to him.

"There's no shame in it, lass," he said. "To enjoy your body is the most natural thing in the world. Society should hang its head for demonizing the most beautiful act between a man and a woman."

"You speak as if you have extensive experience."

"I do," he said. "How else would I qualify to be your tutor? Surely you'd rather learn from a master at the art of coupling—a real man—than fumble in the dark with a mere boy? I would have ye learn the pleasures of your body, lass, so that you might show your future husband how to please you."

Your future husband…

His words tempered her desire. Did he see her as nothing more than an apprentice, to be taught the pleasures of the flesh, then cast aside? Once he'd finished with her, would he move on to the next? Was that what he'd done to Miss MacKenzie, the woman who now clung to him, displaying her desperation so openly?

But he'd made her no promises. Lilah had entered into their agreement willingly. But this man—this beautiful man who loved his homeland, who took pleasure in his privileged life but worked hard for the benefit of others, was in very great danger of making her fall in love with him. Would she be able to safeguard her heart while yielding her body to him?

He dipped his head and placed a soft kiss on her ankle. His touch sent a shiver through her body. Murmuring gentle words of praise, he peppered her skin with small kisses. Then he nudged her thighs apart, and she gave a squeal of embarrassment.

"No, lass," he whispered. "It gives me great pleasure to look at ye. Would you deny me that pleasure before I give you pleasure in return?"

She lifted her hips, and he growled with approval.

"That's right, lass," he said. "Ye're ready for me." His tongue flicked over her flesh, and she gave a low cry.

"Delicious," he whispered. "Perhaps I should place you on the dining table. A rare banquet that would be. Would ye like that, lass, to be spread over my table ready for me to devour whenever I wish?"

His voice had grown hoarse with need.

"Tell me dinner is served," he rasped. "Say the word and permit me to feast."

"Your Grace, I…"

"Just say it," he growled. "Tell me ye're mine for tonight."

"Yes," she said. "Yes, I'm yours."

He dipped his tongue again, a soft, velvet weapon caressing, teasing her, circling her flesh until it found what it wanted—the little nub of pleasure. Then he clamped his mouth over her and sucked hard.

Her body exploded, and she cried out, clutching at the bedsheet as the world shattered around her.

"Good, lass, Delilah…"

His words of praise fueled her pleasure as wave after wave engulfed her. As the waves receded, his caresses grew gentle, while he murmured her name.

The bed shifted, and he moved beside her. His maleness pressed against her side, and a musky aroma thickened in the air. He let out a deep sigh.

She opened her eyes and looked up. The moonlight formed a soft halo around his face as he gazed at her, his eyes glowing in the dark. The aftershocks of pleasure gave way to fear.

Fear that her heart was already lost.

He reached out to touch her face, and she turned her head away.

"Didn't you feel pleasure?"

She forced a smile. "Yes," she said. "You're an able teacher. Perhaps the man I marry will continue my education."

He hesitated, then nodded his head. "You

may compare us if you like, though I'd advise you not to voice your comparison. Sometimes the truth can be painful."

"Yes," she said, swallowing the bitterness in her voice. "It can."

The bed shifted, and he sat up. She reached for the hem of her nightrail, and a warm hand enclosed hers.

"Allow me."

He pulled the garment down, covering her legs.

"I should let you sleep, lass."

He crossed the floor, stopping at the desk where a pile of papers sat—her finished article. He only need lift the top sheet to see the name of the author.

Jeremiah Smith.

"You've been writing poetry?"

"Yes." Her stomach tightened at the lie.

"That's good," he said. "I'm doing all I can to find someone to publish them. May I read it?"

He picked up the top page, and she cried out.

"No!"

Chapter Seventeen

FRASER WATCHED HER on the bed. Moments before she'd been mewling with desire, yet now, she'd withdrawn from him, hurt in her eyes.

She wanted more.

Had he respected her less, he'd have spread her legs and buried himself inside her. But he valued her too much to take her as his mistress. Though she may deny it, she needed to avoid a scandal. She had a bright future ahead of her, and her desire to help the disadvantaged women of London, as well as her talent for writing, were better served with a spotless reputation.

But the need to claim her as his warred with his resolve. What might it be like to have her warm his bed every night? To see her belly round with his child?

He picked up a piece of paper on the desk, and she cried out.

"No!"

"Forgive me," he said, dropping the paper. "I've no right to intrude on your privacy or betray your trust."

She didn't reply, but the stricken expression on her face tore at his conscience.

"I didn't mean to cause you pain, lass," he said, taking her hands.

"You've not pained me."

"I forget how little experience you have of men," he said. "I should listen to Ma's counsel more."

"Your mother?" Her eyes widened. "Does she not like me?"

"On the contrary, she likes you a great deal. But Ma has always told me that a woman's heart is like porcelain, where a man's is made of granite. She said that a man might indulge in as much pleasure as he wishes and be forgiven for it. But she warned me that if a man's *indulgence* brings hurt to a woman, then he cannot call himself a real man."

She wiped her eyes and gave him a smile. "I think tonight's lesson has shown that you're a real man," she said. "I would like to continue my education. Three more lessons remain."

"And do you have a proposal for your next lesson?"

She nodded toward the window. "The mountain."

He lifted her hands to his lips. "Then, lass, I shall bid you good night so you can be sufficiently well-rested to conquer our mountain."

He released her hands, then retreated from the room. After he closed the door behind him, he could swear he heard a cry.

"It's magnificent!"

Miss Hart's joy swept aside any concerns Fraser might have had for her disposition. She seemed to have shaken off her melancholy from last night.

She'd taken to the mountain track with gusto. The drover's road to the pass was relatively easy-going, and she'd refused his help. But when they veered toward the summit, the terrain grew rougher. After some hesitation, she let him take her hand during the steeper parts, and his heart lifted each time she tightened her grip on him.

"I envy you," she said. "If I lived here, I'd climb the mountain every day."

If I lived here…

As if she understood the implication, she blushed. "Does the mountain have a name?" she asked.

"It's called *Benn mo Chridhe*—mountain of my heart."

"Mountain of my heart," she repeated. "I like that."

"My great-grandfather named it," he said. "He fell in love with the land here, almost as much as he fell in love with my great-grandmother."

"He was the one you inherited the title from?"

"Aye, one of that blackguard Jeremiah Smith's cursed Molineuxs."

Her smile disappeared.

"Forgive me, lass," he said. "Today is not the day to speak of enemies, for I'm with a friend, am I not?"

She picked up a stone and held it up. Something glittered in the rock, winking in the sunlight.

"What's this?" she asked.

"Its tiny crystals embedded in the granite."

"It's beautiful. Almost as if the rock were alive."

"It is," he said. "A living, breathing part of the land."

He handed her a flask. "Here, drink."

She wrinkled her nose. "It's not whisky, is it?"

He laughed. "No, it's water."

She took it, then picked her way over the rocks until she reached a large, flat slab that jutted up at an angle, pointing toward the sky. She looked overhead, exposing her throat, and his manhood twitched with the need to taste her skin.

She lowered her head, and their gazes met. Love of life glittered in her expression, and her face glowed with health and happiness.

"Ye look well, lass," he said, "far better than the pasty skin of London. Our land is doing you good."

"Would you prescribe a trip to the Highlands to solve the world's problems?"

"I would. It's the land I belong to, the land I love. Money, titles, it's all nonsense compared to this. The air is fresh, the water pure, and the rocks…"

He moved toward her and held her against the slab of rock—the very same slab he'd envisioned making love to his woman against. He closed his eyes and could almost see the lifeblood of the earth pulsing through the rock.

"We live for the land," he said. "We don't own it. We belong to it. It gives us life and hope. It feeds us, clothes us—the peat keeps us warm, and we have learned to take pleasure from everything around us."

She tipped her face up, and their mouths almost met. Her lips parted, and her sweet breath caressed his mouth. He had only to lower his head to claim those plump lips. The memory of the taste of her swirled in his mind. He longed to hear her little mewls of pleasure once more.

"What do ye think of your third lesson in pleasure, Miss Hart?"

Her tongue flicked out, moistening her lips.

"I enjoyed it very much," she said. "It's rendered me even more out of breath than the second lesson." She lifted her hand and touched his face, rubbing her thumb along the line of stubble at his jaw.

"I find myself in need of my fourth lesson," she whispered. "My thirst for learning refuses to be quenched."

"Then, you must ask for it, lass."

"Your Grace ..."

"No," he said. "Say my name. I want to hear it from your lips."

"Fraser..."

"That's it, lass," he whispered.

"Am I to receive my next lesson?"

"I require payment first," he said.

"With what?"

"May I read the poem you've been writing?"

"You've already seen my work."

"Ah, yes," he said, "but they were written before I began your education. I'll wager your poems have gained depth now you've widened your experience of pleasure."

"How can you be sure?"

"Because it's through experiencing life—the

primal, visceral reaction to the world and its pains and pleasures—that we can voice our emotions. And what is poetry, or any art form, if not an expression of emotion?"

She colored and looked away, and he took her hand.

"May I read it?"

"It-it's not finished."

"But you said last night you'd completed it. Did you deceive us?"

Guilt flickered across her expression.

"Don't you want me to read it, lass?"

"I do, but not yet."

"Is it your best work?" he asked.

Moisture glistened in her eyes, and she blinked, releasing a tear.

"I believe it is."

"Then you shall receive your next lesson when you permit me to read it. How else can I measure your progress?"

He cupped her cheek, and her lips parted. "You only need to say the word."

She hesitated as if in thought. Sadness flickered in her eyes, and she pulled free.

"Are ye well, lass?"

"Perhaps we should return," she said. "I had no idea how cold it would be at the summit."

"Very well."

On the journey back, she said little, giving him short answers to his questions. Most women he'd have believed to be tired, but she seemed energetic, taking the path with light, confident steps. Halfway down the drover's road, the carriage stood waiting. The driver jumped to his feet and opened the door. She uttered a word of thanks and climbed in, and Fraser followed.

She had already arranged a blanket over her knees and placed herself in the center of the seat so he could not easily sit beside her. He took the seat opposite and rapped on the side of the carriage, and it set off with a jolt.

As they approached the castle, her mood darkened, and she seemed deep in thought. She avoided his gaze, focused outside.

The carriage turned a corner, and the mountain disappeared from view. With a sigh, she sat back and looked down at her hands.

He leaned forward and placed a hand over one of hers. She jumped and met his gaze.

"Forgive me," he said. "I spoke out of turn."

Her eyes widened in question.

"Your poem. I had no right to question your honesty over it."

"It doesn't matter," she said, "I…"

"No, let me finish," he interrupted. "You're my guest, and it's my duty and pleasure to make you welcome. I want ye to trust me as I trust you."

His words, intended to comfort, only distressed her more. A tear spilled onto her cheek, and he lifted his hand and brushed it aside.

"Your Grace…"

He squeezed her hand. "Why don't you call me, Fraser?"

"It wouldn't be proper." Her voice wavered. What distressed her?

"Since when have you been ruled by propriety?" he asked. "My wee terrier says what she thinks and believes in herself. I would not have her change."

"Fraser…" she whispered. She lifted her gaze to him.

A ray of sunlight illuminated her eyes. Their rich amber color glowed with warmth and for a moment, they simply looked at each other, as if they were the only two people in existence.

The carriage drew to a halt, shattering the intimacy. He took her hand, and they climbed out.

"It's about time," a female voice said.

Ma stood by the carriage. "Fraser, I've been worried," she said. "You've been out for hours up the mountain. Poor Miss Hart must be exhausted."

"I'm quite all right, Mrs. MacGregor, I assure you," she said. "I wanted to climb *Beinn mo Chridhe.*"

Fraser smiled at her pronunciation but made no attempt to correct her.

"That'll be all," he said to the coachman.

"But make sure the carriage is ready tomorrow morning. We need to leave just after dawn to reach Edinburgh in time for the London coach."

"Aye, sir."

The carriage moved off, and Fraser led her inside. The sun dropped behind the mountain, and a shadow stretched across the ground. He shivered as the skin on the back of his neck tightened. But it was not just the cold. It was the expression in Lilah's eyes. An expression he'd rarely seen in a woman, for too often it was tainted by greed. But he recognized its purity, for it mirrored his own. It was an expression that would only lead to heartbreak.

In her eyes, as she looked back at him, he saw love.

Chapter Eighteen

A FTER ARRIVING HOME in London, her poem was finally complete.

Lilah placed her pen down and picked up the paper and blew on it. The ink glistened in the light, then dissolved into the paper as it dried. She read the lines, her eye following the shapes of the words she'd penned without thinking.

He had been right. At last, she had something worth saying, something from the heart, driven by passion. She had begun to question her beliefs almost as soon as she'd arrived in Scotland. Though he was an aristocrat, a Molineux, he shouldn't be defined by the blood which ran through his veins. Blood and ancestry meant nothing. What mattered was what he did—his beliefs, his love of the Highlands, and his care for the people who depended on him.

Even his admission of his feelings, though it hurt, was, at least, honest.

Lilah only had herself to blame for having fallen in love with him.

Yet her admission of that love had unlocked her heart, and the evidence lay stacked on the desk beside her. A love poem, written from her very soul.

Was that why poets led such melancholy lives? Did they need to experience heartbreak before they could express themselves? Or perhaps they needed to harden their hearts to survive. Lord Byron attracted scandal and left broken hearts wherever he went, but perhaps such notorious behavior had been necessary, to enable him to write such beautiful verse.

Was that what Lilah would have to become in order to survive?

A clock struck in the distance, three chimes. Tea would be waiting in the parlor. And Mr. Stock would be waiting for her in his offices in an hour—waiting for her final essay. Perhaps once she'd delivered the final piece, she might be able to look at *him* with a clear conscience.

She packed the poems into her pelisse, together with her essay, and slipped out of her chamber. She made her way down the staircase and past the longcase clock by the front parlor. The door was open.

"Why don't you come in?" a male voice said.

Sir Thomas sat, reclined in an armchair, his legs crossed.

"That's Dexter's armchair," she said.

He rose to his feet. "And I'm his guest."

"Does he know you're here?"

"Your sister does. She'll be here in a moment."

"Then, shall I pour the tea?"

She picked up a cup, and it rattled against the saucer as her hand shook.

"Are you all right, Miss Hart?" he asked. "Delilah?"

She wanted to admonish him for his familiarity, but concern was etched across his brow—the concern of a friend, and one who, despite his rank, understood her passion for equality.

"Sir Thomas, I…"

He placed his hand over hers. "You seem unhappy," he said, "and you have been ever since you returned from Scotland. Did you not enjoy your visit?"

"I did," she said. "The land was beautiful. Fresh air and mountains."

"Then why do you look so tired?" he asked. "If that's what fresh air does for you, I'd advise you to remain here in London. Perhaps I should send for Doctor Lucas."

She shook her head. "Doctor Lucas is a pompous fool."

Sir Thomas laughed. "He wouldn't welcome

such a description, though he has a reputation for being overly obsessed with the use of leeches. But I do think you should take care of yourself. Or…" he squeezed her hand, "…let someone take care of *you*."

She closed her eyes, but the memory of *him* invaded her mind, of his eyes which had shone with desire when he'd given her pleasure, and full, sensual lips which had kissed and caressed her to unimaginable ecstasy.

Sir Thomas sighed. "I care about you, Delilah," he said. "You know that, don't you?"

"There's no need," she replied.

He stroked her hand and turned it over.

"What's this?"

He tightened his grip and inspected her fingers. "Ink stains? What have you been doing?"

"Writing."

"Again?" He smiled. "Your industry is to be applauded. I do believe a woman needs an occupation to keep herself satisfied and stimulate her mind…" He hesitated and cleared his throat. "…Particularly a married woman."

"I…"

"No, don't say anything," he said. "But let me assure you that *I* would never do anything to make you unhappy. Quite the contrary."

A series of notes rang out from the clock on the mantelshelf, and she rose to her feet.

"What are you doing?" he asked, rising with

her.

"It's half-past three," she said. "I must be going."

"Where?"

"It's not important."

"May I accompany you?"

"I'd rather be on my own."

He withdrew his hand. "Then your wish is my command," he said. "I cannot ask you to honor and obey me—at least not yet. But I hope, one day, you'll always turn to me for help and support."

She dipped a curtsey, then left him alone in the parlor.

⇥⤞✦⤝⇤

"THIS IS WONDERFUL, Miss Hart. Your best yet."

The editor of the *City Chronicle* nodded his approval.

"This essay will cause a stir," he said. "Society will really question the worth of the aristocracy."

"But I've written a balanced article, Mr. Stock," Lilah said. "See the conclusion? It argues that the world we live in can never be completely fair. The fortunes and misfortunes of birth are something we must accept, and we should be defined by what we do with our lives. I trust you won't edit too savagely."

"You must trust me to know my readership best," he said. "But the words will be yours—or, at least, Jeremiah's. I'll merely make the necessary adjustments to fit the tone of my publication. You wouldn't believe the difference that can be made by changing just a few words in every hundred."

"That's what I'm afraid of," she said.

"You trust me, don't you? Nothing I publish is at risk of being branded as libelous. You're safe on that count. I wouldn't want Molineux to lodge a lawsuit against me."

"It's not a lawsuit I'm concerned about. It's your readers and what they might do."

"You've nothing to worry about from my readers," he said. "They're respectable, hard-working men, unlike the Frenchies, who'd think nothing of decapitating a nobleman."

"I'm not sure…"

"Our readership is six hundred, Miss Hart," he said. "Less than half will read my paper from cover to cover, and an even smaller proportion will be sufficiently moved by what you write to take any action. Compare that to the population of London, which is substantially more than one million. Consider how unlikely it is that even two of my readers will pass each other on the street.

"I suppose the chances are small."

"There!" he said. "I knew you'd see sense."

She rose to her feet, and he showed her out. As the clerk ushered her through the door, she spotted a familiar figure ahead of her in the street.

"Sir Thomas! Are you following me?"

His expression betrayed him every time. He'd never be able to cheat at cards.

"Permit me to escort you home," he said.

"I can manage on my own."

"Very well, if you insist, I shall leave you in peace."

Only when Lilah reached the end of the street, did she realize that, for the first time, Sir Thomas had accepted her first refusal.

Perhaps he was beginning to respect her wishes.

Chapter Nineteen

F RASER WATCHED AS Hart flicked through the sheaf of papers.

"Thank you for agreeing to see me, Mr. Hart," he said.

The banker's attention remained fixed on the documents in front of him. Save a slight tic in his jaw, Fraser might have believed he hadn't heard.

No wonder Hart had amassed a fortune. The man possessed two qualities needed to succeed in business. The first was the ability to read what others were thinking while concealing his own thoughts behind an impassive, cold demeanor.

The second was a dispassionate ruthlessness. Hart would think nothing of using the letter of the law to ruin a rival.

But perhaps he could be forgiven. Despite his wealth, Hart was still shunned by most of the *ton*.

Only few exceptions, such as Earl Stiles, saw fit to recognize the Harts in public as acceptable acquaintances.

And Fraser himself, of course. However, Hart was not a man to soften his approach to a business deal on account of an acquaintance.

Or a friendship.

In all likelihood, Hart lacked friends. Any friendship with him would exist purely for the benefit of Dexter Hart. And Fraser doubted whether such a man was in need of anyone.

A pity. Fraser found himself respecting the man, even if he couldn't bring himself to actually *like* him.

Hart set the papers aside. "Your projected profit figures seem impressive," he said.

"So, you'll agree to a loan?" Fraser asked.

Hart shook his head. "Unfortunately, your financial position stands on a knife-edge."

"I'm experiencing a temporary dip in cash-flow until the orders come in," Fraser said. "The term of the loan need not be longer than a year. Two, at most."

"No banker of sound mind would lend you a farthing without collateral."

"I have my London property."

"Which is already mortgaged." Hart rolled his eyes. "Even a man of the meanest intelligence would understand that I'd be a fool to lend you funds on a property to which your other creditors have a prior claim."

"The loan on the house is less than the value of the house itself."

"That's immaterial," Hart said. "The value of a house which you're forced to sell to avoid bankruptcy is substantially less than it would be had you no intention of selling."

"Bankruptcy is a little extreme, don't you think?"

"One of your creditors might agree with you in isolation," Hart said, "but I must consider your debts as a whole." He picked up a piece of paper. "This one, for instance, attracts interest of thirty percent, which falls due next month. How do you intend to service it? Have you persuaded the trustees of the Molineux estate to release funds? There's an entailed property in Hertfordshire, is there not?"

"Yes, Molineux Manor," Fraser said. "How do you know that?"

"I make it my business, Your Grace, to understand the full extent of the risk," Hart said, crisply. "Are you in a position to sell Molineux Manor?"

Fraser shook his head. "The trustees would rather see it crumble into ruin than suffer the indignity of being sold at auction. I can't even sell the silverware inside it. Once the previous duke's debts were cleared, there was no cash left—only the two properties, Molineux Manor and Clayton

House."

"And you saw fit to sink your own funds into renovating Clayton House," Hart said.

"Clayton House is not entailed, so I can do what I want with it."

"You should have sold it when you had the chance," Hart said. "A mortgaged property is just one more fixed cost for you to service."

Hart leaned back in his chair and folded his arms. "I'm sorry," he said. "Much as I'd like to invest, the risk is too great. I cannot see how you'll service the debts you already have, let alone further debt."

He raised his eyebrows as if expecting Fraser to challenge. But the arrogance in his air told Fraser that his mind was made up. A man like Hart was impervious to persuasion, and Fraser wasn't going to give him the satisfaction of seeing him grovel.

"I can service the debts from my business," he said. "I've received sufficient orders for whisky to cover the interest for the next two years, at which point we'll be in a position to deliver and can repay the loans in full."

"And if you aren't?" Hart asked. "What if something happens to halt production? Or if you encounter unforeseen expenses?"

"Then my creditors will enjoy their thirty percent for a little longer," Fraser said.

Hart narrowed his eyes. "I'm still not convinced the population of London will buy the stuff. Personally, I prefer brandy."

"A banker will always have a lower appetite for risk than a businessman," Fraser said.

"Not at all," Hart replied. "I'm merely more capable of weighing the risks against the potential for return."

"And you believe the potential return from my business isn't worth the risk?"

"Not when there's a very real chance of that return manifesting itself as a total loss of one's investment."

A total loss?

Had Fraser suspected Hart to be in possession of emotions, he might have taken his words as an insult and slammed his fist into his jaw to wipe that arrogant sneer off his face. But as it was, Hart was a soulless financier stating what he believed to be a fact and nothing more.

A clock chimed in the distance, and someone knocked on the office door.

"Come in!" Hart called.

A young man entered. Blonde-haired with warm brown eyes and a demeanor to match, he looked the antithesis of the man sitting opposite Fraser.

"Your next client is waiting for you, Hart," he said. "Shall I tell him you'll be ready presently?"

Hart glanced at his pocket watch.

"Tell him I'll be down directly, Peyton," he

said. "I think we're done here."

"Very good." The man disappeared.

"My business partner," Hart said, rising to his feet. "A little too kind for my liking, but he has the makings of an excellent financier."

He held out his hand, and Fraser stood and took it.

"No hard feelings," Hart said, "but business is business. I cannot invest in your enterprise, but I wish you success with it."

"But without your help."

"A man should help himself, Molineux," Hart said. "A lesson the aristocracy will need to learn if it's to survive. But permit me to give you some advice, if I may."

"Which is?"

"I'd minimize your acts of philanthropy until you are more—solvent."

"Philanthropy?"

"From what my sister tells me, you've been using substantial sums of money to support charitable causes. I understand Mrs. Forbes and her establishment have much to thank you for, but I doubt your creditors would agree."

"You've discussed me with Miss Hart?" Fraser asked.

"Naturally," came the reply. "Did you think I'd place my sister's wellbeing in the hands of a man about whom I know nothing? Rest assured, Your Grace, had Delilah given me cause to believe you were a scoundrel, our discussion today would have taken place at dawn, not three in the afternoon."

Fraser's cheeks warmed under Hart's scrutiny as he tightened his grip on Fraser's hand. Had Miss Hart told her brother what they had done in Scotland? They had returned over a fortnight ago, yet the memory of her cries of ecstasy still dominated his dreams. His manhood twitched at the image of her on the bed, her willing body spread out for him like an offering, and he averted his gaze lest her brother read the wicked thoughts in his mind.

Then Hart released his hand.

"I trust there are no hard feelings," he said. "It's a business decision. What say you join me at home tonight, and perhaps you can bring along some of that whisky of yours? I may not wish to become an investor, but that doesn't mean I cannot become a customer."

"I'd be delighted." Fraser's blood warmed at the prospect of seeing *her* again.

"The ladies will be dining out, so we'll have the house to ourselves," Hart said. "Just an informal evening with friends. You already know Sir Thomas, of course."

Sir Thomas—*dear lord*! The last man Fraser wanted was to spend an evening engaging in small talk with his rival.

He caught his breath. Since when had he viewed Sir Thomas as a rival?

Chapter Twenty

W ELL, THIS WAS *awkward...*

Fraser wrinkled his nose at the sickly-sweet sherry under the watchful gaze of his host and the other guest. Were it not for the early hour, Fraser would have cut through the niceties of polite conversation and asked Hart to open the whisky flask he'd brought and be done with it.

Judging by the expression on his face, Sir Thomas was just as delighted—or not—to see Fraser. After issuing the slightest of bows, the man had crossed the parlor in his rather affected little walk—almost as if he were relieving himself in his breeches—and took the seat next to Hart as if to affirm his greater relationship with the man.

Sir Thomas was beginning to reveal himself as something of a shadow of their host, obviously trying to ingratiate Hart by mirroring him in all aspects. Each time Hart crossed and uncrossed his legs, the baronet repeated the gesture. When Sir Thomas scratched his left nostril, almost immediately after Hart had done so, Fraser had to cough to suppress the snort of laughter.

"Is something the matter?" Sir Thomas asked.

"Not at all," Fraser replied. "I'm finding our conversation most insightful. It's a wonder more business isn't conducted in private homes rather than in clubs. A man in his home is less likely to conceal the truth."

"Are you accusing Hart of being deceitful when conducting business?" Sir Thomas asked, nodding toward their host. But other than casting the baronet a sharp glance, Hart said nothing.

"No, you misunderstand me," Fraser laughed. "I'm just saying I'd prefer to discuss business in the comfort of my home, where matters can be discussed less formally."

"Is that why you're wasting all your cash on that mausoleum?" Sir Thomas asked. "So you can conduct your business in it?"

Hart frowned at Sir Thomas, then he addressed Fraser. "Are the renovations finished?"

"Almost," Fraser said. "I should be able to move in next week. It'll be a relief to save on the rent on my lodgings, and it strikes me as efficient use of resources to live and conduct my business in the same building."

"But not a good marriage prospect," Sir

Thomas said.

"How so?" Fraser asked.

"No future wife would relish her home being taken over by offices and clerks," he said. "Ladies value their privacy and should be kept away from matters of business. What say you, Hart? You wouldn't want your sister—any of your sisters—to live in such an environment?"

Could the man be any more transparent?

Hart said nothing, but Sir Thomas rattled on.

"You have an extraordinary approach to business," he said. "A businessman must follow established procedures to succeed. Hart, would you not agree?"

"Perhaps," Hart said. "But I'd argue that undue restriction stunts innovation."

"I don't understand…"

"I think," Fraser said, "our host is saying that in order to evolve, a man must challenge the laws he's expected to adhere to."

Sir Thomas shook his head. "The world would disagree with you."

"That doesn't mean it can't be done," Fraser said. "Consider Edward Jenner, the perfect example of a case where challenging the boundaries of expectation has greatly improved the world."

Confusion clouded Sir Thomas's expression, but Hart nodded in agreement. "He was a fellow countryman of yours, was he not?"

"Aye," Fraser said. "I followed his work with interest and read his obituary in the papers earlier this year. He was derided by the clergy for being ungodly because he tested his vaccine on a child. Yet, that test has saved more lives than any of us could ever hope to do."

"I've never heard of the man," Sir Thomas said. "Was he a friend of yours?"

"He studied at St. Andrews some ten years before me," Fraser said, "but I'd argue that he's a friend to every man, woman, and child, who has been prevented from catching smallpox."

"Quite so," Hart said.

Sir Thomas glanced at Hart, then nodded vigorously. "Oh, *that* Edward Jenner! Of course, yes, exactly so, indeed. A very fine man."

The temptation to indulge in a little sport was too great.

"I see you're a perceptive man, Sir Thomas," Fraser said. "I'd be interested to hear your opinion on some of my own initiatives. In particular, with regards to the provision of benefits to employees in addition to their wage."

"Such as?"

"The right to medical care, for one," Fraser said, "and an annuity for life when they're no longer capable of working."

Sir Thomas hesitated and glanced at their host. "I'd be interested to hear what Hart has to say."

"Naturally," Fraser replied, "but I'm sure we'd both like to hear what *you* have to say first. Mr. Pelham was telling me in Whites only last week that you'd told him how invaluable you were to Hart and that he viewed you as a great proficient."

Hart raised his eyebrows. "Is that so?"

Sir Thomas colored. "Present company excepted, Hart, but Pelham's a typical example of a commoner trying to impress a duke. He must have exaggerated for your benefit, Molineux."

Hart leaned back, seemingly unaffected by Sir Thomas's insult about *commoners*. Fraser doubted whether Hart or Pelham, for that matter, could ever be accused of exaggeration.

Or sycophancy. Sir Thomas had revealed an aversion to the working man. Why, then, had he befriended Hart and followed the man around like a gundog?

There must be only one reason. *Delilah*—and, more to the point, her not insubstantial dowry. Sir Thomas's love of cash, of which Hart had plenty, surpassed his dislike of the lower classes.

Before Fraser could respond, a footman entered, brandishing a silver salver bearing a single card. He approached Hart, who picked up the card and read it.

"Forgive me, gentleman, I must take my leave," he said. "Supper must wait. Please excuse me, it's a matter of urgency." Hart's expression changed to one of satisfaction, and for a moment, Fraser caught a flash of cold triumph in his eyes. Most likely, a business rival was about to be crushed.

He rose from his seat, issued a bow, then exited the room, the footman in his wake.

Sir Thomas gestured toward the decanter. "Another sherry?" he asked. "I could ring the bell for someone to serve us."

"No, thank you," Fraser said. "Now our host has left, I should go."

"Quite so."

Fraser rose and stretched out his hand. Sir Thomas took it, a self-satisfied smile on his face.

"I wish you every success in your business ventures, Sir Thomas," Fraser said, "unless, of course, we emerge as business rivals."

"If we find ourselves in pursuit of the same assets, I believe *I'll* emerge the victor," Sir Thomas said.

"I've no idea what you're talking about."

Sir Thomas tightened his grip, pulled Fraser close, and lowered his voice.

"You must think me a fool," he said.

"Of course not."

"Perhaps you believe your barbaric Scottish ways are more likely to secure the spoils."

"I don't understand you," Fraser said.

"Yes, you do." Sir Thomas's face twisted into a scowl. "Shall I tell you what I think?"

"If you must," Fraser said.

"You should leave her alone."

"Who?"

Sir Thomas let out a huff. "Don't be a fool!" he said. "Leave Miss Hart alone and stop pestering her."

"I wasn't aware I was pestering anybody," Fraser said. "Miss Hart knows her own mind. If she found my company abhorrent, I'd be the first to know."

"She doesn't always know what's best for her," Sir Thomas said. "Women are easily persuaded, which is why you were able to spirit her away to some godforsaken wilderness with none to protect her."

"She had a chaperone all the time she was in Scotland," Fraser said. "Not that it's any concern of yours."

"Then why did she return so downhearted?" Sir Thomas asked. "What did you do to her when you had her in your clutches?"

Fraser laughed. "I believe she rather enjoyed being in my—as you put it—*clutches*, very much. At least it sounded like she did."

Sir Thomas's face turned red. "Why, you damned bloody savage!" he cried. "You come here with your uncouth ways and fanciful ideas. Mark my words, you'll sing a different tune when the mob turns on *you*. As for Miss Hart, she's mine, and if you've defiled her, I'll bloody well…"

"Stop!" a female voice shrieked.

Both men turned.

Lilah stood in the doorway, hands fisted at her sides, her face flushed.

"How dare you discuss me!" she cried.

How much had she overheard?

"Miss Hart," Fraser said, "Forgive me, but…"

She silenced him by raising her hand. "I was speaking to Sir Thomas. Did I hear aright, sir, that you believe me incapable of knowing my own mind?"

"Delilah…" Sir Thomas protested, but she interrupted him.

"How dare you address me with such familiarity!" she cried. "Please leave."

"Delilah, please listen to reason. I have your best interests at heart." He gestured toward Fraser. "This man is a savage whose intentions are dishonorable. He has no claim over you, whereas I…"

"That's enough!" she said. "If you won't be told, I'll summon the servants and have you thrown out."

"I think you should honor the lady's request," Fraser said, "unless you wish to see my savagery unleashed."

"But I'm Mr. Hart's guest," Sir Thomas said, "and he's my particular friend."

"And do you know what else he is?" Fraser asked, raising his hands.

"What?"

Fraser smiled. "Not here."

Sir Thomas stepped back. "You can go to the devil," he said, then he addressed Miss Hart.

"Dearest, Delilah," he said. "I care about you. I…"

"You only care about yourself," she interrupted. "Just go, *Tommie Tiptoes*."

His face darkened into a scowl, then he issued a bow and left. Shortly after, Fraser heard the front doors open and close.

"I thought he'd never go. Miss Hart, I'm sorry you had to hear what I said to him. I meant no disrespect."

She bit her lip and looked away. Had her visit to Scotland made her so unhappy? He thought she'd enjoyed herself. Ma had liked her very much, and she'd seen impressed by the distillery. And her lessons…

Her distress was so thick, he could almost taste it. And another sensation, an unwelcome one, threatened to engulf him. The urge to ease her pain. Not just today but forever.

The raw, base lust he'd first harbored for her had been refined, distilled, then left to mature inside his heart until it revealed the truth.

He loved her.

He loved her passion for life, her advocacy for the downtrodden. But most of all, he loved how she was made for him. She responded to the call of the wilderness in his Highland home as if she belonged there. She was his Highland queen, the one woman who could fulfill him.

The urge to claim her completely had besieged him ever since he'd returned to London. And he could deny it no more.

A tear spilled onto her cheek, and he brushed it aside.

"Where's my terrier?"

A ghost of a smile played on her lips.

"That's better, lass."

"Forgive me," she said, "and forgive Sir Thomas. He spoke out of turn."

She gestured toward the door and gave him a watery smile. "Forgive me, I must be going. Dorothea and I have a dinner engagement, but stay if you wish, until Dexter returns."

"No, I must go," he said. "I shouldn't have come."

Her smile disappeared, and he reached for her hand.

"Miss Hart, did Sir Thomas speak the truth? Did your visit to my home make you unhappy?"

"Of course not," she said. "It was as I expected."

"My own expectations have undergone a transformation since we returned," he said.

"How so?"

He shook his head. "Now's not the time to discuss it."

"Then, when?" Her lips lifted into a smile. "You owe me one more lesson, I believe."

"And what will I get in return?" he asked.

"Will you show me the poems you wrote while you were in the Highlands?"

"I'd be glad to."

"Did you show them to that fool?"

"Sir Thomas?" She shook her head. "No. They're a little too—*personal*. Besides, he has little understanding of beauty."

"I'm sure he's remarked on your beauty many times."

She let out a laugh. "Shame on you, sir, if you think to flatter me. True beauty is far superior to mere aesthetics. If I were faced with such superficiality in a suitor, I'd douse his ardor with a bucketful of ice down his breeches."

"*There's* my wee terrier."

She gave him a smile which, this time, reached her eyes, and his insides tightened with longing.

"I'm afraid there's no time to show my poems to you now," she said.

"Perhaps you could call on me at my lodgings."

"At Clayton House?"

He shook his head. "The refurbishments are not complete. I'm lodging in Curzon Street, so as not to be disturbed by the work. Are you able to visit on Saturday? I can send my carriage to collect you at four."

"I can walk."

"I know you can, lass, but I ask you to indulge me."

"Very well."

He drew her to him, and she tipped her face up. He lowered his lips to hers and flicked his tongue out, tracing the seam of her mouth. Willingly, she parted her lips, and he slipped his tongue inside.

The sensations sent a firebolt through him, and he hardened in his breeches.

"Delilah!" a female voice called in the distance, and she pulled free, her mouth swollen from his kiss.

She called out. "Coming, Thea!"

"I should go," he said.

"Until Saturday."

Saturday. That gave him four days to prepare for the day his life was going to change.

The day he declared his love for Delilah Hart, and offered her his heart and his hand.

Chapter Twenty-One

THE CARRIAGE DREW to a halt in Curzon Street. Lilah stepped out and looked around, but there was nobody about to recognize her. Though she might declare she cared nothing for propriety, she did care about her family's reputation. She owed it to her brother to behave appropriately by not gallivanting around London unchaperoned.

Thea was too old for marriage, and Daisy was a forbidden topic in the Hart household. So Dexter's hopes were pinned on Lilah to marry a title.

Sir Thomas might only be a baronet, but he was the only unmarried, titled man to have shown any inclination toward wanting Dexter as a brother-in-law.

But Lilah found herself wanting another.

She ascended the steps to the townhouse, and the door swung inward to reveal a liveried footman.

"The master awaits you in the drawing room."

He led her inside into a large room overlooking the street. Fraser stood by the window, his back to her. The light of the setting sun caught in his hair, giving it a warm glow.

"Miss Hart, Your Grace," the footman said.

"Very good, Stevenson. Now leave us."

He turned, and her heart fluttered.

A soft smile curved on his mouth as if he understood her body's desires.

"Miss Hart."

His voice, a low growl, resonated through her, and she moved toward him.

"Your Grace."

"I think we can dispense with the formalities, lass." He held out his hand. "Come here."

Large fingers curled around her wrist, and he pulled her close.

"I believe you have something to yield to me today," he whispered.

"Do I?" Her voice came out in a squeak.

"Aye, lass," he said, "something which you have entrusted to my eyes only. Something *intimate*."

His tongue curled over the final word as if savoring the taste of it, and she blushed at the memory of intimacies they'd already shared.

His smile broadened, and he shook his head.

"I mustn't tease you," he said, "though I find myself enjoying the effect."

"Must you be so cruel to one who's in your power?"

"You have equal power over me, lass. You only need learn how to wield it, and I would be in thrall to you, for all eternity."

"Now you're talking nonsense," she said.

He released her hand, and her skin tightened at the sense of loss.

"You do me an injustice, Miss Hart."

"Perhaps we should engage in the real business of the afternoon," she said.

She pulled a sheaf of papers from her reticule and handed them to him. He smiled and placed them on a table.

"Aren't you going to look at them?" she asked.

"Let me get you a drink first."

He crossed the floor to a table laden with decanters. He reached for one, poured a small amount of amber liquid into a beveled glass, then handed it to her.

"Shouldn't you ask me what I want?" she asked.

"Trust me," he said. "Let me give ye what ye *need*. Savor the aroma."

She lifted the glass to her nose and breathed

in the sharp spices, which mellowed and sweetened as she filled her lungs.

"It smells like heaven," she whispered.

"That's because it's forbidden," he said. "It was distilled forty years ago. My grandfather had whisky in his blood. Not only did he turn a blind eye to the moonshine on his estate, he partook of it himself. He set some aside to mature for future generations, knowing that he wouldn't live to enjoy it. This is the only bottle I have left. I keep it with me as a reminder that sometimes a man must be patient. The years have given it character. A soul."

"You speak as if it's a living thing."

"It is, to me," he said. "It's in my veins and in my heart, and is irreplaceable."

"Then it should be preserved."

"Hidden away in the dark? What would be the point of that, lass? It's meant to be relished by those rare souls capable of appreciating it."

She looked at the glass in her hand. It was as if he'd entrusted her with a piece of his soul. Her fingers trembled, and a large, warm hand closed over hers and steadied her.

"Be still, lass," he whispered.

Her senses were assaulted by warmth and spices—the aroma of whisky combined with the woody, musky scent of man. She closed her eyes, and her mind floated in the delicious darkness.

"Yield to me," he whispered. "Feel it. Feel all

of it." His thumb teased her fingers, guiding them across the glass. With her fingertips, she explored the edges of the pattern etched into it. Every ridge, every angle, sliding over the smooth glass as if it were alive. Gently, but firmly, he nudged the rim against her mouth, coaxing her lips open.

"That's it, lass. Part them for me."

Heat bloomed in her cheeks. He tipped the glass up, and she flicked her tongue out. The warm, smoky liquid slid into her mouth, and flavor burst on her tongue.

"Good girl."

Her body tightened at his gentle praise.

"How do I taste?" he whispered.

Soft fingertips caressed her neck, and she swallowed. Liquid fire coated her throat, warming her blood, and igniting the fire in her center. He lowered the glass, and she flicked her tongue out again, chasing the delicious sensation.

"Ah, lass, are ye gaining an appetite for my nectar?"

She gave a squeak of embarrassment as her body strained with need.

"Ye only need say the word, lass, and you could savor the taste each day."

His words thickened the fog of lust, which swirled in her mind.

"W-would you offer me something so precious?" she whispered.

He plucked the glass from her fingers, then

dipped his head and pressed his forehead against hers. His eyes glowed at her, as if stars lived deep inside his soul, and she inhaled the heady, intoxicating scent of whisky on his breath— together with the softer aroma of heather and Highland air.

"Aye, lass, I would."

His expression bore the desire she had come to recognize. But something else shimmered in his eyes. A burning need.

And love.

"Have I earned my final lesson?" she asked.

Raw hunger pulsed in his eyes. "Are ye certain, lass?"

"Yes."

"Do you realize that with the final lesson comes the point of no return?"

"I do," she said. "I can think of no better teacher to…" she hesitated, "…to give myself to."

"Then, I shall treasure your gift, lass, and prove myself worthy of your trust. Come. My chamber awaits."

As Fraser opened the door, small, delicate fingers tightened their grip on him, and the ache in his groin intensified.

Ye gods, she was the most desirable woman

he'd ever known! Not just for her beauty, which shone from within, but her feisty nature, tempered by her caring heart.

The interior of his chamber reflected his tastes, the walls adorned with tapestries and things from home. The huge, canopied bed was covered in a thick woolen blanket bearing the colors of his family's plaid.

He released her hand and motioned toward the bed. Understanding, she sat, reaching out to caress the plaid covering.

"It's beautiful," she whispered.

"Aye," he said. "I've brought my home to London. I'll have the furnishings taken to Clayton House when the work is completed. Even a temporary home must be furnished in comfort, aye?"

Disappointment flickered in her eyes. "Temporary? You intend to leave London?"

"My heart belongs to the land of my ancestors." He sat beside her and placed his hand on her cheek. "But, lately, I find my heart yearning to remain in London."

"Your business must make demands of you here," she said, turning her head away.

He smiled to himself. Did she know that the tone of her voice betrayed her?

"Not just my business, lass," he said, "but the needs of my body and the calling of my heart."

She tensed, and her hands curled into fists.

Stubborn lass! Would she continue to deny her desires? Surely a woman with her intelligence would understand his declaration, even if he were incapable of voicing it directly. Or, perhaps it frightened her? Did she intend, after all, to marry that fool Sir Thomas? She was worth more than that. With her fire and compassion, she was fit to be a duchess.

His duchess.

"*Bean mo chridhe,*" he whispered.

Woman of my heart.

Together they would forge a bond stronger than the mountain—strong enough to withstand the responsibilities which came with his ancestry—both the Scottish and the English. He closed his eyes and pictured his woman—her mouth parted in surprise as he pleasured her thoroughly. And finally, her eyes sparkling with joy as she placed his child in his arms.

His child.

His eyes snapped open. From where had that notion come?

"Delilah…" he breathed.

She turned her head until their gazes locked. Her nostrils flared, the only sign of her anticipation.

And her need.

"Are ye my willing pupil?" he asked.

"Yes," she whispered. "Tell me what to do."

He caressed her face, running his thumb

along her lips.

"What shall I teach ye?"

"Pleasure," she said. "I want you to take command of me." Her face flushed, and she bit her lip.

His hands itched to remove her clothes, to reveal that lush body underneath. But she must come to him. "Strip for me, lass."

She didn't move.

"Must I repeat my request?"

She shook her head, then stood. Arms trembling, she reached behind her gown and tugged at the ties. She gave a little huff of frustration as she fumbled behind her.

"May I be of assistance?" he asked.

He cupped her face and brushed a tear away with his thumb.

"Are ye unhappy, lass?"

"No." She gestured with her hand. "It's just…all this…it-it's too much."

"Shall we stop?"

"No!" she cried.

"There's no shame in giving yourself to me," he said, "but it must be your choice." He reached behind her and caught the ties at the back of her dress. Her body trembled against him.

"May I?"

She nodded, and he undid the ties. Then he released her and watched as she grasped her skirts and pulled her dress over her head.

He reached for her chemise, and she held up her hand.

"No," she said. "Let me."

He backed away and sighed, fighting the disappointment. His whole body throbbed in eagerness to be buried inside her.

Mischief glittered in her eyes.

"I believe you commanded *me* to remove my clothes, Your Grace."

Desire surged in him as she peeled off her undergarments, wearing nothing but her stockings. She reached for the top of one stocking.

"No!" he cried hoarsely. "Let me. Lay back on the bed."

She obeyed, then he took her foot in his hands and lifted it to his lips, kissing the toes through the silk stocking. Then he ran his hand along her leg. Her body trembled, and she let out a soft sigh.

He leaned forward and brushed his lips against the ribbon holding her stocking in place. Her breathing grew heavy as he tugged at the ribbon and hooked his fingers under the stocking. He rolled the stocking down and placed a soft kiss on her bare knee. The skin of her thigh was flushed a delectable shade of pink, and he nearly spent in his breeches at the prospect of her flesh waiting to be claimed.

When she lay naked before him like a delicious offering, he stood back to admire her. Her body was petite yet possessed lovely curves. Perfect breasts fashioned to fit his palms, a delicate waist he could span with his hands, and the flare of her hips with a tempting thatch of curls at the center. She closed her eyes, obviously ashamed of her vulnerability.

"Delilah," he said. "Will ye look at me?"

She opened her eyes.

"Good, lass," he said. "Keep your eyes on me."

He removed his jacket and tossed it behind him. His necktie came next, then he unlaced his shirt and removed it. Her breath hitched, and he gave a soft chuckle.

Her eyes widened as she lowered her gaze to his manhood, which was painfully hard now, almost brushing his stomach.

"Do you like what you see, lass?"

She dragged her teeth along her lower lip, then gave him a wicked smile.

"You forget, sir, I was raised in the country. I've seen many bulls in rut."

The tremor in her voice betrayed her nervousness, yet still, she teased him!

"I ought to discipline you for such insolence," he said. "No tutor would permit his pupil to speak to him in such an unruly manner."

She grinned at him.

He reached for the glass and swirled the

whisky round. Just enough remained for his purposes. He climbed onto the bed next to her.

"No," he commanded as she tried to sit. "Remain where you are so that we may enjoy your lesson." He held the glass up to the light and rotated it, letting the light dance off the facets of the crystal.

"I intend to enjoy this whisky to the full."

He reached over and cupped a breast, relishing the silken skin against his fingertips.

"Is that good, lass?"

"Yes," she whispered. He brushed a thumb across her nipple, and it beaded against his skin.

"So responsive," he whispered. "So needy."

He dipped a finger into the whisky and held it over her breast, a bead of amber liquid dripped onto her nipple, and she gave a little gasp.

"How does it feel?" he whispered.

She shook her head.

"Tell me, lass," he said. "To gain your reward, you must hide nothing from me."

"Hot," she whispered. "Sharp, delicious. It feels like...oh!" She cried out as he took her nipple in his mouth, running his tongue around the tip.

Perhaps this was how the best whisky was to be enjoyed, to enhance the flavor of his woman.

His Highland queen.

He tipped the glass until a dribble of liquid fell onto her stomach.

The finest desserts were enhanced with a dram of whisky, and today he would feast on such a treat. He lowered his head and ran his tongue across her body, following the trail of the liquor, until he met the center of her belly.

"Fraser…"

His name on her lips was almost his undoing, and he gritted his teeth. He placed a hand on her thigh and brushed his thumb against her damp curls. With a sigh, she parted her legs.

"Oh, sweet lord, lass," he groaned. "I can feel you're ready for me." He slipped his finger inside her, and she shivered, drawing his finger deeper in.

"Do you want something, lass?"

"Please!" she cried.

He lowered his head and inhaled her scent, then he flicked his tongue across her flesh and tasted her. Her body bucked, and he lifted his head once more, and she gave a sharp growl of impatience.

"How long shall I make you wait?" he asked, teasing her. "When shall I instruct ye to take pleasure?"

"Now…"

"Are you sure, lass?" he asked. "Are ye ready?"

"Yes!"

He covered her with his body and claimed her mouth.

She curled her tongue round his, and soft moans of pleasure rumbled in her throat.

"Do you give yerself freely, lass?"

"Yes."

Slowly he entered her, marveling at the heat which enveloped him, until he met her barrier.

"Look at me, lass," he whispered.

The trust in her eyes tore at his heart.

"Do you want me?"

"Yes, Fraser," she whispered. "Yes, I want you."

He sheathed himself fully inside her. Her eyes widened, and she let out a cry.

"Good lass," he whispered. "There is only a little pain your first time."

"I felt no pain," she said.

"What did ye feel?"

She blinked and rolled her eyes as if searching for the words. "It was like the sting of the whisky on my tongue," she whispered. "Sharp at first, followed by a delicious warmth. Deep inside."

"And do you want another sip?"

She shifted her legs further apart. "I want to drink my fill."

He withdrew slowly, then eased himself inside her once more, savoring the feel of her body.

"Mmm…" She arched her back.

Her body shuddered, and he struggled to maintain control—he had waited so long for this, had fantasized about her every night.

At all costs, her pleasure must come first.

"Fraser!"

Her body clenched around him. He thrust once more into her, and his own body shattered. Shards of pleasure ripped through him, exploding into stars.

"Oh, lass!" he cried.

He continued to thrust, drawing out every drop of pleasure, then he rolled onto his side, still inside her. She clung to him, her body trembling. He grasped the blanket and pulled it over them both, then he held her.

"Fraser," she whispered. "My Fraser..."

A lock of hair had fallen over her face, and he brushed it aside. Her heart, which hammered against his chest, slowed to a deep, steady rhythm. He stroked her hair, and she sighed like a contented kitten.

She was his soul mate. He had no wish to spend another day without her in his bed.

As soon as he returned her home, he would seek out her brother and ask for her hand in marriage.

Chapter Twenty-Two

L ILAH OPENED HER eyes and reached out. The bed bore his imprint and a faint trace of warmth where he'd lain. A delicious soreness lingered between her thighs, and she blushed at the memory of the pleasures he'd given her. After making love, he'd let her sleep, then woke her, coaxing her to pleasure with expert fingers until she was ready for him again.

But this time, the lesson was different. With gentle instructions, he taught her how to please him, letting her ride him. Lacing his fingers with hers, he guided her as she took her own pleasure while she rocked her body to draw him deeper inside.

The door opened, and she lifted her head.

"Has my Highland queen recovered from her exertions?"

He stood in the doorway, half-dressed, shirt open, revealing a dusting of hair, which she now knew grew thicker lower down.

"How long have you been awake?" she asked.

"Long enough to read these." He lifted his hand, which held a sheaf of papers. "Your poems are beautiful. I've never read the like."

She colored and looked away. Despite the intimacies they'd shared, the mere thought of him reading the words from her soul made her feel more exposed to him than she had ever been.

He approached the bed and took her hand.

"Forgive me," he said. "Was it deceitful to read them without your permission?"

"No."

"You've been nothing but honest with me, lass. I hope you don't think I've betrayed that honesty."

Shame prevented her from meeting his gaze—shame at her deception at having taken financial gain from writing such damning articles about his family name.

"Won't you look at me, Delilah?"

Gentle fingers took her chin and coaxed her to look up. Their gazes met, and his eyes twinkled with a smile.

"There, lass," he said softly. "There must be no secrets between us."

She bit her lip, focusing on the pain to stem

the tears. He traced the outline of her face with his fingertip.

"There's no shame in what we shared," he whispered.

"It's not that," she said. "I…"

"Hush, lass," A wicked glint shone in his eyes. "I hope, one day, to take ye against the hard granite of *Beinn mo Chridhe*. It's time I blessed the mountain of my heart with my woman."

My woman.

She could stand it no longer. The open honesty in his words and voice deserved equal honesty from her. She had to confess whatever the consequences.

"Your Grace…"

He shook his head. "I think we're beyond formalities. You screamed my name, not half an hour earlier, lass. Can you not speak it now?"

"Fraser."

His eyes crinkled into a smile. "That's better."

"There's something I must tell you."

Before he could respond, shouts rose outside, followed by a pounding on the doors downstairs. He lifted his hand in warning and darted to the chamber door, pushing it shut. Footsteps approached and stopped outside, then a man's voice spoke.

"Your Grace? Sir?"

He held his finger to his lips, but Lilah needed

no instruction. To be caught naked in a man's chamber in the middle of the afternoon would result in a scandal. He opened the door a fraction, using his body to shield her from whoever was outside.

"What is it, Stevenson?"

"It's important, sir," the voice said. "Something terrible has happened."

He slipped outside and closed the door firmly behind him. Low voices murmured, followed by a gasp, then she heard his voice growing louder, angrier. Finally, it took on a note of despair and resignation. Then he barked an order, and the footsteps receded.

When he opened the door, Lilah saw a different man to the one who had seduced her just half an hour before. Her heart clenched at the ashen look in his face.

"What's the matter?" she asked.

"I'm ruined."

"Ruined?"

"As good as." He sighed, and his shoulders slumped as if he bore a huge weight. "Clayton House has been destroyed."

"Destroyed?"

"Aye," he said. "A mob ransacked the building and destroyed everything inside."

"That doesn't spell ruination, surely?"

"It does when the house is fully mortgaged." He let out a sigh. "I should have listened to your brother."

"Dexter? Whatever for?"

"He knew I was heading for bankruptcy," he said. "When he refused to give me a loan, I should have listened to his concerns that I was too much of a risk."

"Perhaps the damage isn't as bad as you fear."

"Stevenson is not known for exaggeration."

"There must be something you can do," she said.

"There's nothing!" he snapped. She flinched at the force in his voice.

He took her hand. "Forgive me, lass, it's not your fault. But Stevenson has said that one of my creditors has already called in a loan. News travels fast. The rest will soon be circling me like dogs. The orders I'd hoped would pay for the capital will not now materialize. I pray to God there's something left in Clayton House I can sell to keep the wolves at bay."

He smiled as if to reassure her, but despair had dulled his eyes.

She squeezed his hand. "I wish I could do something."

"You could garrote that bastard for me."

"Who?"

"Jeremiah Smith," he spat out the name, hatred thickening his voice.

Dread curled in her stomach. "What does he

have to do with it?"

He thrust a piece of paper at her.

A pamphlet. Her stomach heaved as she recognized the words. Someone had taken her final article—the one damning the Molineux family line. The final paragraph had been edited to finish with a call to arms.

"Is this from the *City Chronicle*?" she asked.

His eyes narrowed, then he shook his head. "It's a separate pamphlet. Apparently, several were handed out in the taverns around Clayton House last night. It only takes a few drunken dissenters to provide fuel for the fire. Smith's words were the spark that ignited the flames."

"How do you know what happened is related to this?"

"The Runners caught the ringleaders," he said. "They had a copy of the pamphlet on them. Smith has gone too far this time. He cannot hide behind the newspaper." His voice rose in anger. "I swear, I'll hunt him down and bloody well kill him!"

Lilah swallowed her fear and held the bedsheet close. What could she do?

"There's no need to look for him," she said. "I know where he is."

"Do you?"

"Yes," she whispered. "Oh lord, Fraser, I'm so, so sorry."

"You've naught to be sorry for, lass. Come,

let me help you dress, and I can take you home. Then I'll hunt down that blackguard."

"It *is* my concern," she said. "I never thought it would go that far. Mr. Stock has a lot to answer for."

His eyes narrowed, and he withdrew his hand. "How do you know Mr. Stock?"

"I…"

"Do you know Jeremiah Smith as well?"

"I-I don't actually *know* him," she said.

His expression hardened, and she cringed under his scrutiny.

"You said you were sorry, Miss Hart," he said, his voice quiet and cold. "Is there anything, in particular, you have to be sorry for?"

She lowered her gaze to avoid the accusation in his eyes. "I was merely expressing my sympathy."

"There's more to it, though," he said. "Isn't there?"

Her chemise lay crumpled on the bed. She reached for it, but he snatched it and held it out of reach.

"Tell me, Miss Hart," he growled. "Why should you be sorry?"

"I need to dress," she said, her voice wavering. "It's getting late, and…"

"Tell me!" he roared.

She backed away and closed her eyes to protect herself from his fury.

"Jeremiah Smith is me," she whispered. "*I* wrote the article."

He muttered a curse.

She opened her eyes. His face had grown pale, his eyes the color of hard emeralds.

"Would you do me the honor of explaining?"

She reached for his arm, and he jerked away.

"Speak the truth," he said, "but do *not* touch me."

"I'm sorry."

"You can do better than that woman," he said. "You can tell me the truth. Or have you lost all sense of truth, of honor?"

"Don't say that," she pleaded. "I never meant for this to happen."

"Didn't you? How long have you been writing such filth?" He shook his head as if in disbelief. "To think, all the times you spoke to me of honor, of dignity, of doing some service to the world to make a difference. Did it all lead to this?"

"I never wrote a word against you!" she cried. "It was all about the Molineuxs. They destroyed so many lives. Your predecessor treated his wife—my friend—so cruelly. He terrorized me when I was a child. The duke before him was a murderer and was never brought to justice!"

"Foolish woman!" he snarled. "Was this all due to a personal grudge against a man I didn't even know? Did you not stop and think what might happen if your vile words were used to rouse a rabble?"

"I didn't mean to rouse a rabble," she said. "I started to doubt the words I wrote, but Mr. Stock said they were selling well, and I thought there was no harm in it."

He stared at her.

"He promised he'd read my poems once I'd finished the articles," she continued. "Can't you understand that? I wanted my poems published so badly, and nobody would take them."

"So you sold your integrity," he said. "I suppose I'd expected too much when I believed you were different compared to the cold-hearted women of society. But you're the same. Worse, even, for you deceived me into thinking you possessed a shred of honor."

His words, spoken with such cold detachment, tore through her heart.

"Don't say that!" she cried. "You can't think I wanted anything destroyed."

"And yet, I find my home, and most likely my business, destroyed," he said. "You're no better than the revolutionaries of France who tore down the houses of the aristocracy and ruined lives, murdering their way through the country to get their greedy hands on what they wanted."

"How can you say such things!"

She reached for his hand, but he remained

still.

"Fraser, please!" she cried. "Let me speak to Mr. Stock. He can withdraw the article. It was the final one."

"It's too late," he said. "The damage is done."

He threw the chemise at her. "Get yourself dressed."

"Let me explain," she pleaded.

"There's no need. I only want you out of this house."

"You're throwing me out?"

"I'll take you home in my carriage," he said. "I wouldn't toss anyone out on the street, however much they've sinned against me. You have ten minutes to get yourself dressed. I'll await ye by the front door. I care not in what manner you leave this establishment, but it's better for you if you undertake the journey fully clothed."

"What will you do?"

Emotion rippled in his eyes, then he blinked, and it disappeared.

"At this moment," he said, "other than ridding myself of you, I neither know nor care."

"Fraser, please!" she cried. "I love you!"

His eyes hardened. "You don't know the meaning of the word."

"I do!" she said. "You've shown me what it is to love, and that I was wrong to judge others. Does my love mean nothing to you? Do you not care for me? Even a little?"

Regret flickered across his eyes, then he shrugged. "I feel nothing for you, Miss Hart, other than disappointment."

Before she could reply, he left the chamber, slamming the door behind him. Not long after, she heard him bark an order, then silence fell, punctuated only by the ticking clock and the beating of her shattered heart.

Chapter Twenty-Three

AS SOON AS the carriage drew to a halt outside Lilah's home, Fraser opened the door and climbed out. Lilah followed. She slipped on the step, and he tightened his grip on her hand. Hope fluttered in her heart, but it was extinguished when he withdrew as if her touch burned him.

She smoothed her hair, painfully aware of her disheveled look. She hadn't been able to reach the ties of her gown, and she prayed that her pelisse concealed her state of undress. Her petticoat had a small tear near the hem, and several threads in her stocking had been snagged. Sarah would likely remark on it tomorrow unless Lilah mended them herself.

A hand grasped her elbow and steered her toward the door. She tripped on the steps at the quickness of his pace. Did he have to show such eagerness to be rid of her?

The front door opened, and Lilah gave a cry of shame and recognition.

Dorothea stood before her.

"My God! What's happened? You look terrible!" Dorothea glared at Fraser. "What have you done to her, you ruffian!"

He let out a cold laugh. "I've done nothing which she did not beg for. I suggest you ask what *she* has done."

"Delilah?"

Thea's soft inquiry released the tears which had been threatening to spill. With a sob, Lilah pushed past her sister and fled inside. She rushed up the stairs, almost knocking a maidservant sideways, and didn't stop until she reached the safety of her chamber. Only then did she yield to her despair.

He had believed her to be honest, had placed her on a pedestal, praising her integrity.

And she had betrayed him.

She reached inside her reticule and gave a cry of frustration. Her precious poems! She'd left them at *his* house.

But what did it matter anymore? Those poems had been written from the heart—a heart that was now broken. They had been written for the man she loved.

A man who hated her.

RATHER THAN THE relief he'd been expecting, Fraser felt only regret as she disappeared inside. Her hair in disarray, it was only too clear what they had been doing.

Dorothea Hart watched him, her eyes sparkling with intelligence and insight. Were their circumstances different, she might have been an interesting conversationalist. But now was not the time to engage in small talk. He took a step back.

"*Not* so fast, young man!"

Young man? She couldn't be much older than him. But an unmarried woman approaching thirty had little to recommend herself to a suitor and would have resigned herself to spinsterhood. Most likely, Dorothea considered herself the family matriarch. Her voice reminded him of his old nanny who could render him weak and trembling with a single glance.

Damn her! It was not for him to feel guilty.

"I'm busy," he said, his tone as sulky as it used to be when defying his nanny.

"I don't care," she said. "I insist you come inside and explain yourself."

"Don't be ridiculous."

Her lips thinned into a hard line.

"You may have the manners of the savage,"

she said, "but you'll find I am not at such a loss."

Her brow furrowed into a frown, and a determined expression glittered in her eyes, which gave him a jolt of recognition. He'd seen that expression before when Delilah had persuaded him to volunteer at Mrs. Forbes's.

With a sigh, he followed her inside, and she led him into the morning room.

She took a seat and gestured to him to do likewise. She did not offer tea. Instead, she stared at him and lifted an eyebrow, waiting for him to explain himself.

He was not to be intimidated.

"What do you want?" he asked.

She huffed through her nose and glanced upward in irritation before resuming her gaze on him.

"I want to know what you've done to my sister."

"I suggest you ask her."

"I'm asking you," she said. "Or perhaps I should instruct my brother to meet you at dawn? He's an excellent shot."

"I've not got time for this," Fraser said, rising. "I have a business to tend to."

"Sit back down, you cad!" she cried. "My sister is more important than your damned business!"

He flinched at the unladylike curse. Fire blazed from her eyes, and she rose to her feet.

"Your sister has destroyed my business, madam," he said, "and right now, my only concern is to try to ascertain the extent of the damage before it's too late."

She shook her head. "Don't be foolish. Delilah has neither the means nor the inclination to do such a thing."

"You don't know," he said, "do you?"

"Don't know what?"

"Have you heard of Jeremiah Smith?" he asked. "The bastard who's been writing those damned articles in the *City Chronicle* about my ancestry?"

"I've read one," she said. "Rather inflammatory, but considering the political leanings of the *Chronicle*, not unsurprising. But I don't see what some second-rate hack writer has to do with Delilah."

Fraser let out a laugh. "You really have no idea, do you?"

"What's he done?"

"*Mr. Smith* has been distributing pamphlets among the taverns of London, inciting mobs to riot."

"Good God!" she exclaimed.

"The Almighty had no hand in this, madam," he said. "Not one hour ago, I was informed of a riot which has all but destroyed Clayton House."

"And that's destroyed your business?"

"Given my cashflow position, yes," he said.

"My creditors are already calling at my door in anticipation of my ruination."

"Then you're a fool for not better managing your business risks," she said. "I only hope my brother has not been so foolish as to have lent you money."

"No, he didn't."

"Then I salute him," she said. "Can you seek recourse?"

"Who from?"

"Mr. Smith, of course!"

"Precisely."

Her eyes clouded with confusion. "Does Delilah know him?" she asked. "Is that why she's so distressed?"

"No, madam," Fraser said. "Your sister doesn't know Mr. Smith. She *is* Mr. Smith."

"I don't understand."

"She's been writing under a pseudonym and selling her blasphemy to the *City Chronicle*."

"Delilah would never do such a thing."

"She confessed it already."

"And was this before or after you defiled her?"

"Your sister spread her legs for me, Miss Hart. She must live with the consequences of her actions—*all* of them."

She paled at his words. For a moment, he thought she was going to strike him.

"Is that your definition of justice?" she asked.

"No, there's been a misunderstanding. Hotheaded my sister may be, but she'd never go out of her way to harm another."

"Then why do I find myself in such a position?"

"Has your person been harmed, sir?" she asked. "From what you tell me, a few material possessions have been damaged. Possessions can be replaced. But a lady's virtue, once lost, is lost forever. If your business is so finely balanced that a little property damage places it in jeopardy, then I'd suggest the fault lies with you."

He snorted. "Clearly, her lack of integrity has been learned from observing her siblings. Is that how your brother made his fortune so quickly? By ruining others?"

He caught a blur of movement, then felt a sharp pain across his face. Momentarily blinded, he stepped back. Her eyes blazed with fury, and a jolt of recognition ran through him, the memory of the first day he'd encountered Delilah in Clayton House, all fire and passion.

"That's hardly the behavior of a lady, Miss Hart," he said, rubbing his cheek where she'd struck him.

"My behavior is not in question," she retorted. "If Dexter were here, he would have you horsewhipped through the streets for what you've done. Consider yourself fortunate that I will merely warn you never to darken our door again."

"I've no intention of having anything to do with your family again," he said. "I pity your brother but can now see why he works so hard. It's to avoid spending time in a home overrun by harridans."

"Get out," she said, giving him a push.

"With pleasure."

As soon as his feet touched the steps outside, the door was slammed behind him.

His priority, now, was to limit the damage. But would it be so bad if he lost Clayton House to his creditors? Scotland was his home. His soul could wander among the slopes of *Beinn Mo Chridhe*.

Miss Hart might have betrayed him, but perhaps she'd done him a service. He ought to congratulate himself on a lucky escape from being shackled to that family forever.

As he returned to his carriage, he turned and took a last look at the Hart townhouse, his gaze drawn to a first-floor window.

Was she there?

His heart skipped at a movement. Then a face appeared, its features clear in the light of the setting sun.

Sir Thomas Tipton.

"Still sniffing round Miss Hart, I see," Fraser said, though the man couldn't hear him. "Well, you can have her and suffer the disappointment that another got there before you."

Sir Thomas raised his hand as if in salute. Then he smiled.

Sir Thomas's eyes glowed with a sinister look, sparkling with an emotion so strong, Fraser could almost taste it.

Triumph.

Chapter Twenty-Four

ALMOST AS SOON the main doors slammed shut downstairs, Lilah heard her sister's voice outside her chamber door.

"Delilah, sweetheart?"

There was little point feigning sleep. Thea's tenacity rivaled even Dexter's.

"Come in," she said.

Thea slipped into the room. Rather than speak, she took a seat, folded her hands in front of her, and regarded Lilah with a thoughtful expression.

Not long after, Sarah appeared with a tray bearing a decanter of Dexter's brandy and two glasses. At a nod from Thea, she poured a little into each glass.

"Thank you, Sarah, you may leave us now." She nodded toward Lilah's glass.

"Drink, Delilah, dear."

"For what purpose?"

Thea said nothing but took a sip from her glass, then set it aside.

Where Dexter had learned the art of drawing out the truth by asking intimidating questions, Dorothea had learned the subtler form of attack. She created a void of silence, which attracted words and explanations as surely as the dish in Lady Jersey's hall attracted calling cards.

"Forgive me, Thea," she said.

Dorothea picked up her glass again. "Would I be better prepared for your story, Delilah, if I were to drink this?"

Shame elicited the tears which had been stinging Lilah's eyes, and she nodded.

"Did he—*take advantage* of you?"

Lilah shook her head. "H-he didn't..." she stuttered and took a mouthful of brandy, choking at the taste. "I was not unwilling."

Thea sipped her drink. "So he spoke the truth. In that respect, at least."

"Are you angry with me, Thea?"

"Of course not," came the reply. "It takes two to make love."

Thea took another sip. "And the other matter," she said. "Is that true also? What he accused you of doing?"

"You mean Jeremiah Smith?"

Thea let out a sigh. "So, it is true. I shouldn't

be surprised, given how closely your views were aligned with those expressed in his articles." She shook her head. "But the leaflets, Delilah! That was a step too far. Not even your passion to right the wrongs of the world can justify such senseless destruction."

"I had nothing to do with the leaflets," Lilah said. "As for the articles—my views have long since diverged from the sentiments they expressed. I told him that."

"But he didn't believe you."

"No, he accused me of dishonesty."

"In part, he was right, wasn't he?"

Lilah withered under her sister's frown. "I deceived him, yes, but I swear I had nothing to do with the leaflets! The last thing I'd want is to hurt him."

Thea nodded.

"I believe you," she said. "Your only crime is that of naiveté. In truth, you're the most honest person I know. You've never been afraid to speak the truth, even if it causes offense. Such honesty is rare."

Thea's words, meant for comfort, only served to increase her distress. Hadn't *he* said the very same before he discovered her deception?

"Oh, dear God," Lilah wailed. "What will Dexter say when he discovers what I've done? I'm ruined!"

Thea took her hand. "There's no need to tell

him."

"What if Fraser…" Lilah said, and Thea lifted her eyebrows. "What if Molineux says anything?"

Warm, comforting arms enveloped her. "We'll address that problem if and when it arises, Delilah, dear," Thea said. "And if it does, I'll deal with our brother."

"Why are you being so kind?" Lilah asked.

"Because you're already suffering," Thea said. "I can see the shame in your eyes. No amount of punishment Dexter metes out can compare to that which your conscience is already inflicting on you."

"I never meant to hurt him," Lilah said, "and now he hates me!"

"I'm sure he doesn't."

"You should have seen the look in his eyes when he realized what I'd done." Lilah shook her head. "Such disgust—I cannot bear it."

Thea patted her head. "I know, Delilah," she said. "Your intentions were honorable. You were merely misguided. If he's a good man, he'll come to realize that."

"And what if he doesn't?" she cried. "What will I do?"

Thea stiffened. "You love him."

It was not a question.

Lilah blinked, and a hot tear splashed onto her cheek.

"I thought as much."

"How did you know?" Lilah asked.

"You're more concerned with the harm you've caused him than the damage to your reputation."

A sob welled in Lilah's throat, and she yielded to her sorrow while Thea rocked her, whispering words of comfort.

"Hush, little sister," she said. "Everything will be well."

"But Dexter…"

"Our brother will understand."

"But he only cares about our position in society," Lilah said. "He wants me to marry a title, but no one will have me now."

"Haven't you always said you didn't want to be a society wife?" Thea asked. "In which case, consider this a blessing. And if Dexter cares so much about uniting our family with a title, then *he* can marry one and suffer the consequences of a loveless marriage. In fact, I believe he's already set his sights on a lady. He'll be so occupied with courting that he won't have time to admonish you."

"Then, what shall I do?"

"Do what you've always done," Thea said. "But rather than try to change the whole world, why not focus your energies where your talents lie? Sir Thomas was telling me only yesterday what fine poems you write."

"He knows nothing of poetry," Lilah said.

"He's anxious to support your endeavors, and that should be commended," Thea replied. "And there's Mrs. Forbes. She recognizes your qualities and appreciates your help."

Lilah shook her head. "I do so little."

"The most effective way to make a difference is to take small steps," her sister said. "A pebble, when dropped into a lake, causes ripples which extend to every corner of the surface. And if you make a difference to a handful of lives, then for them, you have changed the world."

Thea was right. In her quest for justice, Lilah had believed she could change the world by influencing the minds of many. But all she'd done was help James Stock sell more copies of his paper. And it had not brought her fulfillment— only misery.

But her realization had come too late. By concealing the truth from Fraser, she'd given him every right to hate her, where she had every reason to love him.

Thea kissed her forehead.

"You must rest," she said. "A little sleep will do wonders for your disposition. Shall I send Sarah up with a tray for your supper? Sir Thomas is here. He's dining with us, but I can make your excuses if you're not up to company."

"No, thank you," Lilah said. "I cannot hide. I must face the consequences of my actions."

"You needn't worry about Sir Thomas,"

Thea said, smiling. "There's a lovesick puppy if ever I saw one. He's followed you around since we arrived in London."

"He'll soon stop following once he knows I'm a fallen woman."

"Perhaps, perhaps not," Thea said. "Now get some sleep. I'll make sure you're not disturbed until supper."

After Thea left, Lilah heard voices elsewhere in the house, followed by Sir Thomas's unmistakable little cough. Eventually, the voices faded.

How had Thea described him? A lovesick puppy. Though he couldn't excite her passion, Sir Thomas had been a friend ever since Dexter had brought the family to London. He looked up to Dexter. And he weathered Lilah's sharp tongue.

Perhaps a woman was better protected from heartbreak if she avoided passion altogether. Passion destroyed lives, and now it had broken her heart. Was that why so many people married for convenience rather than love? A woman who never loved was, at least, spared the agony of heartbreak.

Lilah rose from her chair and lay on her bed. She sank back against the pillows and closed her eyes. But sleep eluded her. She had contributed to the ruin of the man she had fallen in love with. A man who matched her perfectly in every way, who believed in hard work and loyalty, and strove to better himself and the lives who depended on him. He let himself be ordered about by her and weathered it all with good grace.

And he had taught her the meaning of pure, unbridled pleasure.

Yet now, he couldn't bear the sight of her.

Chapter Twenty-Five

"SO, TELL ME, Mr. Hart," Fraser said, "why have you asked me to see you?"

One week after Clayton House had been destroyed, Hart had sent Fraser a message, demanding to see him. Fraser had expected to be called at dawn, but Hart showed no sign of knowing that Fraser had taken his sister's maidenhead.

Maybe Hart was about to draw out a pistol from his desk and shoot him.

Fraser glanced at the rug on the floor of Hart's office. The predominantly red background would be perfect for disguising bloodstains.

"I've been looking into your finances," Hart said.

"For what purpose?"

Hart stared at him in the manner of a

schoolmaster, irritated at being interrupted by a particularly weak-brained pupil.

"All in good time," Hart said. His gaze was unsettling, the cold blue of his eyes searching, calculating.

Dexter Hart had the uncanny ability to probe into a man's mind to discover his secrets, then use them to his advantage. Did he apply the same approach to ruling his family?

For a moment, Fraser found himself pitying Delilah Hart. Her brother's iron fist would stunt her free spirit. Had he discovered that she was no longer a maiden? Had he punished her? And if he knew who she'd lain with, would Fraser find his manhood sliced and scattered over Hart's Aubusson rug?

"How bad is my situation, Hart?" he asked.

The banker rolled his eyes. "The news is not good, but you've managed to evade total ruination, at least for now. I took the liberty of writing to the trustees of the Molineux estate, and my lawyer heard from them yesterday."

Why would Hart meddle in Fraser's affairs? Though, if anyone could persuade those old fossils to release the funds to service Fraser's debts, it was Hart.

"Is that why you asked to see me?" Fraser asked.

"It is."

"Did you ask them to help me?"

"Good lord, no," Hart said. "I expect you to be man enough to ask them yourself, though it would be an exercise in futility. The estate is losing money, and the trustees would be fools if they agreed to waste its funds on a failed enterprise run by an incompetent."

Did the man have to be so brutally frank?

"Then why contact them?" Fraser asked. "And why would they respond so hastily? Ordinarily, it takes them weeks to answer my letters."

"That is, I suspect, because your letters are never to their advantage."

"And yours was?"

Hart tapped the surface of the desk with his forefinger.

"I believe I've found a solution to everyone's benefit."

"Are *you* going to fund me?"

The banker let out a cold laugh. "I'm not foolish enough to throwing money at a bad investment either. But my proposal should protect you from bankruptcy, even if it's unlikely to restore your business interests in London in the near future. Though it does require your cooperation."

"What must I do?" Fraser asked.

"Retrench. Abandon your business expansion in London and concentrate on servicing your debts where you are best placed to do so. In

Scotland."

"Abandon London?"

"You must have considered it."

Hart was right. It was the first idea which had come to Fraser's mind. To return to his homeland and concentrate on his own people, where he could not be plagued by…

By what? A little hellion? A wee terrier?

"Yes, I've considered it," Fraser said. "Once I've vacated my lodgings, there's nowhere for me to go, and I have no wish to waste funds on new lodgings."

"Indeed."

"But what does this have to do with the trustees?" Fraser asked.

A flicker of emotion crossed the banker's expression. "As you know, the Molineux estate is losing money at an alarming rate. I've been able to secure an arrangement that will best serve you and it." He blinked, and his expression took on a predatory air. "And myself, of course."

"I don't doubt it," Fraser said.

Hart raised an eyebrow and set his mouth into a firm line.

"What have you arranged on my behalf?" Fraser asked.

"On *my* behalf, actually. The trustees, though not disposed to sell the estate, have agreed to rent it."

"Clayton House is uninhabitable," Fraser

said. "And it's mine outright. The trustees have no right to touch it."

"I didn't mean your townhouse," Hart said. "I was referring to Molineux Manor."

"The country estate?"

"It belongs to the trust," Hart said. "And you're not occupying it. A tenancy seems the ideal solution. It will prevent the trustees from hounding you for funds you don't have and ensure the property is maintained."

"Who on earth would want to live in that damned mausoleum?"

Hart interlocked his fingers and laced his hands on the desk. "I was able to secure excellent terms."

"You?"

A cold smile crept across the banker's mouth.

"Did the trustees see you coming?" Fraser asked.

"They know a good offer when they see one," Hart said. "They've even agreed to release a small percentage of the rental income to you. Not enough to prevent your creditors seizing Clayton House, but it will assist you in restoring your fortunes."

Was this what Hart had planned all along?

Fraser shook his head and sighed. "I always thought it was lawyers who benefited from the misery of others," he said bitterly.

"Bankers are capable of that also," Hart said.

"I'm not a charity."

"At least on that, we are agreed," Fraser said. "Did you have this in mind from the outset when I first asked you for a loan?

Hart's smile slipped. "I may drive a hard bargain, Molineux, but I'm a fair man. Honor does not always walk hand-in-hand with charity."

"Well, if you wish to live in that godforsaken place, I wish you joy of it," Fraser said. "Though I cannot understand why. Unless there's a woman involved."

For a moment, Hart's composure slipped, and he looked away. The urge to discompose this arrogant man was too much to resist.

"I hear the debutante of the season is Lady Atalanta Grey," Fraser said. "Perhaps you're feathering a nest to bag that particular bird. Or the Honorable Elizabeth Alderley, perhaps? The other day, Mrs. Pelham remarked on having seen you riding with her in Hyde Park last week."

Hart's eyebrow twitched.

"My reasons don't concern you."

"In matters of the heart…" Fraser began, but Hart interrupted him.

"I have no heart where women are concerned. Except for my sisters, of course."

Fraser flinched, expecting to be called out. Had Delilah told her brother what had happened?

Hart remained silent and picked up a pencil, which he proceeded to tap on the desk.

"Elizabeth Alderley is the perfect match for you," Fraser said. "Heartless, sour-faced, and haughty. And those are her most endearing attributes, by all accounts."

Hart's eyebrows creased into a frown.

"Her father's just as bad," Fraser continued. "Viscount Alderley snubbed me for being a Scotsman. I can't see him taking kindly to the prospect of a commoner as a son-in-law, no matter how wealthy he is."

The pencil snapped.

"Alderley will learn the error of his ways," Hart said quietly. "We go back a long way, and he'll bend to my will, you can be sure of that. And when his daughter is mine, I will teach him a valuable lesson or two."

Fraser lifted his hand. "I have no wish to know," he said. "You're at liberty to do what you want with Molineux Manor. Have your lawyer draw up the necessary papers, and I'll sign anything you need, especially if it means I can leave London as soon as possible."

He rose to his feet, took Hart's hand in a firm grip, then exited the office.

As he stepped out onto the pavement, he lifted his head and closed his eyes, letting the warmth of the sun penetrate his face.

The image of Miss Hart swam across his vision—the passion in her eyes when he'd first seen her, and the look of horror on her face when he'd introduced himself as Duke Molineux. That passion had softened when she'd spoken of the plight of the women of the world and the forgotten classes. But it had intensified when he'd shown her the pleasures their bodies could enjoy. His blood warmed at the memory of her face, flushed with need for him, lips parted in surprise and wonder when he'd buried himself inside her as if he belonged there.

But passion was a weakness. Perhaps that was why Fraser had failed, where impassive creatures such as Dexter Hart thrived in a world where there was no place for hearts and souls.

But Miss Hart's passion would forever place her in his esteem. No matter what she'd done, he couldn't feel anything but high regard for her. The poems she'd written after they returned from Scotland had spoken to him on a visceral level, such that he couldn't bring himself to give them back. He'd read them each night since the day they'd made love. They rivaled Burns in their beauty and surpassed the bland verses she had penned at first. Such talent needed to be nurtured and rewarded.

But Delilah Hart's passion was not for him. She had betrayed his trust, and he had no wish to experience such betrayal again. Better for them both if they never met again.

Chapter Twenty-Six

LILAH STIRRED HER tea and dropped a lump of sugar into the brown liquid, watching it dissolve. Lately, her constitution had been unsettled, and she'd struggled to finish her meals. Dexter hadn't noticed, but he seemed preoccupied with renting an estate in the country, though he refused to discuss the details. Sir Thomas had remarked on Lilah's constitution when he'd dined with them, but she had told him to keep his nose out of her business. Sir Thomas had laughed it off and defended her when Thea admonished her incivility.

She sipped her tea. The sugar, which she'd once found abhorrent, now soothed her stomach.

She lifted the sheaf of paper she'd been studying and read the words once more. Now frayed around the edges, the poems she'd penned were the only evidence of her love for *him*.

A week after he'd brought her home in disgrace, Lilah's poems had arrived on her doorstep, wrapped in a single bundle, with no message. It was as if by discarding her poems, he had rid himself of the last remnants of her.

And now, two months later, it was as if he'd never existed. There was no sign of him in London, and save the occasional remark from Sir Thomas about barbarians, she could almost have believed that she'd imagined him. Her pitiful attempt to make amends failed at the first hurdle. Her request to Stock to publish a retraction of her last article fell on deaf ears. Instead, he'd laughed at her, then evicted her from his offices, threatening to ensure her work would never be published again.

It had all been for nothing. Instead of justice, her efforts had been rewarded with mindless destruction. Her hopes for a future as a poet had been destroyed as surely as her hopes of a life filled with love and passion.

Now, she must accept her fate and take a pragmatic attitude to life. Not even Sir Thomas's encouragement could lift her spirits. Well-meaning as he was, he knew nothing of poetry, so his praise, though abundant, did nothing to build her confidence. He made all the right noises when he read *Mo Chridhe*, her favorite poem of the set. But he couldn't be expected to understand the meaning behind her words.

She heard a knock on the door and set her cup aside. A footman entered, holding a dish bearing a single card.

"You have a visitor, miss. Shall I let him in?"

She plucked the card from the tray and read the inscription.

Jonathan Sandton
Chief editor, the London Ladies' Weekly

"The *London Ladies Weekly*? I've never heard of it," she said. "Have you, Charles?"

"No, miss."

"Send him in," she said. "Would you ask Sarah to bring another pot of tea?"

"Very good, miss."

Shortly after, Sarah arrived with a tray, followed by the footman and his companion, a short man with a small mustache, neatly dressed in a dark gray coat and cream breeches.

He issued a deep bow. "Miss Hart, a pleasure to meet you at last."

She gestured to a chair. "Please sit. I'm afraid I've not heard of you, Mr. Sandton. How have you heard of me?"

He pulled a sheaf of papers from his pocket. "I've read your work."

"Let me see."

He handed the papers to her. Penned in an

unfamiliar hand were the poems she'd written after her trip to Scotland.

"Who sent you these?" she asked.

"Someone who wishes to remain anonymous," Sandton said. "They asked if I might consider them for publication."

"When was this?"

"A little over a month ago. I take it this is your work?"

"Yes," she replied, "but the hand isn't mine."

"Forgive my tardiness in reviewing them," Sandton said. "I find them excellent, and it would be my pleasure to include them in my journal."

"You want to publish them?"

"Of course," he said. "Our readership is small, but it consists of discerning women who are more appreciative of the world around us than the more—frivolous—pursuits of society ladies. Women of intellect who appreciate matters of the heart. I would very much like to publish *Mo Chridhe* in our next edition. My junior editor and I found that particular poem the strongest of the set. If it's well-received by our readers, then we can make your poetry a regular feature, with a view to publishing a separate volume once we have enough poems to do so."

"Would you give me freedom to write what I wanted?" she asked.

"Within reason," he said. "What attracted me to your work was the passion conveyed within the words. You have a rare gift, Miss Hart. Of course, we reserve the right to discuss any changes to your work before we publish it, but we wouldn't publish anything you were unhappy with."

Lilah hesitated, her experiences with James Stock still fresh in her mind. "I'm not sure…"

"I understand," Sandton said. "If you wish to consider the matter, I'll give you all the time you need. Or, perhaps you might wish to consult another before we discuss terms?"

"You mean a man?"

He let out a chuckle. "It's often wise to get a second opinion from a trusted confidante before making a decision. The sex of that confidante bears no relation on their ability to advise you."

"Then let us discuss the terms now, Mr. Sandton," she said, reaching for the teapot.

The conversation lasted barely fifteen minutes. Sandton seemed genuine, and he lacked the oily obsequiousness displayed by Stock when he'd first shown interest in her articles. After seeing him out, she returned to the morning room, dismissed Sarah, and finished her tea in silence.

Fate had taken an upward turn. At last, the prospect of an independent income. And what better purpose to put the money to than Mrs. Forbes and her charity?

A visit to Mrs. Forbes was bound to lift her

spirits. And an act of philanthropy might help to assuage her guilt over what she'd done to *him*.

"YOU SEEM IN unusually good spirits, Mrs. Forbes."

"That I am." Mrs. Forbes gave Lilah a broad smile as she ushered her into the parlor. "We have that lovely young man to thank."

"Sir Thomas Tipton?"

"No, that young Scotsman. Such a fine man!" Mrs. Forbes let out a sigh. "What a pity his turn of fortunes forced him to leave London!"

Lilah felt the heat rise in her cheeks. "How do you know about his misfortunes?"

"He came to see me just before he left, poor man." Mrs. Forbes replied. "I understand his finances were too delicately balanced to weather even the slightest adversity. And yet, he was still so generous!"

"Generous?"

"Didn't he tell you?" Mrs. Forbes shook her head. "I wondered if you'd persuaded him, but it must have been his own idea. He pledged us a regular stipend and came round with the papers to make it legally binding. Lord knows I need the income. But to take it when I know the benefactor is struggling financially does not sit right on my conscience. I told him so, and do you know what he said?"

"I've no idea."

"He said, 'Och, Mrs. Forbes, I'd be no sort of man if I didn't honor my promises.'"

Mrs. Forbes sighed again. "Ah, yes—*such* a fine man! We can do so much with the extra income."

"I'm able to pledge a little more each month also," Lilah said. "In fact, that's why I came to see you today."

"Lord, thank you, Miss Hart, but I know you give as much as you can. And dear Mrs. Pelham, of course. And your young man's idea is already bearing fruit. I feel so blessed."

"His idea?"

"Did he not tell you?" Mrs. Forbes asked. "He suggested that for each woman I place in employment, if her new employer is satisfied with the appointment, they should pledge to give me a small portion of their wages. I've had one already agree to it—a Mr. O'Reilly in Hammersmith has taken on two girls as chambermaids and will be sending me sixpence each month. And your young man himself took young Rose and her children to Scotland with him to live and work on his estate.

"He took them to Scotland?"

"Two months ago. Rose will work in his factory, and young Will is going to attend school while a nursemaid tends to the baby."

Mrs. Forbes took Lilah's hand. "I have you to thank, Miss Hart. You persuaded him to visit us and to see our work. I owe it all to you."

"You have nothing to thank me for, Mrs. Forbes," Lilah said. "It was all his doing."

Mrs. Forbes smiled. "If I were twenty years younger, I'd be smitten with the man. That is, of course, if he were not so smitten with you. He is indeed a most excellent creature. It's rare to see a man of such high honor these days."

Mrs. Forbes's words only served to increase the pain in Lilah's heart. He had every reason to be bitter and resentful. He faced bankruptcy, yet he still thought of others! To think that such a man had once placed her in high regard.

Would she ever be able to come to terms with what she had lost?

Chapter Twenty-Seven

WHEN LILAH RETURNED home, Thea was waiting for her in the parlor, together with Sir Thomas.

"Ah, Delilah, dear, we've been waiting for you. Do join us."

Lilah looked from one to the other. "This looks serious," she said.

Thea and Sir Thomas exchanged glances.

"Should we ask Dexter to join us?" Lilah asked.

"Our brother has seen fit to go to the country," Thea replied. "It seems as if he has a prospective bride lined up and is planning to rent a property in which to keep her."

"You make it sound like a prison, Dorothea," Lilah said, "with Dex as the jailer."

Sir Thomas frowned, then he turned to Thea.

"Miss Hart," he said. "Perhaps I should address Miss Delilah on her own."

"I'm rather tired," Lilah said. "Perhaps another time."

Thea stood, and Sir Thomas followed suit. "Delilah, I insist you speak with him," she said.

"Oh, very well." Lilah dropped her reticule on the chaise longue and sat beside it.

Thea curtseyed to Sir Thomas. "Please excuse me."

After the door closed behind her, Sir Thomas crossed the floor and sat beside Lilah.

"I've been anxious for the opportunity to speak to you alone," he said, "ever since your *disappointment.*"

"My disappointment?"

"Molineux," Sir Thomas said, his tone hard. "He's a cad for abandoning you. There was nothing wrong with your articles, yet he judges you as if you ransacked Clayton House yourself!"

"How do you know about Clayton House?"

His glance shifted sideways before he resumed his focus on her. "Everyone's talking about it."

"And the articles," she said. "How did you know I wrote them?"

"I'm an avid reader of the *City Chronicle*," he said. "When I stumbled across a scrap of paper in the drawing room, I read it out of curiosity and recognized the words."

"You've been reading my papers?"

"I applaud your talent. Your writing—the articles, the poems—they're worthy of the highest praise."

His gaze shifted as if he had something to hide. Was he the mysterious benefactor who'd passed her poems to Sandton?

"You deserve every success, my beloved Delilah. That cad deserved to be ruined."

Her heart jumped in defense of Fraser.

"What sins has he committed to deserve such a fate?"

Sir Thomas took her hand, then knelt beside her.

"He's made you unhappy," he said. "And I won't have anyone making my beloved girl unhappy."

She tried to free her hand, but he tightened his grip.

"He's a fool for believing you were responsible for those leaflets."

"How do you know about the leaflets?"

His eyes narrowed, and he stiffened.

"I..." he hesitated. "I must have overheard someone mention it at Whites."

He lifted her hand to his lips. "Don't you realize how deeply I feel for you, Miss Hart?" he asked. "Or, perhaps, I may be permitted at last to call you Delilah?"

"Sir Thomas..."

"Call me Tommie," he said. "Or, better still, 'my love.'"

He caressed the back of her hand with his thumb, but rather than the crackle of need which she had experienced at the hands of another, she felt nothing but irritation at his familiarity.

"Don't you know how I deeply admire you, Delilah?" he asked. "You'd make any man the perfect companion. To think how you would shine as Lady Tipton, and how I might prosper with you at my side!"

She snatched her hand away. "Are you hunting my fortune?"

His mouth thinned into a harsh line. "You wound me, dearest Delilah," he said. "Unlike most men, I don't love you for your fortune. And unlike that cad, I'm not merely after your person. Don't you realize I've loved you ever since your brother introduced us? I have loved your intelligence, your wit, and I'd count myself the most fortunate of men to have you as my life's companion. I want you for yourself, dearest Delilah. Were you a pauper on the streets, I would still love you!"

He took her hand again. "Make me the happiest of men, Delilah."

She shook her head. "Sir Thomas, I cannot," she said. "I don't love you."

He opened his mouth as if to argue, then closed it again. "I see I must be patient," he said, "and I'm a very patient man when my heart's desire is before me."

"I have no wish to marry you," she said.

"Nevertheless, I shall ask every day."

"And every day, you'll receive the same answer."

He squeezed her hand. "My love for you is so great that I shall wait forever if I have to," he said. "Nothing can prevent me from believing you're the woman to make my life complete."

He moved to embrace her, and she pushed him away. "Please, don't touch me."

"Of course." He stood and gave her a bow. "I am your servant, Miss Hart. Now and always."

He bowed again and left the room.

Delilah waited for her sister to return. Most likely, Thea had been listening outside, eager to hear the outcome of Sir Thomas's proposal and demanding to know why Delilah had rejected him. And when Dexter returned, doubtless he'd question her, too. And give her a lecture on the benefits of obedience and raising the family's position in society.

But even if she'd wanted to marry Sir Thomas, it was impossible. When he discovered her secret, he'd want nothing to do with her.

As she reached for her reticule, another bout of nausea rippled through her, threatening to expel her tea.

Delilah could no longer deny the truth. She was pregnant with Fraser's child.

Chapter Twenty-Eight

"I'D LOVE TO see that delightful young woman again, Fraser," Ma said. "I can't think why you didn't bring her with you when you returned home."

Fraser pushed his soup bowl aside and winced as hot liquid splashed onto his hand.

"How can you say that after what she did, Ma?"

"She penned a few articles," Ma replied. "I suspect the world has forgotten about them by now." She turned to their dinner guest. "What say you, Miss MacKenzie?"

Jennifer scowled and said nothing.

"She did more than that," Fraser growled. "I was almost ruined because of her."

"I agree," Jennifer said. "I always thought her a deceitful creature. There was something in her eyes I didn't trust."

"Surely, you can't blame a woman and her pen for the actions of a bunch of dissenters," Ma said.

"If I recall, Ma, you told me Jeremiah Smith was the worst sort of man," Fraser said. "Has your opinion changed merely because that man has turned out to be a woman?"

"Perhaps."

"Ma, if a woman writes a man's words, then she should expect a man's consequences."

"And so, should you," Ma said. "Your affairs wouldn't be in such a sorry state had you taken a more sensible approach to your business. Tell me, when should I expect your numerous creditors to turn up here and seize Glendarron from beneath my feet to pay your debts?"

"Ma!" Fraser cast a glance at Jennifer. "We have a guest."

"There's no harm in Miss MacKenzie knowing," Ma replied. "After all, you've known her so long, she's practically family." She dipped her spoon into her soup. "Didn't you tell me Miss Hart's brother had found a solution? I'll hazard a guess she asked him to make amends on her behalf."

Fraser shook his head. "Hart knows nothing of the matter, trust me. His sister has not told him."

"What makes you think that?" Ma asked.

The fact that Fraser hadn't found himself with a bullet through his heart for debauching the man's sister made him think that.

He leaned back while the servants cleared away the soup and began serving the entrée—the Scotch beef ragout which Miss Hart had remarked on as being the finest beef she'd ever tasted. Ma smiled at him across the table. Had she deliberately chosen the menu tonight to remind him of *her*?

"Hart's a businessman," he said. "He's renting Molineux House for a pittance, just enough to stave off my creditors for a few months. Believe me, he's not doing it out of kindness. I doubt the man understands the meaning of the word."

"You can say what you like," Ma said, "but I think it a shame she won't be visiting again."

Fraser sighed. He might have left London behind, but he couldn't free himself from the memory of her. Not when Ma wouldn't stop blethering about her.

As for Hamish—if he asked Fraser one more time when he'd next see the 'lovely wee lassie,' he'd remove the man's ballocks and gift them to Ma as earrings. Perhaps then, they'd stop plaguing him.

Hamish had taken quite the shine to her and said she had the Highlands in her heart. Fraser would have laughed at such a preposterous notion, had he not read the beautiful words she'd penned in her poem *Mo Chridhe*.

The water of life to carry thee home…

Whatever her sins were, her passionate heart deserved to be fed and nurtured. He would forever admire Delilah Hart, the poet. As for Delilah Hart, the woman, whatever passion she ignited, he couldn't trust her.

"I daresay the lass's absence explains the sour expression on your face, lad," Ma said.

"That's enough, woman!" he roared.

"Fraser!" Jennifer exclaimed. "If London has had such a detrimental effect on your disposition, then I was right when I said last year that no good would come out of your going there."

"Then rejoice in the fact that you were right," Fraser said. He nodded toward Ma. "Forgive me, I meant no disrespect."

He sliced through the beef. The knife scraped against the plate, and he shuddered at the sound. He looked up to see Jennifer staring at him, the hint of a smile on her lips.

"Is the food not to your liking, Miss Mackenzie?" he asked.

"On the contrary," she replied.

"Well, there's no need to stay when dinner is finished."

Her smile disappeared.

"I apologize for my son, Jennifer, lass," Ma

said. "He reigns triumphant when his business prospers but lacks the maturity to accept a downturn in his fortunes without bitterness."

Ma was right. He was behaving like a brat. Better to say nothing than argue. Ma was not one to back down when they disagreed, and if the creditors were to come calling, he'd need her support and forgiveness.

The meal continued in silence, after which Ma made her excuses and retired, leaving him alone with his former lover in the drawing room. He poured two glasses of whisky and handed her one.

"You seem out of sorts, my love," she said. "I daresay that *delightful young woman* is to blame."

"How do you know that?" Fraser asked.

"So, I'm right," she said. "Didn't I say she'd lead you to ruin? You should have heeded my warnings."

Warnings fueled by petty jealousy.

"I always said she was too particular in her attentions toward you," Jennifer continued.

"That's not true," Fraser said.

"Oh, but it is. Didn't you first encounter her snooping in your London townhouse? For what purpose would she be there other than to pry into your affairs? Who is she? Nobody! An upstart of inferior birth."

He drained his glass to dull his senses to her onslaught, but she continued, relentless in her criticism of her rival.

"I always thought she was a hellion, Fraser. And now you're on the brink of ruination, and she's nowhere to be seen! Whereas, I am always here for you."

"What do you mean?"

"It's perfectly simple," Jennifer said. "My fortune is at your disposal if only you'd be willing to offer for it."

Dear God—not that!

"Well?" she prompted.

"Well, what?"

"Don't you think it's time we did what our mothers have always expected?"

"A lady should wait to be asked."

"We've known each other too long for niceties, Fraser," she said. "Despite London's diversions, you must admit your heart is here. And my fortune would restore your business."

"Forgive me, Miss MacKenzie…"

"Jennifer, please," she interrupted.

"Miss, MacKenzie," he said. "I must speak plain. I will always care for you. But I'm the last man who could make you happy."

"Who are you to determine what would make me happy?" she asked. "Don't you know I've always loved you?"

"You love the idea of being my wife, Jennifer," he said, "which is a different thing altogether."

She took a sip from her glass.

"It's *her*, isn't it?"

He didn't need to ask who she referred to.

"This has nothing to do with Miss Hart," he said.

"She's known you for a matter of weeks, Fraser, whereas I've known you for years," she continued. "Who is she? My family dates back centuries, as does yours. But the Harts are nothing! No lineage, no quality, and no manners. She's nothing, Fraser—nothing!"

She was wrong.

Delilah Hart was everything.

"Miss MacKenzie," he said, "do not speak so…"

"I'll say what I like when I see the man I love being duped!" she cried. "Did she spread her legs? Is that it? It seems that friendship cannot secure your hand, whereas whoring will always prevail."

He leapt to his feet. "That's enough! You know nothing of her. She may not be able to trace her family back to the thirteenth century, but that's of no detriment to her character. She's bright, kind, and passionately devoted to helping others. As a woman, she knows the obstacles she faces in the world are that much higher, that much harder to climb, yet still she persists! Not for personal gain, but because it's the right thing to do. Can *you* compare to that?"

She rose to her feet, trembling. The shock in

her eyes tempered his fury.

"Forgive me, Jennifer," he said. "I've no wish to cause you pain. You deserve a man who loves you. And I am not he. I cannot pretend otherwise, for it wouldn't be fair."

"Very well," she said. "But you'll regret not offering for me. There's plenty of men hereabouts who'll happily take me—and my fortune."

"Then I wish them good fortune and happiness."

"If only I could bestow equal good wishes on you," she said, "but I find I cannot. Not when you've broken my heart."

"Then, I ask your forgiveness," he said.

She shook her head.

"What can I do?"

"Tell your man to send for my carriage," she said. "Don't bother to show me out. I know the way."

After she left, he retired to his chamber. Ridding himself of Jennifer, at last, had only served to increase his burden, for now, he'd added regret at having broken her heart.

He didn't love Jennifer, but neither did he wish to see her unhappy.

Ye Gods—since when had he grown into a milksop who cared for the feelings of others, even those who sought to take advantage of him?

He rolled onto his side, the bed creaking beneath his weight, and closed his eyes. But it could not dispel the memory of her—the feisty lass who had taught him compassion and unlocked his heart.

He hardened almost instantly. He could almost smell her and hear her little mewls of pleasure, which turned into cries of ecstasy as he'd thrust himself deeper into her warm, welcoming body.

Picturing the expression in her eyes and her lips parted of surprise, he fisted his manhood as if he was, once more, a lad of sixteen hiding beneath the bedsheets.

If the memory of Miss Hart was all he had, then he must be content with that.

Chapter Twenty-Nine

L ILAH FLICKED THROUGH the volume of poems, which had arrived from Mr. Sandton that morning. "Now my dream is finally being realized," she said. "I find it gives me little pleasure."

Her nausea from her pregnancy had gone, and save for a slight thickening of her waistline, it was not yet visible. But she could not conquer her melancholy.

As he'd promised, Sir Thomas had proposed almost daily since her first rejection of him last month. Of Fraser, there was no news other than general gossip about the failure of his enterprises in London. She suspected Dexter knew something, but her brother remained tight-lipped, spending every working hour either at his bank or with his lawyer.

Clayton House had returned to the sorry state in which it had been the day Lilah had met Fraser. With one exception. The birds had gone. They'd flown away the night the house was ransacked and the aviary destroyed. The poor creatures stood little chance of survival in the wild.

More lives affected by her foolish ambitions.

Yet, still, she took tea in the afternoon with her friend, as if nothing had changed.

She tossed the volume aside and sighed.

Anne set her teacup down. "Are you quite well, Delilah, dear? You seem out of sorts."

"Yes, I'm well," Lilah said.

"Are you sure? You've not been yourself lately."

She looked away, avoiding her friend's perceptive gaze.

"I thought as much," Anne said. "How long have you been in love?"

"Don't be ridiculous!" she snapped, then immediately regretted her outburst. "Forgive me, Anne." She reached for the sugar and dropped four lumps into her tea, blinking back tears.

"Since when have you taken that much sugar in your tea?"

Lilah shook her head and picked up the teacup. Her hand shook, and the cup fell to the floor with a clatter, splashing hot liquid onto her gown. She jumped and placed a protective hand over her belly.

Anne shot to her feet and rang the bell. Shortly after, a maid appeared, and her friend helped the maid to clear up. Lilah stood, but Anne waved her away.

"Sit down, Delilah," she said. She addressed the maid, "You may go now."

"Yes, Mrs. Pelham." The maid bobbed a curtsey and disappeared with the tray, leaving the door ajar.

"I should tend to my gown," Lilah said. "The tea will stain."

"Other things can leave marks."

Lilah shifted in her seat as her cheeks warmed.

"I'm no fool, Delilah," Anne said. "I have children of my own." She nodded toward Lilah's hand, still placed over her stomach, "...and *that* confirms my suspicions."

"Anne," Lilah said, "I don't know what..."

"Pay me the courtesy of speaking the truth."

Lilah bent her head and closed her eyes, but she could not stop the tear, which splashed onto her hand.

"Very well," she said. "I'm pregnant."

Anne let out a sharp breath. "Is that why Sir Thomas has been proposing to you each day?" she asked. "If he wishes to stand by you, then you must let him."

"But I don't love him," Lilah said.

"Perhaps you should have thought of that before you…"

"Sir Thomas isn't the father!"

"Good heavens!" Anne exclaimed. She looked at Lilah, a thoughtful expression on her face, then she nodded. "I suppose that's why he left for Scotland. I didn't take him for a cad."

Lilah brushed the skirt of her gown where the tea had already soaked into the material.

"He doesn't know I'm pregnant," she said, "and it wouldn't do any good if he did." She sighed. "How did you know it was Molineux?" she asked.

"I didn't," Anne said. "You've just told me. I suppose that's why you've been refusing Sir Thomas's advances. At least you won't have to worry about Sir Thomas offering for you again. Once he knows, he'll give up on you."

"That's where you're wrong, Mrs. Pelham," a male voice said.

Lilah looked up and let out a cry.

Sir Thomas stood in the doorway next to Thea. His expression conveyed a hint of triumph, whereas Thea's showed shock.

Sir Thomas recovered first. "Miss Thea, Mrs. Pelham, would you be so kind as to grant me an audience with Miss Delilah in private?"

"No," Lilah said. "There's nothing you can say to me which cannot be said in front of others."

"You owe him an audience, at least," Thea said. She turned to Sir Thomas. "But my sister is distressed. If you upset her further, I shall hear of it."

"Believe me, ma'am, my intention is to secure her happiness," he said.

Anne joined Thea at the door, and they exited the room, closing it behind them. Sir Thomas crossed the floor and sat beside Lilah.

He said nothing but reached for her hand. She made no attempt to resist. Silence fell, broken by the occasional noise outside—the sounds of London and its inhabitants going about their business.

"Did you hear much of my conversation, Sir Thomas?" Lilah asked. "It's ungentlemanly to eavesdrop."

"I couldn't help overhearing," he replied. "The door was open. But perhaps that's for the best. My dear, Miss Hart—beloved Delilah—let me renew my offer of marriage."

"What makes you think my answer has changed?"

"Your condition."

"My *condition* is as it was," she said. "The only difference is that you're aware of it. Do you still want to marry me, knowing I carry another man's child?"

He flinched, then nodded. "Of course."

"And you'd marry a woman who'll never

love you?"

"You'll learn to love me," he said, his voice rising. "I love *you*, despite what you've done, and I'll promise to keep you. That must count for something. Can the same be said of *him*? He can't even keep his townhouse."

"What do you mean?"

"Clayton House is to be sold. Your brother is making the arrangements as it seems that some of the Scotsman's creditors are clients of Hart Bank. It sounds as if his business is going the same way." He smiled. "I've a mind to purchase it myself. It could be a wedding gift for my wife."

"W-what about the child?" she stammered. "If it's a boy, he would be your heir."

"I'm willing to risk that," he said. "Besides, it might be a girl."

"And would you raise it as your own, knowing whose child it is?"

His body stiffened, and he tightened his grip on her hand. "We won't speak of it. Naturally, I'll want children of my own. You've proven you're capable of conceiving, so you can furnish me with my own children once we're married. But rest assured, I'd never refer to your child as a bastard. Not even when we are alone."

His words, spoken with cold practicality, struck a frost in her heart. He lifted her hand to his lips. "I love you, Delilah," he said, "enough to forgive your past indiscretions."

"I don't know…" she hesitated.

"Well, I do," he said. "Think about your family. Your brother's position in society depends on your marrying well. Despite your not insubstantial fortune, do you think you'll secure another offer of marriage now you're a fallen woman?"

"Ah, my fortune," she said. "Are you offering me respectability in exchange for cash?"

"Dearest Delilah, I'm not marrying you for your fortune. If you had nothing, I would still want you. What other man could possibly compete with that?"

Her life stretched before her, split into two paths. The first led toward ruination where she found herself alone, unloved, and with an illegitimate child in tow, her family's reputation ground in the dirt, and her brother's hopes dashed. The second led to a marriage of convenience to a man she didn't love but who would give her respectability and her child a title.

Determined not to look back or to regret the paths which were now closed to her, Lilah curled her fingers round Sir Thomas's hand and nodded.

"Very well," she said quietly. "I'll marry you."

The words were like chains, securing her imprisonment in a society marriage. But it was the least reprehensible course open to her.

"Dearest, Delilah!" he cried. "You make me

the happiest of men!" He took her face in his hands and pulled her close for a kiss, but she pushed him away. A flash of irritation sparked in his eyes.

"I'll give myself to you once we're married," she said, "but I'd ask you to respect my wish to be left alone until then."

His lips thinned, and he nodded, the benign smile returning.

"Of course, my love," he said. "I shall look forward to it. But you must, at least, grant me leave to announce our betrothal in the newspapers. I shan't leave until you agree."

He pouted in the manner of a small boy. Perhaps he thought it endearing, but it only rendered him petulant. But if it rid her of him today, she'd agree to whatever he asked.

"Very well."

"Capital!" he cried. He jumped to his feet and opened the door, and after a suspiciously short time, Thea and Anna appeared. But while Delilah held her betrothed's hand and weathered their congratulations, her mind could not help but wander north to the Highlands.

To *Beinn Mo Chridhe* and the man she loved.

Chapter Thirty

"M ISS DELILAH! WHAT the devil are you doing here?"

Mr. Payton, Dexter's partner, stood in the office doorway. "Is your brother expecting you?" he asked. "He's rather busy, I'm afraid." He glanced at the longcase clock by the window. "In fact, he's due to meet a client now."

"A Mr. Samson?" she asked. "To discuss an investment proposition?"

"*You're* Samson?"

"How else can I see my brother?" she asked. "He always refuses my requests to visit him here."

"He's a busy man, Miss Hart," Peyton said. "He won't appreciate a social call."

She snorted. "I know Dexter well enough to understand *that*. But I'm here on a matter of business."

"I don't know…"

"My fortune is invested with the bank, Mr. Peyton," she said. "It is unentailed. I am of age. I can do what I want with it—including withdrawing it in its entirety."

Peyton smiled, warmth in his eyes. "Then I shall hinder you no more and wish you good luck," he said, "though perhaps it's your brother who needs it."

He led her to a thick oak-paneled door and knocked.

"Come in!"

The voice on the other side reeked of authority. Peyton gave Lilah an apologetic smile, then opened it.

"Mr.—er—Samson, to see you."

"Bring him in."

Sunlight streamed from the office window, leaving the room's occupant in what must be an almost permanent shadow.

He moved into the light, and his clear blue gaze fixed on her.

"What are you doing here, Delilah? I'm busy."

"I'm here on business."

"I'm expecting a Mr. Samson. Not you."

"Think about it, brother," she said. "Haven't you read the Book of Judges?"

He rolled his eyes. "I've no time for riddles."

"Aren't you going to invite me to sit, Dex?" she asked.

"In my place of work, I'm addressed as Mr. Hart."

Mr. Peyton cleared his throat, and Dexter gestured to the chair opposite the desk.

"Sit," he said, "before Peyton here accuses me of being unchivalrous."

"I can't imagine anyone here criticizing you," she replied. "I suspect frankness is not a quality conducive to the longevity of a man's tenure in your employment."

She sat, and her brother dismissed Peyton in a gruff voice.

"Now we've concluded the *pleasantries*, tell me why you're here," Dexter said. "Shouldn't you be simpering over your trousseau or skipping in the park with your betrothed?"

"Until I'm shackled to Sir Thomas, I'm my own woman," she said, "and can do as I please."

"Which is what?"

"I have a proposition relating to the loans secured on Clayton House."

His face remained expressionless, but his body stiffened.

"I cannot discuss my clients' financial arrangements."

"I wish to make a financial arrangement of my own," she said. "But before I do, have you sold Clayton House yet?"

"Not yet," he said, "but that's none of your business."

"What if I could persuade you not to?"

"Delilah, I run a bank, not a charity."

"I, of all people, know that," she said. "I want you to draw up a loan agreement for me. I was considering something in the region of…"

"Stop there, you fool!" he interrupted. "This is why I maintain that women and business don't mix."

He made a dismissive gesture with his hand. "What in the name of all that is holy, makes you think my bank would lend you money?"

She waved her hand in a perfect imitation of his gesture. "This is why women are disadvantaged in a world of men. We're not even permitted to complete our sentences. I don't want to borrow money."

"Then, what do you want?"

"I wish to invest a sum of money in the form of a loan to the owner of Clayton House so that he might retain it and continue to further his business interests."

His eyes widened. "What sum were you thinking?"

"I don't know how much is needed," she said, "but I have twenty thousand at my disposal, deposited at this very bank."

"That's your dowry!"

"It's not entailed," she said. "I was thinking of

a loan, with terms generous enough such that he'd accept it, but not so generous as to arouse suspicion."

"Generous terms?"

"Minimal interest and no security."

"You'd be a fool to consider it," he said. "Molineux is not a good prospect. The market for whisky is yet untested. You may not see your money back. And don't think I'd be foolish as to settle another twenty thousand on you should you lose it."

"It's a risk I'm prepared to take."

"And is Sir Thomas?" he asked. "He won't want a penniless wife."

"He's told me several times that he loves me, and he doesn't care about my fortune."

"Men make pretty speeches when they believe the bird—or the fortune—is in the bag," Dexter said. "Go home, Delilah. You may have good intentions, but this is not your province. As your banker, I would caution you against this. As your brother, doubly so. You're a young woman…"

"If you're about to tell me that my sex renders me incapable of making rational decisions, I'll throw you out of that damned window," she said. "I'm not asking for your advice. I'm instructing you to make the arrangements."

She scraped her chair back. "Of course, if you won't accommodate me, I'll ask Mr. Peyton to withdraw my funds today so that I might approach another bank to assist me."

"Do what you wish," he said. "I care not. But you'll find the banks hereabouts are not disposed to accommodate the wishes of a woman."

"Don't be silly, Dex," she said. "There are plenty of women in the city who deal with bankers."

He rose to his feet, his tall form giving a menacing air.

"Let me clarify for you," he said quietly. "I will *not* accommodate your wishes. In fact, I'll do everything in my power to instruct my colleagues in the other banks to refuse to admit you."

"You wouldn't dare!" she cried.

"Try me, dear sister."

He gave her a smile of triumph, which she longed to wipe out with her fist.

But words would have more of an impact, for they could more easily strike the center of the target.

"Then I have no choice but to announce my condition to the world," she said.

He paled. "Your—condition?"

"Yes," she said, placing a hand over her belly. "I'm with child."

"Don't mock me, Delilah," he said. "You'll regret it if you do."

"Ask Thea if you don't believe me." She grasped the hem of her skirt. "I can reveal the evidence if you like. It's just beginning to show."

His hands curled into fists. "What the devil have you done?"

"Rather an inane question, given your extensive experience of the act," she said. "Perhaps the *Times* could mention it in their society pages."

He placed his fists on the desk and leaned forward, his nostrils flaring.

"You wouldn't dare."

"Try me, dear brother."

For a moment, they stared at each other. Then he sat, resignation in his eyes. Had she believed him capable of emotions, she would have thrown her arms around him and begged him to understand.

"All right, you've made your point," he said. "I can issue an offer to Molineux. As to the terms, I'd suggest a term of no more than two years and a yield of no less than twenty percent, which is an acceptable rate given the level of risk."

"Five years and fifteen percent," she said. "I believe those are appropriate terms for enterprises of moderate to high risk. And it goes without saying that I remain anonymous."

He sighed. "Very well. If Molineux accepts the offer, I'll ask my lawyer to prepare the documents."

"Thank you."

She stood, and he followed suit and offered his hand. She took it, and the ghost of a smile played across his lips.

"Careful, Dex," she said, "or I might believe you have a heart."

"Then you'd be wrong," he replied. "But for the sake of the man who professes to have given his heart to you, I would ask that you tell him what you have done before you marry."

"What I do with Sir Thomas is none of your business," she said. "Just as what you do with your women is none of mine."

His head snapped up. "What do you mean?"

"Aren't you courting someone?" she asked. "You must be very proud of her if you're keeping her a secret from your own family."

"I don't court," he said. "I claim."

"So it's true," she said. "You've been feathering a nest in the country for a particular bird. Have you bagged her yet?"

His smile disappeared, and he withdrew his hand.

"You have, haven't you!" she cried. "When are we to wish you joy? We could have a double wedding to save on the expense."

"It's time you left," he said through gritted teeth. "Forgive me for not showing you out."

Evidently, she'd struck a nerve.

He remained standing while she left, but any trace of warmth in his expression had disappeared.

Perhaps marriage to Sir Thomas was not the

worst fate to befall a woman. She found herself pitying the woman unfortunate enough to secure Dexter's hand in marriage.

Chapter Thirty-One

FRASER SHOOK HIS head in disbelief. "Simpkins, is this some kind of joke?"

"Of course not, Your Grace," the lawyer replied. "The document is legal and perfectly clear. An unsecured loan of twenty thousand at a competitive rate of interest for a period of five years, or an earlier date as the debtor sees fit."

"And the creditor?"

"Wishes to remain anonymous, according to Mr. Hart," the lawyer replied.

"Doesn't he wish to be thanked?"

"In my experience, investors prefer a dividend to a hearty thank you, Your Grace. One cannot live off the latter."

Only one person could have made such a generous offer. Harold Pelham was the only man of Fraser's acquaintance—and his only friend—

with access to such funds. Affable as the man was, he wouldn't have made a decision driven by sentiment. He stood to gain if Fraser's business succeeded, for who would Fraser turn to in order to distribute his whisky?

Nevertheless, the terms were generous, and it was the best offer Fraser could hope for. And Pelham's request for anonymity had removed that degree of awkwardness, which would have prevented him from accepting.

When the time came, he could swallow his pride and thank his friend in person.

He stood and shook the lawyer's hand. "Write to Hart directly and tell him I accept. Now, please excuse me. I have much to do."

He ushered the lawyer out, then headed for the distillery.

He found Hamish in the main building chatting to Rose, the young woman who'd arrived from London yesterday with her son, Will, and baby daughter. He found himself eager to hear an English accent again. Though his heart belonged to Glendarron, he missed London.

Five months had passed since he left, but his mind still wandered there, during those periods of silence when his thoughts were subject to the influence of his heart. And now he had reason to return. His business prospects reignited, he could restore Clayton House and rebuild the aviary. He could furnish Mrs. Forbes with enough supplies to feed and clothe every starving mouth in her shelters.

He would do it to prove himself worthy.

Worthy of *her*.

"Hamish!" he hailed. "I have good news!"

Hamish turned and waved. The young woman dipped into a curtsey.

"There's no need for that, Rose," Fraser said. "How's your Will settling in?"

"Ever so well," she said. "He's already made a friend at school and has been learning his letters."

"A friend?"

"Aye," Hamish said. "Old Alistair's grandson, Callum."

"Such a polite boy," Rose said. "I can't thank you enough, sir, for taking us in."

"I should be thanking you, Rose," Fraser said. "We're always in need of good workers, and Mrs. Forbes has nothing but praise for you." He turned to his foreman. "I trust she's settling in well, Hamish?"

"Aye, sir, very well, indeed."

"Then, Rose," Fraser said, "with your permission, I'll write to Mrs. Forbes to let her know."

"May I send her a letter, too?" she asked. "I'm anxious to hear about the wedding."

"Is Mrs. Forbes getting married?"

"Lord, no, sir!" Rose laughed. "I meant Miss

Delilah."

Fraser's throat tightened at the mention of her name.

"Miss Hart?"

"We were glad for her when she told us," Rose said. "Mrs. Forbes made a special tea for us all to celebrate."

She clasped her hands to her chest. "I'm that happy for her! To think—she'll be Lady Tipton!"

Lady Tipton…

Invisible cold fingers clenched his stomach, and he swallowed the bile rising in his throat.

"Are you all right, sir?" Hamish asked.

Fraser nodded, but the cold tightened his chest until he struggled to breathe.

He'd lost her. Because of his stupid pride, anger, and resentment, he'd dumped her on her brother's doorstep and fled to Scotland to lick his wounds.

Which had paved the way for that fool to snatch the spoils.

But perhaps it was not too late. If he left today, he'd reach London in four days—five at the most.

"When's the wedding?" he asked.

"I believe it's tomorrow," Rose said.

The nugget of hope died. Not only was he too late, but he'd have to endure the day of her marriage, knowing there was nothing he could do to stop it.

DELILAH SMOOTHED THE skirt of her wedding gown and looked at her reflection. The woman staring back did not look like a bride. Her belly protruded through the delicate lace, and no amount of work on Madame Dupont's part could disguise her condition.

Tomorrow she would be married. Sir Thomas had insisted on restricting the guests to close family only, 'to preserve sensibilities,' and Dexter had agreed. They'd even kept her from going to church while the banns were being read.

To prevent attention being drawn to you, Delilah. There's plenty of time to parade yourself round London once you're Lady Tipton.

What Dexter had actually meant was that she'd be permitted to present herself in public once an appropriate period of time had elapsed after her child was born, so as to prevent the gossips commenting on the fact that her child would be born three months after her wedding.

The chamber door opened. Dorothea's face appeared in the mirror, and she placed a hand on Lilah's shoulder.

"You look beautiful, Lilah," she said. "My

little sister, the prettiest bride in London."

Lilah lifted her hand and placed it over her sister's, interlocking their fingers. "Hardly that," she sighed. "I'm marrying a man I don't love to prevent my child from being born a bastard."

"Delilah!"

"Forgive me, Thea," she said. A tear splashed onto her cheek.

"Society marriages aren't based on love," Thea said. "You're a strong woman—stronger than me. And clever. You'll have him bending to your will in no time. Think of it, Lilah! A home and children."

"I suppose it's the least reprehensible option," Lilah said.

"It could be worse." A look of sadness crossed Thea's expression, then she smiled. "Sir Thomas is not a bad man. He loves you, and your fortune is guaranteed to enhance that love."

"Except I have no fortune."

"What do you mean?"

"I've invested it," Lilah said. "Though, according to Dexter, I've as good as given it away."

"Good heavens!" Thea cried. "Does Sir Thomas know?"

"He's said he's not marrying me for my money."

"That's not what I asked," Thea said. "It's easy for a man to declare he has no need for something when he doesn't expect to be deprived of it. You must tell him, Delilah. It's only fair."

"I promised Dexter I'd tell him," Lilah said, "and I will."

"Tell him before tomorrow. He has a right to know that your fortune is no longer at his disposal."

"You think a marriage should be founded on funds?"

"At the very least, Delilah, it should be founded on honesty," Thea said. "You, of all people, should understand the consequences of deception."

Thea was right. Lilah's dishonesty had driven away the man she loved.

The man I love…

"Delilah? Are you all right? You've gone dreadfully pale."

"I'm well, Thea, but perhaps I've been standing too long."

"Let me fetch you some water."

"No, I'll be better once I'm out of this gown," Lilah replied. "Would you send Sarah to help me?"

"Of course." Thea dropped a kiss on her shoulder and withdrew from the room.

Lilah drew in a breath. The bridal gown restricted her movements, tightening against her chest, holding her captive.

Instead of this choice, she could still retire to the country, then return once the child was born under the guise of a widow. If she stayed away for long enough, a year or two, society might believe it.

But no—she couldn't do that to Sir Thomas on the day before their wedding. It would be cruel to hurt his feelings when he'd professed to love her.

After Sarah had helped her into a day gown, Lilah slipped downstairs. Voices came from the morning room, and as she pushed open the door, Sir Thomas stood by the window, Dorothea next to him.

He rushed toward Lilah and took her hand, his grip a little too tight.

"My beautiful bride-to-be." He bent his head to kiss her, and she turned away. A flash of annoyance crossed his expression, then he patted her hand and smiled like an indulgent parent. "There's plenty of time for that tomorrow," he said, "when we can start a new life together. And I promise, upon my heart, that I will never let you down."

Thea shot Lilah a pointed look and raised her eyebrows.

Tell him, she mouthed.

"Dorothea, would you excuse us for a moment?" she asked. "I have something I need to speak to Sir Thomas about."

"Of course."

After her sister had left, Lilah took Sir Thomas's hand. His smile broadened, and he squeezed her hand affectionately.

"What is it, my love?"

"I'm afraid I'll disappoint you."

He lifted her hand to his lips. "Dearest, Delilah, nothing you do could ever disappoint me, and nothing will prevent you from becoming mine tomorrow."

Chapter Thirty-Two

FRASER CLIMBED OUT of the carriage outside Clayton House and hunched his shoulders against the wind. A light dusting of snow covered the streets of London, which were deserted. The weather had driven the people indoors.

How London was considered the center of the world when they couldn't stomach a little cold was beyond him. At Glendarron, blizzards clutched the landscape with icy hands for weeks at this time of year, but they never conquered the spirit of the people.

The butler opened the door, and Fraser stepped inside. Clayton House was unrecognizable from when he'd first seen it so many months ago. The garden, once overrun with weeds, was neatly trimmed, the ornate plants replaced with simple shrubs. The interior replicated Glendarron—soft oak paneling had replaced the cold marble of his predecessor, and antlers adorned the walls, together with tapestries depicting the highlands.

"Mind how you go!"

The butler barked orders as two footmen lifted Fraser's trunk from the carriage, then he bowed to Fraser.

"Welcome home, Your Grace."

"Thank you—Baldwin, isn't it?"

"That's right, sir," the butler replied. "Will you require tea?"

"No, thank you, Baldwin. After being cooped up in that carriage, I'm in need of a walk."

"In *this* weather?"

"There's nothing better than a crisp, cold afternoon for a constitutional."

"Very good, sir." Baldwin issued a stiff bow and shuffled off, his body vibrating with the stiff disapproval thinly disguised beneath the stoic exterior of an upper servant.

Fraser could almost hear the man's joints creaking as he crossed the floor. From where had his agent excavated that old fossil?

Miss Hart would have said something about him having blocks of ice in his breeches.

His mouth creased into an involuntary smile at the thought of her laughter and delightful wickedness, before the memories of their last encounter doused his pleasure.

She was no longer Miss Hart. She was Lady Tipton and had been for two months. Was she, even now, residing in some dreary little mansion somewhere, servicing the needs of that little fop, and looking forward to the prospect of having ten of his brats tugging at her skirts?

He thrust his hands into his pockets and strode along the drive. The servants continued to unload his belongings. By the time he returned, a fire would be crackling in the drawing room, and he could indulge in his whisky without the need to pander to society.

Without anyone to contradict his every word and fight him at every turn.

Without the passion and release his body had been craving these past months.

Damn it—would he never be free of her? A piece of her even resided in Clayton House. *Mo Chridhe, a volume of poems*, had already taken permanent residence in the library.

"Hey! Watch where you're going!" a voice cried out.

He jumped back as a hackney carriage thundered past with the crack of a whip and rattled into the distance. He lifted his hand in a gesture of appeasement, then set off in the opposite direction.

By the time he reached the familiar street, the light had already begun to fade. The low winter sun cast its rays over the buildings, giving them the soft purple hue, which often signaled the onset of snow.

Most of the houses on the terrace were occupied. Lights flickered in the windows, and silhouettes moved about. The occasional pale face looked out from the top floors—servants taking a glimpse of the world outside before being summoned to service the shivering creatures who employed them.

None of the houses held any interest for him, save one. Three houses from the end of the street, its dark windows gave it the forlorn appearance of an abandoned orphan. The last time he'd seen the building, it vibrated with life and passion—the anger of a matriarch, the despair of a young woman, and the triumph of a rival.

He looked up, searching for evidence of life. But other than the reflection of the sunset winking in the top windows, the house showed no sign of it.

Perhaps it was for the best that the house was empty. What would he have said to her if she'd been there?

Was she happy? Or had that freedom of spirit, that fire, been doused by the cold waters of reality?

Would there ever be a woman to measure up to her?

Light footsteps approached, and he hunched

his shoulders and stared straight ahead as if to render himself invisible.

A hand touched his arm, and a female voice spoke. "It *is* you! I thought as much."

Clad in a scarlet, fur-trimmed jacket, her blonde hair peeking out from beneath her bonnet, Anne Pelham stood out among the harsh winter landscape.

He issued a bow. "Mrs. Pelham."

"I'm so glad to see you," she said. "London is frightfully dull this time of year, but there's nothing to compare to excellent company."

"You're too kind," he said. "But if you dislike London, why do you stay? Don't you have a house in the country?"

"Harold is here," she said, "and I'd rather be by his side." She blushed and smiled, the epitome of the well-satisfied and well-loved wife. Harold Pelham was, indeed, a lucky bastard.

"Tomorrow, I stake my claim on him," she continued, "and we leave for Hertfordshire."

"Then I count myself fortunate, having seen you today," he said. "It seems as if all houses in London are empty."

"All, or just one?" she asked, her gaze lingering on the townhouse before them. "Most houses on this street are occupied."

"I suppose they are."

"But the one in which you have a particular interest is not."

She nodded toward the Hart residence.

"It's been unoccupied for a month," she said. "Mr. Hart is in the country with his new wife."

"He's married?"

"Just last month. A rather hasty affair, so I heard, and a most unsuitable woman."

"And…the rest of the family?"

"Miss Hart's in Bath," she said. "She's taking the waters for her health."

"I didn't know Miss Dorothea was unwell."

"No, I meant Delilah."

"Oh," he said. "Lady Tipton."

"Oh, good lord!" She cried. "You've not heard?" She shook her head. "I suppose being half a world away, the news didn't reach you. The marriage never took place."

Glendarron was hardly half a world away.

"What happened?" he asked. "Did she break off their engagement?"

"No, he did. The night before the wedding." She lowered her voice, "Her dowry never materialized. Apparently, she invested the money—rather unwisely, it seems."

"Invested it?"

"I don't know the particulars, but Harold overheard mention of it in Whites. I'll never understand why gentlemen accuse ladies of idle tattle when they're equally at fault. But if men believe that gossip over brandy in a smoke-filled clubroom is akin to an intellectual conversation, then who am I to shatter their illusions?"

"And Mr. Pelham?"

"My husband knows better than to discuss *his* business openly. His ability to keep an open ear among so many loose tongues, serves him well."

"And he trusts you with the secrets revealed in Whites?" Fraser asked.

She smiled. "There was little to relate other than the disappearance of twenty thousand pounds."

He froze. "How much did you say?"

"Twenty thousand," she said. "If you ask me, Delilah was at liberty to do what she wanted with her fortune, and if Sir Thomas spurned her as a result, then she's well rid of him."

Twenty thousand! It couldn't be a coincidence.

She curled her lip into a sneer. "Sir Thomas is making a speedy recovery from his ordeal."

"How so?"

"He's been seen paying compliments to Lady Atalanta Grey, who's still in town," she said. "I wish him well in his endeavors. If he prefers a soulless debutante, then he never deserved my friend."

"The cad!" Fraser cried. "Why didn't Hart challenge him?"

"Other than soundly ejecting Sir Thomas from his home, he did very little."

Fraser shook his head. "If I were her, I…"

"You'd what?" she asked. "Run after him

through the streets of London, beg his hand, and further your humiliation?"

"He deserves a bloody good thrashing!"

"And you're the one to do it?"

"If I must," he said. "If there is none other to fight for her."

She raised her eyebrows at his vehemence.

"Tipton must be brought to justice," he said.

"I agree," she replied, "but society would argue that he acted within his rights. A marriage is like a business agreement, with obligations and expectations on both sides, and the marriage settlement he was expecting never materialized."

"Surely, you don't see Miss Hart as a commodity, who should come with payment to compensate for the obligation of keeping her?"

"Of course not," she said, "but I don't make the rules of our world. Besides, I believe she only wishes for peace, given her condition."

"Is something wrong with Miss Delilah's health?"

She blushed and shook her head. "I've said too much. She's in perfect health but needs a little rest after a trying few weeks. Would you be so good as to escort me home?"

He held out his arm. She took it, and they set off. Before they reached the end of the street, he turned and took a final look at the Hart townhouse.

"I should visit her," he said.

"Please, you mustn't. I doubt you'd be welcome, and she's not accepting visitors."

"Why not?"

She hesitated. "Dorothea is very particular about guests."

"That doesn't sound very accommodating."

She turned her head away, but not before he caught the blush on her cheeks.

"Something's the matter," he said. "Isn't it? If you don't tell me, I'll find out myself."

She let out a sigh. "Harold wouldn't want me to say anything, but neither do I wish to hear you've been tattling in Whites and arousing suspicion. If I tell you, will you swear never to breathe a word?"

"I swear."

She cast her gaze about the street, as if expecting to see eavesdroppers hanging out of every window, then she lowered her voice.

"Delilah is with child."

"She's *what?*"

"Keep your voice down," she hissed. "She's to remain in Bath with Dorothea until her confinement is over."

Dear Lord! Had Sir Thomas taken advantage of her before abandoning her?

Hypocrite…

Hadn't Fraser done exactly that?

"And—the father?" he asked.

"Isn't it obvious?

"Perhaps she loved him," he said, wincing at the bitterness in his voice. "Perhaps he planted his seed to secure her dowry. How disappointed he must be to find his efforts were in vain!"

She withdrew her hand and gave him a resounding slap on the face.

"How dare you make light of my friend's circumstances!" she cried. "She'll be shunned by society, and her brother is furious with her. What hope does she have now of securing a living or a home of her own?"

Fraser's cheeks warmed with shame at the part he'd played in her downfall. He closed his eyes but could not dispel the image of her supple little body laid out for him to feast on.

Oh, Delilah—my Lilah!

"Your Grace?"

He opened his eyes. Mrs. Pelham stared at him, understanding in her eyes.

"Is there something you should tell me?" she asked.

"I love her," he said, his chest tightening. "I always have."

She reached up and caressed his cheek where she'd struck it. "Forgive me," she said. "I had no wish to hurt you. I did wonder whether there was an understanding between the two of you, but when you left for Scotland, it was as if you'd never existed. She never spoke of you, just grew silent, and threw herself into helping Mrs.

Forbes."

"It's I who should beg forgiveness," he said. "I shouldn't have left. I'm the cause of her ruination."

They rounded a corner, and she pointed ahead.

"There! We're almost home. Won't you join us for supper? Harold would be glad to see you, I'm sure."

Her affability was too much to resist, and he was in sore need of congenial company after the revelation.

But as soon as dinner was concluded, nothing would prevent him from traveling to Bath. If Baldwin thought his master eccentric, then an unexpected journey at first light tomorrow would confirm his suspicions.

Chapter Thirty-Three

CHILDREN'S VOICES PENETRATED Lilah's dreams, and she opened her eyes. Though the air was cold, the furs kept her warm, like a cocoon. Thea's voice carried across the wind, punctuated by squeals of merriment as she played with the housekeeper's children.

Free from the confines of London society, Thea's personality came to the fore. She loved children, and though she was deemed too old for the society marriages Dexter wanted for them all, she was looking forward to becoming an aunt.

Dexter had rented them a house on the outskirts of Bath, close enough to enable Lilah to take the waters if she wished. And it came with a sizeable garden, which enabled her to enjoy the fresh air away from the judgmental eyes of the world.

The lawn stretched toward a line of trees leading to a pond, where the occasional ripple of a fish disturbed the surface. In the center of the lawn, an armillary sphere stood atop a stone pillar surrounded by rose bushes. Frost covered their leaves as if they'd been dusted with sugar.

But despite the cold, spring filled the air. Bright green shoots poked through the frost and would soon burst into vivid colors.

The season of rebirth and new beginnings.

Dexter had offered to find Lilah a husband. Despite having warned her he'd not give her another dowry, he promised he'd ensure she was provided for. She had expected her brother to be angry with her, but his anger and disgust were directed at Sir Thomas. Dexter had begun to suspect that he had been involved in producing the leaflets inciting the riot at Clayton House. But, where Lilah may originally have wanted to see the man brought to justice, she now only wanted to forget he'd ever existed.

As to finding a husband, she was done with placing herself at the mercy of a man. All that mattered was her child. Where she'd planned to battle the world, she now had a new challenge— that of nurturer and protector. The world would have to wait.

She shifted position to ease the ache in her back and placed a hand on her belly, whispering a greeting as she felt the child move.

Ruined she may have been, but out of that ruination, had come a life. Whatever *he* thought of Lilah now, the child had been conceived out of love.

Her love.

"I cannot wait to meet you, little one," she whispered. "And you will be loved. By so many people. Your aunt and uncle…"

Laughter erupted behind her, the uninhibited squeals of young souls who knew nothing of the world.

A tear formed in her eye, and she wiped it away. But she had no right to wallow in self-pity. Her child would want for nothing. What was a little scorn from society compared to the hardships many other women endured?

And what did it matter if she surveyed the landscape before her and found it wanting, compared to the rugged mountains and hillsides of the Highlands?

No—she had no desire to see the mountain again.

None at all.

Not the wild, wide-open spaces, nor the fresh air, the cries of the eagles, or the majestic peaks which stretched toward the heavens…

Moisture stung her eyes, and she blinked.

She heard raised voices—a man's voice, pleading, and Thea's sharp tones. Lilah closed her eyes.

Thea must be admonishing the butler again, Lilah smiled. Her sister always took the housekeeping too seriously. She'd never forget the years of poverty they'd endured before Dexter made his fortune.

A familiar, rich voice invaded her mind. She bit her lip, but it persisted, as unyielding as the Highland rocks against which he'd almost claimed her.

The voice grew louder. Angry, indignant—as it was on the day he'd cast her out.

The voices stopped. Footsteps approached, but she kept her eyes closed and tipped her face toward the sun, relishing the warmth on her face and the soft pink glow through her eyelids.

A shadow passed over her.

"Delilah."

The soft whisper, filled with love, resonated through her bones. She smiled, and the touch solidified as strong fingers interlocked with hers. Warm, soft lips caressed her skin.

She opened her eyes and looked into a clear blue ocean.

Unable to forget the anger which had darkened those eyes the last time she saw them, she withdrew her hand and pulled the furs up to her chin as if to protect herself. But he grasped her hand again, and she surrendered. Her body responded to his touch, and shivers of need tightened her skin as he caressed her hand with his thumb.

"Did I hurt you so badly that you shrink from my touch?"

How she'd longed to hear his voice again!

"I never meant for any of it to happen," she said.

"I know, lass. I curse the day I let my anger rule my heart—and I doubly curse the day my pride drove me to Scotland—away from you. But now I've found you, I have no wish to let you go again."

"How did you know where I was?" she asked.

"Mrs. Pelham told me where to find you," he said. "I happened across her not long after I returned to London."

"You're in town?"

"I was," he said, smiling, "but I'm now here, in the presence of a goddess. I also find myself in a much-improved position financially, thanks to an anonymous investment."

She tried to withdraw her hand, but his grip, though gentle, was not to be denied.

"I hope one day to meet my investor," he said, "to admonish them for their lack of sense."

His eyes crinkled into a smile. "Fifteen per-cent is a poor yield given the risk the investment posed. Perhaps I should sell Clayton House and pay the capital early to preserve the investor's reputation. They must be the laughingstock of London."

"No!" she said. "You can't do that. Not when you went to such lengths to restore it."

"I'm prepared to reconsider if the investor agrees to my terms."

"Your terms?"

"A trifle, really." He smiled and looked round the garden, seemingly fascinated by the surrounding trees. The silence stretched, filling the air until she could no longer bear it.

"Might I know your terms?" she asked.

"If you wish," he said. "Though I'm perplexed as to your level of interest. My terms are that I wish to know the name of my investor, so I might thank them personally. I cannot continue to accept the generosity of a stranger."

Mischief shone in his eyes.

He was teasing her!

"Perhaps your investor has a good reason for anonymity," she said.

"Anonymity can lead to disaster."

She cast her gaze down in shame at the memory of what her anonymity had done to him. He caught her chin with his hand and gently tipped her face up until their eyes met.

"Forgive me," he said. "I didn't mean to distress you. But if you'd favor me with an answer. Was it you?"

She nodded.

He closed his eyes and drew in a sharp breath. When he opened them again, the pupils were dilated until they were almost black.

"Why did ye do it, lass?"

"I had to make reparation after what I'd done."

He shook his head. "It wasn't your fault. The fault lies with the blackguard who incited the riot. And with me, for thinking you could have done such a thing."

"I should have been honest with you from the start," she said. "I'd hated the Molineuxs for so long, and I wanted to hate you so badly. But, infuriating man that you are, you made it impossible for me to do anything but love you."

"You loved me?"

"I tried not to. I wanted to make a difference to the world, but I lost sight of the impact my actions had on others. My own selfish desire to have my words read by the world led to your ruination."

"No!" he said. "My ruination was inevitable. I'd overburdened my business with debt, on the strength of too optimistic an outlook, and I lost sight of the need to set aside enough to weather the storm. That the storm came was nobody's fault. We cannot prevent bad weather. We can only prepare ourselves to survive the consequences."

He held her hand against his heart. "It wasn't *I* who suffered ruination and disgrace."

She lowered her gaze to her swollen belly.

Did he, like the rest of society, see her as nothing more than a sullied woman, despite the part he'd played?

She snatched her hand away, and this time, he released his grip.

"I didn't lend you the money, seeking gratitude," she said coldly. "A fifteen percent return will pay handsomely for my keep. After all, my needs are small."

He made no attempt to take her hand. Instead, he knelt before her.

"What are you doing down there?" she asked. "You'll get your knees wet."

"Infuriating woman!" he laughed. "Aren't suitors supposed to kneel before their intended before they bare their souls? Didn't that Tipton fellow do the same?"

She gritted her teeth at the mention of Sir Thomas. The pain and humiliation of their last interview still lingered—his angry words on discovering her dowry was not his for the taking, the insults for laying with another man, and finally the accusations of entrapment and dishonesty.

The man at her feet covered both her hands with his.

"Forgive me!" he cried. "I should not have mentioned that scoundrel's name. He's a cad, to take advantage, then abandon you! I'll hunt him down and shoot him if you wish."

"What good would that serve?"

"It would make me feel a damned sight better."

She shook her head. "*You* did nothing wrong."

"And neither did you," he said. He gestured to her belly. "Let me share your burden. Say you'll be mine, and we can start anew. This time with no secrets, but sharing each other's lives, thoughts, and deeds. A marriage of equals."

Equals? Why, then, did he refer to her child as a *burden?*

"What will happen to my child?" she asked. "It would be born too soon after any marriage to be considered respectable."

"What does that matter?" he asked. "In the eyes of the law, it will be mine."

"Would you accept another man's child?"

"Oh, lass, don't you realize how much I love ye?" He lifted her hands and kissed her knuckles, one by one. "All that I have would be yours, and all that you have would be mine. Your child is a part of you and, for that, I will love him as my own. If you're in any doubt, I shall drive you to my lawyers to draw up a document declaring him my heir. I shall teach him to run my distillery and to weather the burden of being a duke."

"And if it's a girl?"

"Then she shall rule over the distillery better than any man. And I'll take great delight in fending off prospective suitors with my pistol, like any doting father."

"And if I told you that I have lain with none but you?"

His forehead creased into a frown, and he cocked his head to one side. Then understanding flickered in his expression, followed by unbridled joy.

"Ye're a saucy wench to deceive me so," he said. "Did you mean to test the strength of my love?"

He pulled her into his arms, then placed his head on her shoulder and sighed.

"I've missed ye," he whispered, his warm breath tickling her neck.

"I have yet to answer your question," she said.

"Witch!" he teased. "If you weren't in a delicate condition, I'd take you over my knee and spank ye raw."

"If I recall," she said, "you made that same promise the day we met, and you have yet to honor it."

He gave a low growl which vibrated against her body. "Then, my feisty wee terrier," he said, "I'll take great pleasure in proving my honor when the time is right—when I take ye against the hard rock of *Beinn Mo Chridhe* and claim you as my Highland queen."

A wicked pulse of need coursed through her.

He lifted his head and swiftly captured her mouth. At her gasp of surprise, he slipped his tongue in—teasing, probing, seducing.

The child gave a sharp kick, and she let out a cry.

"Did I hurt ye?"

"No." She took his hand and placed it on her belly. The child kicked again, and a smile of joy illuminated his face, his eyes sparkling with pride.

"Oh, lass," he said, "will you not end my torment? It gives me such pleasure to see you round with my child. Make me the happiest of men, I beg ye."

"Would you grant me freedom, Fraser, if I asked it?"

"Freedom from what?" he asked. "From me?"

"Freedom to live my life as I chose," she said. "To help the world, to write…"

"I have no wish to be your jailer," he said. "I offer my heart, my name, and my protection, and I ask nothing in return. As for your writing, I would never stifle such talent. Sandton said…"

He broke off, a blush coloring his cheeks.

"It was you, wasn't it?" she asked. "You approached Sandton on my behalf."

"Had I not made a promise that I'd do all I could to help you?" He smiled. "I approached several publications until the *London Ladies Weekly* showed interest in your work."

"And you approached him after we—we

parted?"

"I promised to help the woman I love, did I not?"

"You love me?" she asked.

"Lass, I've loved you almost from the moment I first saw you, even if it took me months to admit it to myself," he said. "I'm so proud of you, my love, and my life would be complete if I could have you by my side for always. But even if you tell me to leave and never see you again, still I would be proud of ye, and love you until I draw my last breath."

"Then," she whispered, "nothing would make me happier than to be with you for always. As your wife."

He bent his head and placed a kiss on her belly. "Did you hear that, little one? You are witness to your ma's consent."

She giggled, and he kissed her again. "Come, lass, let me take you back inside before your sister slices my ballocks off and feeds them to the fish in that pond."

"Did she say she would?"

"Had those children not been present, I think she'd have tried it the moment I arrived. But if I see her running toward me with an urn in her hand, then I know I'm in trouble. Isn't that how the Hart sisters attack unsuspecting men?"

"Am I ever to be forgiven for smashing that vase over your head?"

"My dear lass, I will never regret the day a feisty wee terrier accosted me with a vase. I believe that was the moment I fell in love with ye."

He helped her up and wrapped a fur around her as if she were as delicate as a bird's egg. Then, hand in hand, they returned to the house.

Epilogue

Glendarron, Scotland
Six months later…

DELILAH CLUNG TO her husband as his breath came in shallow pants, puffs of warm air against her neck. Still inside her, their bodies sticky with sweat, he held her as if his life depended on it. The hard rock against her back was still warm from the afternoon sun, and her body trembled from the aftershocks of her climax. She could still hear her screams of ecstasy echoing across the mountainside.

She shifted position, and a shock of need coursed through her nipples.

"Not yet, lass," he murmured. "Let me hold ye against the rock for a while. Too long have I dreamed of this moment, that I wish to savor it, to etch it into my memory."

"I trust this won't be our only memory, Your Grace."

A wicked glint shone in his eyes, and he grasped her wrists and pinned her against the rock. "*Your Grace*, is it? That wasn't what you were screaming earlier as I buried myself inside ye."

He ground his hips against her. A flare of pleasure pulsed deep inside, and a cry escaped her lips.

"Greedy lass," he said, his voice hoarse. "Perhaps I should spend every day here, giving ye a good, hard tupping against the rocks."

"You're a beast!" she said, laughing.

"Aye," he growled, "I'm a stag in rut, eager to please his mate. Perhaps this beast should mark his mate so none other can claim her."

He lowered his lips to her neck and nipped the sensitive flesh, sending a shock of pleasure through her. When he lifted his head once more, his eyes pulsed with desire and love. He planted a soft kiss on her lips, then eased himself out of her. Once again, she felt that brief moment of loss, each time he withdrew.

He took her left hand and kissed the wedding band on her finger.

"We should return," she said. "Flora will wonder where we are."

"Our daughter will either be fast asleep or in Nellie's care."

"Or your mother's."

He chuckled, and his body vibrated against hers. "I swear young Nellie is turning out to be a feisty lass. I've never seen anyone battle so hard with Ma for a baby's attention. She's blossomed much since Mrs. Forbes sent her to us."

"I'm sure your mother enjoys the challenge," she said. "She told me the other day what a help Nellie was around the house. She also said she hopes to see Flora furnished with brothers and sisters for her to indulge and spoil."

His eyes darkened with lust. "I shall enjoy making them," he said. "Perhaps, even today, you may be carrying my son."

"Do you wish for a son?"

"If I have no sons and a hundred daughters, I should be delighted. I care nothing for preserving the Molineux line, and a daughter can run the distillery as well as a son."

He kissed her once more. "A wife, also," he said. "Hamish tells me your idea of providing verse to adorn the labels of each bottle of whisky has attracted more orders. I'm pleased to see my wife's talents are now being used to my benefit rather than my detriment."

She swatted his arm, and he grinned. "There's my hellion! I'd much rather battle with you than endure a biddable wife any day. Besides, I know you'll sheathe your claws at the end of our battles and permit me to sheathe…"

"That's enough!" she laughed, "or I'll begin to believe the rumors that all Highlanders are barbarians."

"Barbarians we may be, but we appreciate beauty nonetheless," he said. "Did I see a package arrive this morning from Sandton?"

"You did," she said. "My second book of poems has gone to print, and he's written to ask if I'd be happy to write a third."

"And will you?"

She gestured around her. "With this world at my fingertips, how can I not be inspired? I wish to spend the rest of my life here."

"Just wandering?" he teased, "or rutting?"

"Fraser!"

"Ah," he rumbled, "that's what ye were screaming when I parted your thighs and thrust deeper inside ye."

He planted a kiss on her lips. "I'm afraid, my love, it's time to return to the house. This is the furthest you've ventured since Flora's birth, and Ma said she'd slice me open if I didn't return ye before dark."

He buttoned his breeches and tucked in his shirt while she pulled her skirts down.

"We must look like peasants," she said. "What will your mother think of us!"

"That we're a couple unafraid to indulge our love," he said, "by rutting against the hard rock of the mountains…"

He planted a kiss on her forehead. "...or when I mount ye over the desk in my study..."

His lips brushed against her cheek, then followed a path toward her mouth. "...or when I feast on ye in my bed while ye lay open and ready for me, your sweet flower luscious and pink, and..."

"Fraser!"

He cupped her face in his hands.

"Perhaps we might..." she hesitated. "Just once more?"

"Oh, lass!" He laughed. "When a man has thoroughly pleasured his woman, he must be given time to recover. But let me promise you here and now—tonight, when all have retired, I shall bring ye to the heights of pleasure such that ye shall scream my name and soar through the sky to join the eagles in heaven."

"I must be content with that."

"Ye'll be more than content, lass."

It was a promise she knew he'd keep.

He reached out his hand, and she took it, and let him guide her along the mountain path. In the valley below, Glendarron Castle shone in the light of the setting sun.

Her home in the foothills of the mountain of her heart.

The End

About the Author

Emily Royal grew up in Sussex, England, and has devoured romantic novels for as long as she can remember. A mathematician at heart, Emily has worked in financial services for over twenty years. She indulged in her love of writing after she moved to Scotland, where she lives with her husband, teenage daughters and menagerie of rescue pets including Twinkle, an attention-seeking boa constrictor.

She has a passion for both reading and writing romance with a weakness for Regency rakes, Highland heroes, and Medieval knights. Persuasion is one of her all-time favorite novels which she reads several times each year and she is fortunate enough to live within sight of a Medieval palace.

When not writing, Emily enjoys playing the piano, hiking, and painting landscapes, particularly the Highlands. One of her ambitions is to paint, as well as climb, every mountain in Scotland.